ROOM SERVICE

LINDSEY POWELL

Content copyright © Lindsey Powell 2023
Cover design by Wicked Dreams Publishing

All rights reserved. No part of this book may be reproduced or utilised in any form, or by any electronic or mechanical means, without the prior written permission of the author.

The characters and events portrayed in this book are fictional. Any similarities to other fictional workings, or real persons (living or dead), names, places, and companies is purely coincidental and not intended by the author.

The right of Lindsey Powell to be identified as the author of this work has been asserted by her in accordance with the Copyright, Designs and Patents act 1988.

A CIP record of this book is available from the British Library.

Except for the original material written by the author, all mention of films, television shows and songs, song titles, and lyrics mentioned in the novel, Room Service, are the property of the songwriters and copyright holders.

Books by Lindsey Powell

The Perfect Series
Perfect Stranger

Perfect Memories

Perfect Disaster

Perfect Beginnings

The Complete Perfect Series

Part of Me Series
Part of Me

Part of You

Part of Us

Part of Me: Complete Series

Control Duet
Losing Control

Taking Control

Games We Play Series
Checkmate

Poker Face

Dark Roulette

A Valentine Christmas

End Game: A Valentine Wedding

Games We Play Complete Series

Wreck My Heart Series

Wrecking Ball

The Untouchable Brother

<u>Stand-alone</u>

Take Me

Fixation

Don't Look Back

Too Much, Not Enough

Room Service

Chapter One

ELISE

I enter room twenty-nine of the hotel I work in, sighing as I carry the clean sheets over to the bed. I put them down on the table that sits to the side and look at the mess before me. Sheets pulled off and creased, the duvet is lying on the floor in a heap, the pillows askew, with two over by the window, and I can only guess that they have been flung there at some point.

My eyes move to the bedside table, where a couple of open condom wrappers sit, the tops torn off and thrown on the floor. At a quick scan, I count five empty packets, and my eyes widen a little. Jesus… five? I've never been fucked five times in one night, I would be lucky to get it once, seeing as my husband of five years is a lazy prick who is only concerned about getting himself off and then rolling over, because apparently that's his job done. Wanker. It also doesn't help that I don't find him attractive in the slightest and the thought of him touching me makes my skin crawl. I hate him. I truly, truly hate him. I never really liked him in the first place, but my parents pushed me to marry him, because back when I did, he had a decent job, seemed to want to look after me, and they piled on the guilt for me to just do it and save myself from a life of poverty—which is exactly what we had all been living since I could remember.

He uses me when he wants something, and other than that, he sits on his arse and glugs beer whilst watching any old crap on the TV. My parents keep piling on that guilt for me to stay, and I am so fucking sick of feeling guilty all the damn time. It's my life, and I'm the one working my arse off as a fucking cleaner to make ends meet, so I wonder why on earth they urge me to stay with him? I mean, shouldn't they be telling me to run far away and make a better life for myself? I know that if it were my daughter, I'd be helping her, not drumming into her that there is no other option.

There is always another option.

And I already have a plan in place.

I save a little of my wages every month, putting it in a savings account until I have enough money to get the hell out of there. I've already made my peace with the fact that my parents will never forgive me, and for that, I can't forgive them. We're not close anymore, because they have driven me away with their constant put downs and ridiculous demands. I did what they asked, and they just moan at me anyway—nothing I ever do will be good enough, I know that now. Took a while for me to truly grasp that concept, but I've come to a point in my life where I no longer give a damn.

Look out for number one. And that is exactly what I have been doing for the last six months. I have no one to rely on but myself, and I will get myself out of this loveless marriage if it's the last thing I do.

I've managed to save a few hundred pounds so far, by working overtime and walking to and from work rather than catching public transport. Every little bit of spare change goes into my secret kitty, and every time I add a little money to it, I smile and know I am one step closer to being free.

It's going to take me a little while longer, but as soon as I have enough money for a plane ticket and have any paperwork in place that I need, then I'm out of here. I've already researched hostels I can stay in, and I have no problem with not having my own place, because I know that will come later down the line. Eventually. But even if I have to wait, so be it, because anything is better than my current situation.

I'm being proactive as much as I can be.

With another sigh, I start to strip the sheets, balling them up and throwing them into a heap on the floor, and I'm so lost in my thoughts that I fail to notice anything until there is the sound of someone clearing their throat behind me. I shriek loudly and throw the pillow that was in my hands in the air. My eyes are wide as I whip around, my heart beating a million miles a minute, and I'm met with a guy dressed in nothing but a towel.

Good fucking God.

"Umm…" Words fail me as I take in his toned abs, olive skin, and muscular arms. Where the hell did he come from? Is he a mirage? Is my mind conjuring up beautiful men now? Am I that fucking desperate in my pathetic life for it to do that? I close my eyes and open them, but he's still there. Okay, not a mirage then.

"I didn't realise housekeeping were due today," he says, his face deadpan. Oh shit.

"I… I'm so sorry," I mumble, as I feel my face getting hotter and hotter by the second—probably look like a fucking beetroot. I quickly move myself into action, bending and picking up the sheets that I've torn off the bed to take to the laundry room. "I'll just… umm…" My voice fades off as I nod towards the door and start to move.

"So, am I expected to sleep on the bare mattress?" he questions, and I stop in my tracks, turning back around to look at him. He's even more stunning to look at a second time, and when my eyes connect with his grey ones, I feel something weird happen inside of me. What is that? Like a flutter, only it's pulsing and making its way down to my… *Enough, Elise. That's enough.*

"No, of course not," I say, averting my eyes from his, because they feel like they're boring into me and trying to see into my soul. "I'll just go and get the clean sheets and then I'll be out of your way." I turn and leave the room, the sound of the door clicking closed behind me seeming to echo all around.

I throw the dirty laundry into the trolley I have stationed in the hallway, and I take a couple of deep breaths. I put my erratic heart beat down to the fact that he scared the crap out of me, and I wasn't expecting anyone to be in the room, ignoring all the other reasons that it could be. I double check the chart to make sure I was supposed to clean the room today, and it shows that it should be vacated. Guess I'll be reporting the faux pas to my manager then, because I sure as shit am not getting the blame for walking in on a guest—a very wealthy guest, I might add. You don't stay in the Blue Diamond Hotel if you don't have money. And yes, the name really does reflect the standard of clientele that come here. We get paid minimum wage whilst the owner rakes in the big bucks. I've never met the owner, but I imagine he's a smug prick that deems everyone to be beneath him. I probably shouldn't be so judgemental, but I've lived a life where I am judged at every turn, so fuck it, while I'm stuck here, I'll judge others in the same way they do me.

I gather myself and go to pick up the fresh bedding, when I remember I already took the clean sheets in the room, so I make my way back to room twenty-nine, shaking my head at how I'm so flustered and distracted by the handsome stranger. I use my key card to open the door, and when I walk in, there is no sign of the handsome stranger. I breathe a sigh of relief and quickly get to work, remaking the bed and praying that I get out of here before he appears once again. I presume he's in the bathroom as the door is shut, and I presume that is where he came from before, because there are no other doors except for the wardrobes, and I hardly think he managed to teleport his way in here. I chuckle quietly to myself as my brain goes off on a tangent. It's the only way to survive some days—let my brain think silly thoughts to amuse myself.

I finish putting the bottom and top sheet on the bed, and I'm just making sure the duvet is all straightened out, when the handsome stranger emerges from the bathroom and walks across the floor to the table and chairs that sits right beside the floor-to-ceiling windows and takes a seat in one of the plush chairs. And I mean *plush*. So fucking plush it's like a treat for your arse. I may have taken a few moments break on occasion, when no one else has been around, just to imagine that I'm one of the rich guests. It's a wonderful fantasy for someone like me. Helps keep the dream alive that maybe, one day, it could be. You never know what life is going to throw your way. You just have to make the best of it until then.

I busy myself putting the new pillowcases on and plumping the pillows, keeping my back to him as I do, but it's like I can feel his eyes burning into me, through me, watching me as I work. I don't know whether to be offended because he's monitoring my work, or whether to be flattered that he may just be checking out my arse. *Yeah, okay, Elise, in your dreams.*

When I'm finished, I finally turn to face him. "I'm sorry about the confusion this morning, sir. I will make sure it doesn't happen again," I tell him, somehow sounding more confident than I feel. "Is there anything else I can do for you before I go?" It's the polite thing to do, and I'm hoping this means he may not report me for the intrusion, even though it's not technically my fault.

He studies me for a moment, his finger brushing over his lips as he does.

I feel the tension in the room ratchet up a notch. Do I just leave? No, that would definitely mean being reported to my boss, who is a bitch and seems to hate me—she always relishes in having to tell me off, or so it seems, anyway.

"What's your name?" he asks me, his deep voice doing nothing to quiet whatever the hell is going on inside me.

"Elise."

"Elise what?" He speaks with such authority that it makes me gulp.

"Elise Woods, sir."

He continues to hold my eyes, and for reasons I can't fathom, I can't seem to look away. Minutes tick by before he stands, sliding his hands into his trouser pockets. His shirt showcases his biceps, and with the cuffs rolled up, he looks like something out of a dream. A very horny dream.

He walks towards me, and I have to remind myself to keep fucking breathing.

"Well, Elise," he says as he comes to a stop in front of me. "I'll be seeing you again soon."

"You will?" I say, my voice a mere whisper.

"You can count on it." And then, just like that, he turns and goes back to his seat, turning his attention to the laptop on the table.

What the hell just happened?

I've never really had any communication with guests, except for the odd demand here and there and a polite 'hello' to most others as I pass by them in the hallways, so this weird interaction has left me feeling… flabbergasted? Is that the right word? I have no idea as I remind myself to move and get back to work.

My legs feel shaky as I go, and when I get to the door and open it, I make sure I don't look back, even though I could feel his eyes on me again every step of the way.

Chapter Two

DORIEN

Elise Woods.

A nice surprise on a Monday morning, and one I am going to fuck.

Chapter Three
ELISE

"Girl, what is with you today?" Celeste remarks as I walk into the break room, looking all kinds of frazzled. "You ran out of room twenty-nine earlier like your arse was on fire."

"Nothing, except for the fact that I had a run-in with the most gorgeous guy I've ever laid eyes on," I tell her as I flop down onto the shitty plastic chair. No plushness for our arses in here.

"Oooo," Celeste says as she puts her phone on the table and sits forward on her seat, giving me her full attention. "Tell me more."

I let out a quiet chuckle and roll my eyes. Celeste is always down for a bit of gossip in this place, and she's been my friend since day one. I trust her implicitly, and she is the only one here that knows how dire my home life is. I try to keep everything private from the others, but most of them form their own conclusions on their colleagues' lives, like it's some kind of fucking game show and whoever guesses right wins a prize. Not for me. I'd rather have one good friend than fifty shitty ones.

"There's not much to tell other than the fact he walked in wearing nothing but a towel whilst I was stripping his sheets."

"Is that it?" she says, looking disappointed that my frazzled state isn't because of something juicier.

I throw a half smile her way. "He said he didn't think housekeeping was due, and I quickly changed his bed and apologised for the intrusion, before he looked at me like he was trying to burn my clothes off with his eyes and then asked my name and told me he'd be seeing me soon. Oh, and he really is the most handsome guy I've ever seen in my life. Like, seriously hot on another level."

"Okay, that's better," she comments. "How handsome are we talking here?"

"Stupidly so. A ten plus."

"That good, huh?"

"That fucking good," I tell her.

"So, what's his name?" she asks.

"I have no idea."

"You didn't ask?"

"Why the hell would I ask his name? That would just be weird."

"He asked yours," she states.

"Yes, and he's a paying guest, so it's different. If I'd asked his name, it would have just been awkward."

"If you say so," she says with a wave of her hand. "I'd have asked his name."

"Yeah, right before you'd have flirted your way into his bed, I'm sure," I say, but I inject humour into my voice, because Celeste is a free spirit who goes with the flow and sticks her finger up to what others think. She's my breath of fresh air, and I'm going to fucking miss her when I leave.

"Elise Woods, I'm offended by the insinuation," she says as she dramatically opens her mouth, as if she's shocked, but really, we know she isn't.

"You wouldn't be if you saw him," I mutter, conjuring up an image of the man in question and thinking about how I wish I weren't married and if only I could be more like Celeste.

"He was really that good-looking?" she questions, interrupting my thoughts.

"He really was," I say on a sigh.

Silence passes between us for a few moments, until Celeste says, "You really need to get laid."

"I got laid about two years ago, and I don't wish to repeat it anytime soon," I tell her, even as the mere mention of it makes me feel icky. I shouldn't feel that way about my husband, I know that, but he's just so… cringe. My body was just a vessel for his small dick, once upon a time. And yes, I am fully aware that I would be telling anyone else to get the fuck out, but like I mentioned, I'm trying, and I have my plan in place. Until then, I'll just continue to put up and shut up.

"That's not a lay, that's just some lazy prick lying on top of you and grunting in your ear while you're bored stiff," Celeste comments, and if it weren't so fucking tragic, I'd laugh. "I mean, you need to *really* get laid, by a guy who isn't all about himself and who knows what to do with it."

"If only, Celeste."

"What's stopping you?" she asks, and I look at her in disbelief as I hold my hand up and point to my ring finger. "Girl, please, people have affairs all the time."

"Well I'm not one of those people," I tell her. She knows my feelings on infidelity, it's a no-go area. I may be miserable as sin, but I still have my morals.

"I'm just saying… not everything is black and white. People seek comfort in others for all sorts of reasons," she continues, unfazed by what I said. "And who says anyone has to know?"

"Oh my god, stop," I tell her as I shake my head from side to side.

"What? You know it makes sense."

"Maybe to you, but not to me."

"So what? The alternative is to be fucking miserable until you leave his arse in the dust?"

"Yes," I state.

"Elise, listen to me. You don't love him—you never have. Your heart never truly let him in, so would you really be betraying him? Or are you just betraying yourself by denying yourself the chance to really live?"

I'm stumped as her big brown eyes stare at me. I can see that she's hurting for me, hoping and praying that I just get the happiness that I crave, or a little excitement until I do, anyway. I get it, I really do, but could I really even think about cheating on my husband? Could I be a person that does that? I've never even entertained the idea before.

Celeste clearly takes my silence as food for thought as she carries on. "You're twenty-five years old. You've been married since you were twenty. You settled down with him when you were eighteen, and your parents forced your hand to put that ring on your finger, making you feel like you had no other choice. I'm not even going to pretend to know what that feels like, but, fuck, Elise, you're no longer connected to any of them"—she puts her hand over her heart—"in here. You once said that you let them go a long time ago, so I'll ask you the question again. Would you be betraying him, or are you betraying yourself?"

I feel the tears prick the backs of my eyes.

She's right.

I did say I'd let them all go and that the only thing stopping me from disappearing is money. Once I've got that, I'll be able to go. I'll be free.

I bite my bottom lip and blink furiously as my eyes divert to the clock on the wall. My break is over in two minutes, and I've never been happier for my break to end. I need a minute.

"I need to get back to work," I tell her as I stand and move around the table. When I get a couple of feet away from her, she speaks.

"You know I'm right, Elise."

Yes, I do, but it might just hurt me more to admit it.

Chapter Four

ELISE

I close the front door behind me, leaning wearily against it as I kick off my shoes. I worked in a daze for the rest of the day, keeping myself busy to stop my mind from thinking about... well, everything. If I don't think about it then I can keep pretending to be content with my lot. If I don't think about it then I can't get upset. And I certainly can't be letting the image of the man from this morning infiltrate my mind—not any more than it has done so far, anyway.

"Where the hell have you been?" I hear Derrick, my husband, shout from the lounge. I already know that when I walk in he'll be laying on the sofa with a couple of empty beer bottles on the coffee table in front of him. I take a few deep breaths, placing my workbag on the floor and shrugging off my coat before making my way down the short hallway of our house.

"Sorry, the bus was delayed," I tell him when I walk in, to which he snorts. Sure enough, there he lays, beer bottle in one hand and the other down the front of his boxers as he scratches his nuts. Lovely. Just lovely.

"What's for tea?" he asks.

"I'll go and throw something together now," I say, stifling a yawn.

"Don't be too long, I'm starving," he informs me, and I simply roll my eyes and walk to the kitchen. I try not to be in the same room as him for too long, other than our bedroom, of course, because I haven't thought of an excuse that he will buy in regards to why I no longer need to sleep in the marital bed.

I open the fridge and see that we're running low on supplies, so I'll have to go shopping tomorrow after work. He won't mind that, because any night I have to go shopping he's guaranteed pizza, just because it's quick and easy to do when I get in later than normal. I close the fridge door and move to the freezer. Things aren't fairing much better in here, but I do have one portion of lasagne left, so I pull that out for him and grab the bag of chips to go with it. I gave up trying to make him eat healthy a long time ago. Considering he's nearing forty-five, you'd think he would look after himself more, but no, that would require effort. And yes, he's twenty years older than me, and I can only assume that my parents saw that as a golden ticket to having a better life. I'd like to think it was for my own sake that they convinced me to say 'I do', but I know it's more for the pension pot they thought he was squirrelling away and the fact he had his own house and used to work as a successful investor—that is until he screwed up royally because his own arrogance refused to pull out of several deals that went pear-shaped and resulted in his downfall and his two year unemployment. I think he prefers the life of a slob, or he seems to, anyway.

With that downfall came my calling card. I had to get a job, any fucking job, to keep our heads above water. I didn't work before that because I was at university, trying to get an art and design degree. I've always loved fashion, and I was so happy to be learning, designing, doing anything regarding my passion. So, when he got fired and he quickly showed that he had no intention of trying to get another job, I quit Uni and found the first job that I could. That was to become a maid, because I had zero qualifications from being a drop out and the bills needed to be paid. My pay has never gone very far, just covering the bills and necessities, but Derrick doesn't care. I've tried talking to him about it several times, but he always pushes it to the side and dismisses me.

And when I went to my parents to talk to them about how much it hurt me to quit Uni and stay with a man that never suited me in the first place, they told me to suck it up and get on with it, in so many words. No sympathy, only disappointment, as if it had been my fault that he had lost thousands and thousands of pounds at the company he worked for.

That moment hurt more than I can ever explain. I almost grieved the loss of my parents then, because it was like they had died. The mother and father I thought I knew had gone, only to be replaced by two strangers. I allowed myself to hurt, and it took months for me to fully accept that they meant every word they said. I kept expecting them to change their minds, to come to me and apologise for pushing me to marry him in the first place, but there was nothing. No remorse, no emotion, nothing. And over time, I still let their guilt trips influence me, eat away at me, because I had always craved their approval. Until six months ago…

"Honestly, Elise, what are you doing with yourself?" my mum, Karen, says as I sit at her kitchen table, sipping the shitty coffee she's put in front of me. "You think that being a maid is the best life can offer? You need to get your man in a better mood to get back out to work."

I stare at her incredulously. Is she for real right now?

"I mean, when you married him, I thought that was it. All of our worries would be over. But no, you managed to mess that up too."

My mouth drops open as I continue to stare at her.

"To think, after all of the effort we went to…"

My brows furrow at her words. What is she talking about? I rarely question my parents, because I'm just the good little daughter that does as she's told, but this time, I can't help myself as I say, "What do you mean? Effort for what?"

She whirls around to look at me, my mother, the woman who should love and protect her child no matter what, but all she does is look at me with that disappointment I've become accustomed to. "Honestly, Elise, do you think you got Derrick to marry you of your own accord? A man who had a good job and was willing to give you the world?"

"I'm not sure I'm following," I tell her, because fuck, is she saying what I think she's saying?

"We set it up, so you'd have a smoother road than we ever had. We made sure the marriage happened, and that we wouldn't have to worry about our future. But now… now everything has gone to pot. And what for? For nothing, it seems."

She speaks like what she's just announced is no big deal, but it very much is. To me it is, anyway.

"Mother, are you saying that this was some kind of arranged marriage?"

"Don't be so ridiculous. Of course not."

"Then what the hell is it?" I question, feeling anger rising inside of me.

"Don't speak like that to me, young lady. I'm your mother," she scolds.

"Yes, you're my mother, so you should only want the best for me," I tell her, my voice getting a little louder.

"I do want what's best for you—"

"But only so you can get the best for you and Dad too, right?" I say, cutting her off and standing from my chair, the shitty coffee forgotten about on the table. "You made it so that Derrick married me. You made it happen by fuelling me with guilt, guilt that I never should have felt. You encouraged me to marry a man that I never loved, and barely even liked. You have made me feel like a failure at every turn, and for what, Mother? What was the end goal for you?" I am raging. I've never been so angry at her.

"Watch your tone," she warns me, but I don't give a fuck about my tone right now, I'm too pissed at her.

"Tell me, what was the price for pimping out your only daughter to a man old enough to be her dad?" I say, my eyes narrowing as I refuse to back down.

"I did not pimp you out. Don't be so vulgar."

"Then what would you call it?" I ask.

"Ensuring you have a better life than—"

"Yeah, yeah, better life than you and Dad, I got the memo. It's all I've heard for years. Don't worry, it's well drummed in, but that still doesn't answer my question."

The silence stretches between us, my eyes boring into her as I wait for her to give up the answer. And when she does, I feel like my whole life has been a lie.

"He bought our house, and he made sure we had enough money to live off for a few years."

"Oh my god," I say on a breath as it whooshes out of me. "And let me guess… that money is running out."

Her silence speaks volumes.

"Unbelievable," I say as I grab my coat off the back of chair and put it on. I need to get out of here. I need to get away from the very person who should never have even thought to do this to me. But there is one last thing I need to ask her before I go… "Are you even sorry?"

She holds her head high, nothing but a hard look in her eyes. "I did what I had to do, and when you've seen sense, you'll realise that too."

"Except it hasn't panned out the way you wanted, has it? The guy I married is broke and I'm working as a goddamn maid to make sure I keep a roof over my head. I gave up my hopes of a career because you were too selfish to let me forge my own path."

"He was a good man once, and he can be again. You just have to work a bit harder to make it happen."

Fucking hell. She's not got a clue.

I don't say another word as I leave, shutting the door quietly behind me and making my way to the park to try and process the shitshow that is my life.

I sat in that park for hours, but the only conclusion I kept coming to is that my mother and father just wanted what was best for them and fuck the consequences. Having already grieved the loss of my parents' love, I just became numb. Numb to them, numb to Derrick, numb to anything to do with my personal life. It didn't even hurt like it should have, because they'd already hurt me previously. It was more like the final nail in the coffin. So, I made my plan, and I will see that plan through. I have to. For me, and only me. I blocked out that conversation with my mother, we've put a fake front over it, and this is the first time in a long time that I've let myself remember it for what it is—a fucking betrayal.

And yes, I may have let Derrick fuck me back when I was truly trying to give the marriage a shot, but it meant nothing. I felt nothing. It was just sex—really crappy sex.

I know people would judge me for that alone, but they haven't lived my life. They wouldn't have the first idea about how I've felt and dealt with all the crap thrown my way. They don't get to belittle me because I don't tell them anything. It's easier that way. Celeste is the only person I've ever truly let in, and it will stay that way until I'm able to work through all of the emotions stored up inside me and really let them go.

I'll get there, but for now, I need to cook this food for Derrick, and then I can retire to bed, where I'll dream of a future that looks a little less dark.

Chapter Five

ELISE

Room twenty-nine.

I've stood outside it for the last five minutes. It's on my list for today. Bugger. I already double checked with the schedule coordinator to make sure it definitely required housekeeping this morning, and they confirmed that it does.

I hope that means he's vacated the room and isn't in there in all his manly glory to make me feel like a goddamn teenager with a crush.

With a deep breath, I open the door and see the room is empty. That means nothing though, as I thought it was empty the other day, so I strain my ears and listen for any sounds coming beyond the bathroom door. I wait several seconds, but there's nothing.

Okay, get in, get out. Simple.

I have no idea why I'm acting so bloody erratically about this guy, but the sooner I'm out of here, the better it'll be for my bloody sanity.

I quickly strip the bed, noticing another three condom wrappers on the side table as I do. It figures he'd be a bit of a player. I can see why women would fall at their feet for him—hell, I almost had myself.

I gather the wrappers and throw them in the small bin next to the side table. Why on earth they couldn't manage to throw them in the bin themselves, I have no idea, it's not even that far to go, for goodness' sake. I go about my business, making everything clean and fresh, admiring how the room seems to glisten now I'm done. Feeling pleased with myself, I gather up my supplies and make my way to the door, only for it to open and fly straight into me. I let go of everything I'm holding, and it splatters to the floor as I struggle to remain upright.

"Shit," I blurt out as I struggle to regain my balance and start to fall backwards. I close my eyes, waiting for the inevitable thump to sound as I hit the floor, but it doesn't come. Instead, I feel a body behind me, arms going around me, and the distinct feel of someone's breath on the side of my neck as they hold me in position.

And not just anyone's breath. Not just anyone's arms. Not just anyone's fucking body.

His.

It's him.

Tingles shoot down my spine from the contact. My cheeks feel like they're on fire. My legs want to give out and allow me to collapse against the man behind me, and my heart is racing like never before. Time seems to stop as his arms tighten a little around my waist and he makes sure I'm standing upright.

Fucking breathe, Elise.

I expect him to let go, but he doesn't. Instead, he keeps his body pressed against my back and puts his lips by my ear to whisper, "Careful, buttercup."

Buttercup? Never thought that could sound hot, but coming from him, it absolutely does.

"I'm so sorry," I say breathlessly as I pull my body from him, even as it screams for me to stay pressed against him. I put my head down and glue my eyes to the mess on the floor, to see that some of the cleaning products have leaked amidst the cleaning cloths, and the rubbish bag has managed to land upside down, the contents in a pile at my feet. How the hell did I manage to make this much mess from a door knocking into me?

I drop down and crouch as I scurry to grab everything and try not to cry from sheer embarrassment.

But then he crouches too, in front of me, placing his hand on top of mine as it reaches for one of the dusting cloths. I freeze, my eyes on the back of his hand. His very nice hand that adorns a simple single silver ring, and I realise that I've never studied someone's hand so intensely in my whole life. I've never seen a hand as attractive, but his definitely is. *Good God, I'm a hot mess.*

"Elise." He says my name with authority, and my head snaps up to look at him. Fuck me, his eyes are so beautiful I could get lost in them. "It's my fault," he continues, his thumb now starting to run back and forth over my hand. "I shouldn't have opened the door so quickly."

Why is he running his thumb over my skin?

Why is he being so nice right now when I'm the one that's made a mess?

Why is he blaming himself?

"I apologise," he finishes, and damn me for feeling my eyes well up. "Are you okay?" The look of concern on his face has the tears pushing from my eyes and down my cheeks.

"I'm fine," I say with a shake of my head as I quickly pull my hand from his and stand up. "I'm sorry, I'll get someone to come and clean this up, I just have to…" I let my voice trail off as I turn for the door and rush out, leaving the mess behind, along with the first man to show me any sort of kindness in… well, ever.

I feel like an absolute fool as I tear down the hallway and head for the stairwell rather than the lift. I can't be waiting around when I'm in this sort of state, the other guests wouldn't like it. Hell, he may not have liked it, but I couldn't hold back. I couldn't contain the sheer emotion that bubbled up within me from his actions. Simple actions. Compassionate actions. From a guest. Fuck my life. Is this really what it's come to? Is this really who I have become?

I race down the steps, willing them to carry me faster to the staff toilets. We have to use the designated toilets for staff, the closest to me being on the second floor, and I wish it were bloody closer as I make it down the fourth set of steps. Two more to go.

"Elise," I hear shouted from above, and damn me, I pause and look up, only for my eyes to collide with his.

"I'm fine, thank you, I just need to do something," I manage to say before I resume my steps. Two more flights of stairs and I'll be on the right floor. I block everything out as I pull the door to the second floor open when I reach it and rush along the corridor, being careful not to plough into any guests. I know I'll be in deep shit for my behaviour, but I fail to care at this moment in time.

When I burst into the toilets, I go to the end cubicle and lock the door behind me. And then I let it all out. I let myself cry. I allow myself this moment to just fucking hurt. I thought I was done with the hurt, but something feels like it's slicing through my heart and reminding me how helpless I've really been all of these years. I sob for the young girl who took the wrong path and never had the right people in her life to guide her. I have some kind of breakdown in the middle of my shift, and I can't for the life of me stop it.

"Elise, is that you?" I hear from the other side of the cubicle door, and I inwardly groan. Hayley. My boss. Bitch boss, to be accurate.

"Yes," I manage to squeak out, as I desperately try to rein in my emotions once again.

"Could you come out here, please." She may be saying please, but really, she doesn't mean it. She's the most uncaring woman I've ever met, apart from my mother, for obvious reasons. I grab some tissue and wipe my face before opening the door, to be met with the ice-cold exterior of Hayley. Oh boy. This is all I need.

"What on earth is going on?" she asks as she stands there with her hands on her hips and one of her feet tapping impatiently on the floor. She's only a few years older than me, so you'd think we might have some things in common, but I quickly found out that she lived and breathed her job, and I concluded from her chilly manner that we would never be friends.

"I'm sorry, I just needed a minute," I say, and she scoffs.

"You just needed a minute," she repeats. "On work time."

"I didn't mean to—"

"Whatever is going on outside of these walls needs to be left there. There is no room for error, or for guests to see you in this state."

"I apol—"

"I don't want to hear your excuses. I will be docking your pay by fifteen minutes for the inconvenience."

"Please don't do that," I plead. I need every penny, and fifteen minutes will be money taken from my savings.

"Don't beg, Elise," she bites. "It's most unladylike." And then she turns and walks to the door, but before she pulls it open, she says, "Clean up your face and get back to work. I don't pay you to be sniffling in the toilet." Then she's gone, the door closing loudly behind her.

"Bitch," I whisper, feeling more angry than upset after that little showdown. Although, it can't really be called that, seeing as she didn't let me get a fucking word in.

I go to the sink and turn the tap on, leaning over to splash some cold water on my face. It doesn't matter how much water I splash on there, it's not going to cure my puffy red eyes, and I don't have any make-up on because I don't wear it to work, so I can't even try to hide it with anything. I'll just have to look like a wreck for the remainder of the day.

With a sigh, I make my way out of the toilets and back down the corridor, to return to the floor I was working on. As I walk near the lift, it opens, and out walks the man who made me crumble—through no fault of his own.

He stops and stares, and I feel a small smile grace my lips, in appreciation of his kindness.

And what does he do?

He winks at me. Fucking winks at me, sending all of my lady parts into chaos. And then he walks out of the lift and turns to go down another corridor.

Huh. I wonder where he's going? His room isn't on this floor. But I shake my head and realise that it's none of my damn business.

I push the door for the stairwell and make my way back up to the seventh floor, thinking about how I'm going to end up staying late tonight, to make up for those fifteen minutes, and hopefully add a few more.

Chapter Six

DORIEN

She's like glass. Fragile.

I've never been a fan of glass.

It's not a challenge to break.

But something tells me there's a fire inside of her that is yet to be coaxed out.

And I'm going to enjoy being the one to light it.

Chapter Seven

ELISE

My back aches and my feet hurt, but I stayed and made up for my fifteen minutes, and worked an extra two hours after that. I'm exhausted, but it's kept my mind busy and kept me away from home for a little longer, so it's not all bad. I know I'll be going home to a whinging husband, because how dare I stay to work late and not have time to go shopping and cook him dinner, but fuck it, I need the money.

I take the last rubbish bag to the chute and throw it in, looking to the window to the left of me, seeing that the stars are shining brightly, glittering, looking so beautiful. I appreciate the little things. The simple things. The true beauty of things that other people take for granted.

It helps me in ways I can't explain. The world is such a wonderful place, if you just take a moment to really look at it.

I wrap my arms around me and walk along the corridor, ready to get my things and go home. Home… shame it doesn't feel like that. I'm a maid at work, and I'm a maid in my own house. It's pretty much all I do. Pity party for one over here.

I go to the ground floor and into the staff room where my locker is and open it, taking out my bag and changing into my trainers. I close my locker and turn around, only for the door to fly open abruptly. Oh great, it's Hayley. As if I needed to have a run-in with her again today.

"Elise, you're still here, thank God," she says, and for the first time since I've worked here, she sounds somewhat relieved by my presence.

"Is something wrong?" I ask, my brows furrowing.

"Yes. I need you to stay," she informs me.

"What? Why?" I question. She's asked me on a couple of occasions before to stay, but never with the same urgency.

"I need an extra pair of hands to waitress a private function, and I need the room cleared after."

"I've already worked an extra two hours tonight and I'm beat," I tell her honestly.

"I'll pay you double time."

Okay, that's got my attention. "And how long would you expect me to stay?"

"I don't have a cut off time. The party could go on for a while."

"I don't know—"

"Triple time and I'll have a room free for you to stay in once it's all finished and cleaned up," she says, cutting me off.

Triple fucking time and a bed to sleep in after? Jesus, she must be desperate.

"Why the urgency?" I ask, because my curious mind needs to know. It's not like she's doing a favour for me, I'm well aware that I am a mere speck in her world.

"Because it's for the directors of the hotel. Everything has to go smoothly. And as much as I don't want this to go to your head, you're the best cleaner I have here," she admits, and I can't stop my mouth from dropping open. Well fuck. "So, is that a yes?" she continues, pushing for an answer.

"Wait a minute," I say as I realise that she didn't just ask for a cleaner. "Did you say you needed a waitress too?"

"Yes."

"Don't you have agency staff for that?" I ask.

"I do, but to get someone here in the next half an hour is going to be a challenge."

"But I'm just a cleaner."

"So be more than a cleaner for one night," she says, and there's a different look in her eyes... like she can almost see that I could be more, be better... but I quickly shake my head from side to side and dismiss that idea. She's as cold as ice and is only doing this to save her own arse from the big boss man.

Triple time is something I can't afford to turn down, and I also wouldn't need to tell Derrick about the extra money either. Not to mention I'd get a night away from him, on my own, once I'd finished working, of course.

"So, is that a yes?" Hayley says, interrupting my thoughts.

"It's a yes," I tell her, and I see the hint of a smile on her lips, but she quickly schools her face and puts her icy exterior back in place.

"Good. Now, follow me to my room and we'll get you into something more appropriate for the party. You can hardly serve drinks in a maid's uniform."

"Oh... uh... okay... but I need to call my husband first," I stammer, completely thrown off by the turn of events.

"You have two minutes. I'll wait outside." And then she turns and walks out, closing the door behind her as I dig my phone out of my bag.

"I'll only need thirty seconds," I mumble as I press the call button and wait for him to get his lazy arse off the sofa to answer the damn phone. Eight rings later, he's managed it and grunts down the line.

"Who is it?"

"It's me. I'm just phoning to say that I won't be back tonight, they've asked me to work late and do clean up after a party, and they're giving me a room for the night because they don't know what time it will finish," I ramble.

"What? What about me? I'm fucking starving, Elise."

I roll my eyes at his predictable response. "There's a pizza in the freezer, I'm sure you can manage to turn the oven on," I respond sarcastically.

"Fine," he grits out.

"See you tomorrow."

"Whatever," he says before he cuts the call, and I turn my phone off and throw it into my bag, which I quickly put back in my locker.

A night away from Derrick is like heaven, even if it is for work.

I open the door and walk out to see Hayley on her phone, tapping away as she waits for me.

"Oh good, you're ready. Let's go," she says, and then I'm following her down the corridor and to the lifts. I know she's on the first floor, so she's close enough to the reception area for any problems that may arise with check-ins and customer complaints.

We ride the lift in silence, and when the doors ping open, I scuttle along after her like a good little worker.

She stops outside room number three and unlocks it with her key card, announcing, "Welcome to my humble abode," as we enter.

Humble abode? Yeah right.

It's as magnificent as the rest of the hotel rooms, but slightly bigger than the rooms I usually clean, with two doors to the right rather than just one for a bathroom—probably because the room is like a mini apartment, except there's no kitchen. We're in the lounge area, and I know the other two doors lead to the bathroom and also a separate bedroom.

"Now, I figure we're about the same size, so I'll grab you the appropriate attire for you and then we can get to the penthouse."

"The penthouse?" I ask, shocked, because I've never been to the penthouse before. Shocking, I know, but it's never been listed on my cleaning duties, and there is no other way I'd ever get to go in there.

"Yes, Elise. The penthouse. That the directors use when the owner allows." She stares at me pointedly and says, "Please close your mouth, you look like you're trying to catch flies."

I promptly shut my mouth and she opens the door to, I presume, the bedroom and waltzes inside, appearing a few moments later with an armful of clothes, and a pair of shoes on top.

She stops in front of me, holding the items out for me to take, and then she ushers me into the bathroom to get changed. I sure hope this shit fits.

Five minutes later, I am surprised that it does, perfectly, so Hayley was spot on about us being the same size. My maid uniform lies on the floor beside my feet as I stare at the difference a nice outfit makes. The white shirt covers my modesty but hugs my curves beautifully, while the skirt with a minimal slit just above the knee pairs nicely with the sheer tights and the black high heels.

"Are you done?" I hear Hayley shout—as patient as always, I see.

"Yeah," I call back, and the door opens as she walks in and takes in my appearance.

"Better," she states before she's behind me and taking my hair out of the clip that keeps it off my face and proceeds to fluff it before grabbing a brush.

"Uh, I can do my own hair, you know," I tell her as she fusses around me.

"We don't have much time and I need you to look like you belong," she tells me, to which I scoff.

"Gee, thanks for the pep talk," I reply sarcastically.

"This is serious, Elise. The directors are the ones who control everything around here, and if they don't see everything as being up to scratch, then they have the power to make changes, and I'm sure we all want to keep things the way they are."

I get the impression she's talking about the possibility of jobs being lost if they don't approve, and I sure as shit don't need the stress of trying to find something else—I'm guessing she doesn't either.

"Just a touch of make-up and then we can go," she says as she pulls open some drawers, taking out whatever she intends to put on my face.

"Aren't there spare waitress uniforms for me to wear?" I question, because it seems strange that she would dress me in her personal clothes.

"There would be if the agency staff returned the items as

requested," she retorts, clearly annoyed, and I decide to keep my mouth shut and not ask anything else. Who am I to question the way she does things? She must be well thought of, because she's been here as long as I have, and to my knowledge has never been reprimanded for anything.

Ten minutes later, I'm looking at a very different version of me. I haven't worn make-up in years, not seeing the need to bother anymore, and the result is... I look like the old me again. The one where the light was still in her eyes and she had a zest for life, despite the constant guilt from her parents. That version of me had hope. She had drive. And I know that she still lives inside of me, urging me to be who I want to be and not the shitty version I've been moulded into.

"Right, let's go," Hayley announces, like I'm not having some sort of fucking epiphany. "Now, Elise," she shouts from the other room, and I quickly rush out, wobbling a little on the heels as I do, because it's been a fucking lifetime since I last wore a pair of shoes that weren't flat. "Sort that out before we get there. The last thing I need is for you to fall flat on your face," she comments, but I don't have time to reply as she marches forward, a woman on a mission it seems, whilst I concentrate on not toppling over. "Quick, quick," she quips.

It's like the next ten minutes are a blur as we get in the lift to go to the penthouse and Hayley fills me in on everything I need to know. No sooner has she finished speaking and the doors of the lift open, and then she walks me down a short hallway and opens a door, which leads straight into a large room, massive actually, already filled with people.

"Don't screw this up, Elise," she warns me, before she's walking into the room and disappears into the crowd.

Right then. *Show time, Elise.*

Chapter Eight

DORIEN

Business functions bore me, but I have to be here to show my face and smile at all the smug arseholes here that will be hoping for a share of the millions I have stowed away in the bank, and I smirk on the inside knowing that they won't see a fucking penny more than I deem necessary.

I don't usually hang around at the hotels I'm in the process of merging my company with for long when I visit, so as soon as this is done, I'm out of here. Everything seems to be running perfectly, and the hotel manager, Hayley, has shown that she does indeed run a tight ship. Something she promised me she would continue to do when I become the sole owner of The Blue Diamond chain, like she is guaranteed the job. And speak of the devil…

"Dorien," she says, her pouty mouth pulling into a smile as her eyes lock with mine.

"Hayley." I give her a polite nod in greeting. She seems to be good at her job, but that's as far as it goes, no matter how much she's liked to try and fucking flirt with me when I've visited.

"Everything is running smoothly," she informs me.

"I can see that," I state, because why is she stating the obvious? "It's what you're paid for."

"Oh, yes, of course," she mutters, the smile fading a little. "I just wanted to let you know."

"Noted." I have no inclination to have a conversation, getting through the evening is bad enough without catering to Hayley's need for confirmation she's doing a good job.

"I'll just…" Her voice fades off as she starts to walk backwards, and then she's disappearing between the groups of people.

There are many well-known guests in here, as well as potential investors, and of course, the directors. I've been in this game long enough to know that they're only here to try and line their own pockets, and unlike them, I don't need the money, and I don't need the status—in fact, I keep my face out of the limelight as much as possible, because I don't like people and I don't need the drama that people bring. I've never been introduced to the staff here, there has been no reason to be, not at the moment, because until this merger goes through, there is no need for me to know their names or what part they play in the running of the hotel. But when I take ownership of this chain, I'll be making it my business to know certain staff members… My mind drifts to the maid in my room earlier today, the same one that turned up the other morning and almost took my fucking breath away.

The one I know has a fire inside of her.

The one I want to break.

The one with the dark brown hair that was tied back, had curves that would feel fucking fantastic to run my hands over, and those eyes… like deep pools to the ocean. Simply stunning.

And the one that is walking through the penthouse right fucking now, carrying a tray of champagne and looking like she would rather be anywhere else but here. That makes two of us.

I watch from the side, hidden by the dimness of the lighting.

She's wearing make-up. She doesn't need it, but fuck does it make those lips look plumper than they already are. And her hair is down, framing her face perfectly. Don't even get me started on those long legs and that skirt that shows off the roundness of her arse. Lord, give me strength.

As she nears where I'm standing, I move through the sheer black curtains that cover the open doors behind me and onto the balcony, stepping to the side so I'm hidden in the shadows and away from prying eyes that may venture out here and come over to make meaningless small talk with me.

I have no intention of letting Elise Woods know I'm about to be the owner, not until I've had my wicked way with her, anyway.

I take in the night air, breathing deep and wishing this night would just fucking end already. I need to bury myself in a woman and forget about the stress that plagues my life. It's how I deal with things. Fuckboy, hardly. I'm thirty-nine years old and do what the hell I want, when I want, and I answer to nobody. I keep my private life private. I have one close friend who has been in my life since high school, and also his wife—the family I chose. I fucked my actual family off years ago when they made it clear they only wanted to know me for the money I could pass on to them when they were strapped for cash. I had a mother that didn't love me as she should, and a father that drank himself to death at the ripe old age of fifty. Stupid fuck. I had no role models. I made myself who I am today. I lived in a shitty neighbourhood and was bullied daily as a kid, having to try and defend myself even though I was scrawny and packed about as much punch as a wet fish. I craved my parents' acceptance for years, until one day, before my father died, I heard them talking about me. They saw what I was doing in the world of business, and they wanted a piece of my pie. They took money from me when they claimed they were desperate, and like an idiot, I fell for it, because they were my parents and I loved them. But after hearing them talk about me as nothing more than their cash cow, I checked out, and I haven't spoken to them since—well, my mother, seeing as my father is no longer around.

I went to my father's funeral, but I only observed from afar. I watched as he was lowered into the ground, my mother stood to the side with a stoic look on her face, and only three other people to grieve the passing of a waster.

So when I say I need to relieve my stress, I mean in the business sense. Sex makes me forget, so if I want to fuck a woman three times in one night, then I will. But I always remain discreet. I only ever fuck them in hotels, none of them getting to come back to my home. And I never give them my name, preferring to eat their pussy to keep them from continually asking.

Some may call me damaged. I call me realistic.

If you don't let people close, then they can't fucking hurt you.

And the last thing I would ever do is let a woman in to screw me over. So, I screw them and then move on. One night is all they get, and my arrangement has served me well for the past… well, a long time.

A pair of heels clicking grabs my attention, and I turn my head to see the beauty I've been fantasising about since Monday morning walking through the open double doors. She's looking straight ahead and goes over to the balcony railing, her hands now free of the tray that was carrying the drinks I saw her with just moments ago as she grips onto that railing and takes a deep breath.

I become fucking mesmerised by her actions. The way her head tilts up slightly, the way her hair falls down her back, slight wisps moving in the gentle breeze. The way her hands mould around the railing, and the way her eyes close as she inhales.

A devilish thought occurs to me, but… do I dare?

It seems I do as my feet move quietly of their own accord, careful not to alert her to my presence, and I thank fuck for the curtains covering the open doorway.

I sidle up behind her, until I am inches away from touching my chest to her back. Her scent is like some kind of fucking nectar as I breathe it in, and then I make my move before I frighten the shit out of her, placing my lips next to her ear and saying, "I didn't expect to see you here, Miss Woods." And then I quickly realise my mistake as she jumps and shrieks at the same time, her body jolting forwards as my hands land on her hips to steady her—well, that's the excuse I will use anyway, but the reality is that I just wanted to fucking touch her.

"Calm down, buttercup," I soothe, my lips returning to her ear and my body pressing lightly against hers.

"You scared me," she whispers, but she doesn't sound scared. She sounds… breathless, in a good way.

"You never know who lurks in the shadows, Elise," I say, my voice low. I can feel her body tense at my words, her back going straight, and I push my chest against her a little more. Christ, she fits against me like a goddamn glove.

"What are you doing?" she asks, still whispering.

I smirk at her question. "Warning you about the dangers of the dark."

"I need to get back to work," she says abruptly as she pushes herself back against me more, trying to move away, but all she does is push her arse against my dick, and I groan deep in my throat, my hands still on her hips, holding her in place.

"Room twenty-nine in thirty minutes," I say before I let go and step back from her, my hands already itching to be back where they were a few seconds ago, but preferably on her bare skin rather than her fully clothed self.

She whirls around with her eyes wide. "I can't do that, I'm working."

"And I'm a paying guest that needs room service," I tell her.

"But… but…"

"But nothing, Elise. Thirty minutes, and don't keep me waiting." With that, I turn and walk away, confident enough to know that she'll come.

Chapter Nine

ELISE

What the hell was all that about? What bizarre universe am I in?

A gorgeous guy is showing me attention, albeit a very small amount, but still, he's making me feel… awkward, uncomfortable, and worst of all, desired, like he wants me in ways he'll never be able to have me. I don't know how he's managing it, but I'm pretty sure he's good at getting women into bed, if the condoms on the nightstand the last two times I've cleaned his room are anything to go by.

He's older than me, for sure, and he's definitely so far out of my league that it's laughable. I don't even know the guy's name. And let's not forget the fact that I am fucking married, even if I can't stand my husband.

There is no way I'm going to his room in thirty minutes.

No way at all.

Chapter Ten
DORIEN

Thirty minutes.

That's what I told her. And she hasn't shown up, but I tell myself that she'll be here any second now. And if for some reason she isn't, then I'll go and fucking find her.

Chapter Eleven

ELISE

The party finally comes to an end at half twelve, and the last guest leaves five minutes later. I was on pins as the night went on, expecting the mystery guy to show up and rat me out for not going to his room, like some kind of booty call—which I guess is what he wanted. I may think he's gorgeous, but there is no way I want to be another notch on his bedpost, it's not something I would do, and that would apply even if I wasn't married… I think.

I throw my hands in the air as my mind spins with questions, doubts, and ridiculous answers.

"You did good tonight, Elise," I hear Hayley say as she enters the room, looking just as perfectly put together as she did at the start of the night. Meanwhile, I probably look as frazzled as I feel, the tiredness creeping over me now that the night has ended.

"Here," she says as she stops in front of me and thrusts me a key card. "Room number fifteen is yours until the start of your shift tomorrow morning at eight."

I take the key card and refrain from groaning at the thought of how knackered I'll be all day tomorrow. Dead on my feet is what I'll be.

"I trust that you'll have all of this cleared up before you retire to your room?" she questions, but we both know it's not really a question at all.

"Yes," I tell her, and she gives me a satisfied nod in return.

"Your maid's outfit is in the bathroom, ready for you to change into, and you can make sure my clothes are taken to the laundry room and cleaned tomorrow," she orders.

"Sure thing," I respond, stifling a yawn.

"Eight a.m. sharp, Elise," she barks at me as she waltzes away and opens the main door that we came through at the start of the night, disappearing from sight seconds later as she closes it behind her, leaving me on my own to work my magic on this room. She didn't even look like she'd done a full day's work with her blonde hair still perfectly in place, not a hair falling out of the bun she seems to prefer, and her make-up looking just as it did first thing this morning.

I sigh and look around at the many empty glasses and platters of food that have been half-eaten. I best get to work so I can go to my room and get a decent night's sleep without Derrick's snoring interrupting me intermittently throughout the entire night.

I start to collect plates up and take them through to the kitchen area which is at the end of the main room, where I begin to place them in piles on the side before I load the first lot in the dishwasher. It's going to take about three loads to complete it all, and then I guess I'll have to stay to dry it and put it away, otherwise Hayley will be on my arse first thing in the morning.

Once all the plates have been stacked, I load the dishwasher and set about collecting any rubbish lying around as my mind wanders to the handsome stranger that I just keep seeming to run into this week. If he were a regular guest, surely I'd have seen him before now?

My thoughts are halted as the lights go out and the whole apartment is shrouded in darkness, save for the very dim moonlight coming in from the open doors to the balcony. I opened the curtains a little while ago, to let some fresh air filter through as the bodies began to disperse.

"Shit," I curse quietly as I reach out in front of me to try and feel my way around to get to the phone which sits just beside the large TV on the very far wall. Although, if the power is out, there's no point in trying to use the phone.

I've never been scared of the dark, it's just frustrating that I don't know my way around this place well enough to go and alert the reception that maintenance need to get up here, if they don't already know, of course.

I seem to be doing okay as I continue to try and get to the phone, just to check that it isn't working before I attempt to find my way out of here.

I walk a few more steps, my eyes straining to try and make out any shapes at all, and then I feel my toe hit something and I curse out loud, my leg giving way as I begin to tumble to the ground. I close my eyes, holding my hands out in front of me and waiting for the impact of my body hitting the floor, but it doesn't come. Instead, two arms wrap around me from behind and haul me backwards until I'm standing up straight, my body flush against theirs, my heart beating erratically, and my mind instantly wondering if I'm going to fucking die in this room, because what the hell?

"Shhh," is whispered in my ear, and my heart nearly fucking stops.

It's him, again.

What is his deal?

I breathe in and out as he holds me there and I wait to see what the hell he thinks he's doing.

"You didn't come to my room," he says in a low voice, his breath making my skin prickle.

"I told you I was working," I reply, and damn me for sounding all breathy and shit. Ugh.

"Not good enough."

"We don't all have the luxury of money, Mr Whateveryournameis," I respond before I can stop myself, and I immediately want the ground to swallow me up, but then I remind myself that he's the one that's come in here and put his hands on me. He's the one holding me against him right now, invading my personal space. He's a guest where I work, but I don't have to be treated like this. It is not in the fucking job description.

So why aren't I pulling away?

Why am I still stood in his arms, with his breath continuing to tickle my skin?

"I don't like being stood up," he says, his lips now whispering over the shell of my ear as I fight my body's urge to just melt against him.

Is this what I have become? Craving the attention of a complete fucking stranger who could be a goddamn serial killer? He could be anything, and here I am, letting him touch me, hold me, and make me feel things I haven't felt… ever.

Christ, what am I doing?

"I didn't stand you up, I had to work," I tell him, butterflies swirling around inside me as one of his hands moves to lay flat on my stomach. "What is this? What are you doing? And who the hell are you?" The questions rush out of me all at once, and I suddenly find I need all the answers.

"So many questions, Miss Woods…"

"It's Mrs," I whisper.

Silence descends.

Seconds tick by.

Did he hear me? But I already know the answer to that as I can feel the tension in his body.

Oh Christ, is now the part where he goes deranged psycho killer on me because this isn't going to go the way he planned?

What was the plan?

Is he going to hold me here all fucking night?

I'm about to ask that very question, but then I'm being hauled backwards as he moves to the balcony, pushing me out until I get to the railing where he turns me around and cages me in with his arms either side of me.

"You're married?" he questions.

"Yes," I answer pathetically, wishing I could give any other answer instead, and I feebly hold up my hand to show him my ring. He stares at it, like it's the most vile thing he's ever seen—and I'd have to agree with him. I usually don't wear it during work hours, with the excuse that I don't want to lose it or damage it, but really, it's because I can't stand wearing it. It's usually hidden in the pocket of my uniform, but tonight I had to put it on when I changed from my maid's uniform to the clothes that Hayley gave me to wear, because I didn't have time to put it in my locker and there are no pockets in the skirt I'm wearing.

"Do you love him?" he asks, and I drop my hand and frown, because that was not at all what I was expecting.

"What?"

"I said, do you love him?" he repeats.

"I'm sorry," I begin with a shake of my head. "Do I know you from somewhere previously and my mind has just decided to forget? Because you ask pretty personal questions for just being a stranger."

"The first time I ever saw you was on Monday," he confirms.

"So what is this about? Why does it seem like I keep running into you? Why have you come here now? And why did you want me to come to your room? Because, and forgive me if I speak out of turn seeing as you're a paying guest here, I am struggling to understand what the hell is going on," I admit, my confusion and frustration getting the better of me.

"I'm a man that goes after what he wants, Elise, and what I want is you," he says, not stuttering, no timidness, just the straight up truth. I don't even know why I feel he's telling the truth, because I don't even fucking know him—hell, I still don't even know his name. But something inside of me seems to want to trust his words. Trust his truth. Trust that this is real.

Oh my god, I need to get a damn grip. This is madness. He's got me pinned against the railing, and he could quite easily be a psychopath and throw me over the damn side so I plummet to my death, but again, I know that he won't do that.

Call me fucking crazy.

"We don't even know each other," I say, voicing my thoughts.

"Do we need to?" he counters.

"What?" I whisper, but he doesn't answer, and instead he just stares at me, his eyes penetrating mine.

Do we need to know each other?

Do I need to know his name?

Can I really do this?

I'm fucking married. But I don't love him, never have. Forced to wear a ring to please my parents. Forced to live a life I hate.

Don't I deserve a little fun? A little crazy? A fucking orgasm that I haven't given myself?

Haven't I suffered enough?

Haven't I given enough?

Don't I deserve to be selfish just this once?

"Are you married?" I ask, because I'm stalling while my mind continues to argue with itself.

"No."

"Girlfriend?"

"No."

"Explain the empty condom packets then," I say before I can bite my tongue.

"I like to fuck, Elise."

"Oh." I want to slap myself on the forehead. Fucking oh? My God.

"This would simply be that. A fuck. Sex. No feelings, no emotions, no baggage. Just me and you."

"But I'm—"

"Married. It's why I asked you if you loved him. So, I'll ask again. Do you love him?"

"No," I say quietly.

"Does he fuck you hard and make you scream?"

I should be appalled by his questions, disgusted, in fact, but I'm so fucking wet right now it's ridiculous.

"No," I admit.

"Does he fuck you like he hates you?"

"What does that even mean?" I question, and he smirks.

"You'll find out," he answers, and there's a large part of me that wants to find out right now, but can I really cheat? It's adultery. There is no grey area here. If I do this then I'm an adulterer, and there is no turning back.

"I... I..." I stutter as I struggle to find the words I need, my body at war with my mind. I can feel his chest pressing against mine, his lips so close that if I move forwards even a fraction, we'd be kissing.

My husband has never made my heart pound as much as this guy does. He's never made me wet without touching me. He's never made me breathless from just his words alone.

This is a whole new sensation, a whole new everything.

And the only thing standing between me and this man are my morals.

Do I have morals anymore?

Haven't I crossed an unforgivable line already?

My heart never checked-in when it comes to my marriage, but I've been loyal and worked myself to the bone for Derrick to sit on his lazy arse all day for months. I've already checked out of everything, it's just my body that's still there, not my spirit. My spirit is waiting for me to flee, and it's waiting for me to start living again.

Do I live now? Start early? Put a bounce back in my step?

It's just one night... right?

Chapter Twelve

DORIEN

I can see the tug of war playing out in front of me. Her eyes telling me so many different things as she remains silent.

I wish I could help her, but I can't. She has to make this decision on her own. But it's the first time I've met a woman who is so desperately trying to do the right thing, even if she doesn't love her husband. Most jump on my dick pretty quickly, but she's different. She's torn. And something inside of me wants to repair that tear and make her believe again.

I lean in until my lips are by her ear as I whisper, "If your heart has already checked out, then what have you got to lose?"

"My morals. My dignity. My beliefs," she answers, her voice quiet.

I hear her words, and it makes something twist inside of me. Morals. I have none. Dignity. I own my shit and make no apologies. Beliefs. I lost my belief in anyone but myself years ago. It's just how the dice rolled.

"This world is full of people that hold onto their beliefs until their dying day, but most I've come across are miserable and full of regret, not going after the things they wanted most and putting other people's needs before theirs. And then they throw themselves a pity party on their death bed. I've witnessed it, and I refuse to live it, so I do as I please and fuck what anyone else thinks, because they'll always have an opinion, and someone will always think you're in the wrong somewhere along the line."

I let my words hang in the air between us as I pull back and study her face once more. Her delicate features, her silky hair just begging to be wrapped around my fist as I fuck her ruthlessly from behind.

"I've never thought of it like that," she says on a breath, her eyes looking at me like I just handed her the moon and the fucking stars all at once.

"Well, start, because you only get one life to live, Elise, and from what I can see, you're not living one little bit."

"How do you do that?" she asks in disbelief. "How can you pinpoint what I am without even knowing me or having a proper conversation with me?"

"I'm very good at reading people." She doesn't need any more details, and this is the most conversation I've had with a woman in years. It's as far as I'm willing to take it, too. I don't do pillow talk, and I don't do heart-to-hearts.

"But... if I do... this... with you... then I'll know that I've lied and cheated. I don't know if I could live with that kind of guilt..."

Fuck me, she's killing me here. My dick is ready to impale her, and my head is wondering why on earth I'm still here when it's clearly not something she's totally into.

"I can't answer that for you, Elise," I tell her honestly. Her decisions have to come from her, and from her alone.

"Tell me your name," she says, changing the subject briefly.

"Why?"

"You know mine, so it's only fair I know yours." She's attempting to stand her ground, and I find that I quite like it as she looks up at me with something of a twinkle appearing in her eyes.

"Dorien."

"Dorien," she repeats. "Dorien what?"

"It's not important."

"It is to me," she says, and fuuuuuuck, the way she looks at me as she says it has me wanting to break more of my boundaries than I already have around her.

With a sigh, I shake my head.

"This was a mistake," I say as I push away from her and take a few steps back.

"What?" she asks, like I've just given her whiplash.

"I apologise if I crossed any lines, and I assure you it won't happen again," I say before I turn my back on her and walk away. The door shuts loudly behind me, and I make sure that I restore the electric before I leave the floor and return to my room, suddenly wondering if she may be my first regret in years.

Chapter Thirteen

ELISE

He just walked away from me. Like nothing significant had happened. Like what he said didn't mean a damn thing.

The rage that has been coursing through me all day at work is like an inferno building inside of me, waiting for the moment when it can really blow off steam.

Celeste has asked me several times if I'm all right, but I've just shrugged her off and told her I'm tired after working late last night—which isn't a total lie. I am exhausted, but I have enough anger inside of me that it's been keeping me going all day long.

And now, I get to walk into the house in front of me, to a husband that I wish would just fuck off.

I truly am a horrible person, and yes, I am very aware that I am throwing the most depressing pity-party for myself—much as Dorien implied people did when they refused to go after what they want.

Dorien. Such a striking name, and it really does suit the very striking man.

I don't know why he's had such an impact on me in less than a week, and I guess I'll just put it down to one of life's strange curveballs.

I didn't see him today, and I kept away from room twenty-nine, even though it was on my schedule and I'll most likely go back tomorrow for a bollocking from Hayley. I'll worry about it when it happens, because right now, I fail to care.

I open the front door and close it quietly, kicking off my shoes and padding my way along the hall. But I stop when I hear Derrick muttering and then laughing.

"Grab them, push them together for me, baby," he says, and I frown. What the fuck?

"That's right, now open those legs and show me what you're hiding from daddy."

Daddy?

Open those legs?

The shock running through me leaves me standing on the spot, half scared and half hopeful that he's having an affair and I can end this shitty marriage instead of running away like a lost lamb.

"Stroke it… that's right… up and down… tell me how good that is…" And then I hear him grunt, and I feel the bile rising in my throat.

I walk to the lounge door and peer around, to see Derrick on the sofa, his cock in his hand as he strokes it up and down slowly, his eyes glued to the laptop, and some drool dripping from his mouth. And on the screen is a woman, spread before him, her fingers brushing her pussy as she lies back for him.

"Oh my fucking god," I say out loud, and Derrick immediately lets out a yelp and sits up as quickly as he can, because he's got a stomach that's growing by the day getting in the way.

"Shit, Elise," he says as he reaches over and shuts the laptop screen with a thud. "It's not—"

"What it looks like?" I interrupt. "Because you had your dick out whilst watching some woman play with herself on the damn laptop, Derrick." I look down at the offending penis and make a face. "Fucking put it away, for Christ's sake."

He tucks his todger back into his jogging bottoms and huffs as he pushes himself off the sofa to stand.

"I didn't mean for you to walk in," he says sheepishly.

"Really?" The sarcasm is very apparent in my voice. "Is this what you do when I'm not here? Pay for services like that?" I point to the laptop, disgusted.

"You're home earlier than normal," is his feeble response.

"Oh, I am sorry, I'll just go so you can finish," I say, and I turn on my heel and go back to the front door.

"Where are you going?" Derrick asks as I put my shoes back on.

"Away from you," I spit.

"But you can't just go, what about my dinner?"

I finish putting my shoes on and stare at the utterly selfish bastard as he looks at me with shock and surprise.

His fucking dinner?

Christ, I am the biggest moron to ever walk the face of the earth.

"It's over, Derrick," I tell him, feeling a weight lift from my chest as soon as the words leave my mouth.

"Pfft. You can't leave me."

"I can, and I am. I can't stay in this sham of a marriage any longer."

"Sham? I fucking looked after you, cared for you, gave you a home," he sneers.

And with that, the inferno inside of me blows. "Oh really? And where was the part where you cared for me? Hmm? Where the fuck have you been for the last couple of years whilst I've worked as a goddamn maid to make ends meet? I gave up my dreams when I married you. I gave up my life because my parents made me feel like I had to, and what for? For this shitty existence where I hate coming home to you and where I feel like I'm failing at every turn? An existence where I'm twenty-five years old with no future in sight if I stay here with you? An existence where you jack off to some slut on a laptop while I clean bathrooms and cater to rich people who look at me as if I'm some kind of speck on their shoe?

"I'm fucking done, Derrick. I don't love you, and let's be honest, you've never really loved me, not as a husband should love a wife. This was a mistake from the word go."

My chest is heaving as I release everything that has been pent up inside of me for years. It feels fucking good to unleash it.

"It was a good deal at the time that went bad," he states simply, and those words should hurt, but they don't. They should rip me from the inside out, but they just make me feel freer.

"Never have you spoken a truer word," I say as I turn and open the front door.

"You'll be nothing without me," he shouts as my feet land on the first step.

I pause and turn my head to the side as I say my parting words to him. "You're wrong. I'll be everything without you." And then I slam the door and make my way back to the hotel to try and catch Celeste before her shift finishes. I should make it, she'll be there for another half an hour, and I'll ask her if I can crash at her place tonight.

I walk quickly, the breeze brushing against my face, making me feel fresher than ever before. It's funny how alive I feel even though my marriage has just ended.

Some vows are made to be broken, and sometimes it feels utterly fantastic to break them.

Chapter Fourteen

DORIEN

As I pack my stuff in my suitcase, I feel something of a lead weight deep in my stomach. It's the first time I don't want to just up and leave because of a woman. A woman I haven't even tasted, haven't even forged any kind of connection with... except, I can't stop thinking about her. Elise Woods.

There's something wildly enchanting about her, and it's messing with my mind.

I've thought of nothing but her since last night, and maybe I shouldn't have walked away. Maybe I should have had my wicked way with her and fucked her on that balcony, but like I said before, she's different, and I can't put my finger on why she is the exception to the rule I live by. So, the best thing to do is just to get out of dodge and get back to business.

I put my last items in the suitcase and close it, moving it by the door, ready for when my car service arrives in the next fifteen minutes.

I could go and see if she's here. I could go and get her file from HR and look at every little detail they have about her, but that isn't what I do, not to mention it's bordering on stalker level. It's so unlike me, I'm more of a fuck 'em and chuck 'em kind of arsehole.

A knock sounds on the door and I grab my wallet off the side table, ready to tip the porter who will be taking my case downstairs. I don't need a porter to do it, but this is a high-class hotel and it's the way things are done, not to mention I will own the fucking place soon and every visit here has resulted in me receiving the kiss-my-arse treatment. As far as I'm aware, Hayley is the only member of staff 'in the know' about my possible takeover, so I can only presume that this is just how things are done, and I can see why the rich and mighty choose to come here. It's the fucking arse-licking service they all crave, clearly.

I sigh and open the door, ready to reel off instructions, when I'm stopped in my tracks. Because it isn't the porter at my door. No. It's Elise. She's stood there, her chest heaving, her hair a little wild and some falling from her ponytail around her face.

I'm not sure what she's expecting by showing up here, not after the way things were left last night, but I can only assume she's come to give me a piece of her mind.

I step back and she walks in, closing the door behind her, keeping her eyes on me the whole time.

"Did you mean what you said? That we don't need to know each other to… you know?" She's timid as she speaks, but there's something slightly different in her stance—confidence. It was lacking before, but it's there, simmering under the surface.

I nod at her, wondering where she's going with this. But then her next words almost knock me on my arse.

"I want you to fuck me, Dorien. I want you to fuck me like you hate me. I want you to make me feel nothing but you."

I have no idea what's happened in the last twenty-four hours to turn her head, but she's standing there, opening herself up to me, to this, to us, for one night. And I'm not about to question it.

Chapter Fifteen

ELISE

I didn't even try to find Celeste when I got here. I just came straight to room twenty-nine to see if he was still here, and luckily for me, he is. I have no idea where the words I just spoke came from, but I know I want this. I want him.

My morals have held me back for years, the guilt that plagues me keeping me from leaving Derrick sooner, but the minute I saw him stroking his dick to a woman on a screen, I knew it was my time to put me first.

So, here I am, opening myself up to a complete stranger who I don't know. And I'm okay with that. I don't need flowers and chocolates, or the hassle of dating. There is no romance, not in my life, anyway. What I need is raw passion, one night to do as I please and have a man take control, showing my body just what he can do.

I thought I would feel shame coming here, be embarrassed by my words, but all I feel is free. I'm letting my wings spread, and if that starts with a good hard fuck, then so be it.

He's still looking at me, and a part of me thinks he may reject me and then all of this will have been for nothing. But then, suddenly, he's pushing me against the door, his body flush with mine and his lips so fucking close that I could just push forward and touch them with my own.

"You sure you want this, Elise? Because I'm not about to go easy on you," he says quietly, warning in his voice, as if he is trying to deter me whilst wanting me to stay.

"I want this," I say firmly. "Do your worst, Dorien."

He smirks, and it makes my heart pound. I watch as he takes his phone out of his pocket and hits a few buttons on the screen before putting the phone by his ear. "Cancel the car, and the porter. I won't be needing them," he barks before he ends the call and throws his phone on the table beside the door.

"Buckle up, buttercup," he growls before he stands back and barks, "Get undressed."

I gulp as my hands move of their own accord, going to the buttons on my maid's uniform. I slowly undo each button, focusing on the man in front of me, the one dominating the entire room. And when the last button is undone, he tells me, "Drop it to the floor."

It's like I'm on autopilot as I push the material over my shoulders and let it drop down the bottom half of my body, until it's pooling at my feet, leaving me in nothing but my underwear, socks, and shoes. I inwardly cringe at still having my shoes and socks on, and before he can tell me to remove them, I quickly bend down and do it, kicking my shoes off to the side and throwing my socks right along with them.

"Did I tell you to take your shoes off?" he asks, his face deadpan.

"N... No," I stutter, feeling all kinds of foolish.

"Get on your knees," he barks, and I slowly lower to the ground, my whole body trembling with nerves, and also excitement of what he might do.

"Good girl," he says as he walks towards me and circles me like a predator sizing up its prey. "Take off your bra."

"But..."

"But what, Elise?" he asks as he stops in front of me, looking down on me and making me feel... I'm not sure. Small? No, that's not right. I mean, I want to be here, but how I can already feel the wetness between my legs when he hasn't even touched me? How can I possibly be thinking this is the hottest thing to ever happen to me when he hasn't even done anything but make me get undressed? When he's made me kneel before him?

"I… What about you?" I ask, because I wouldn't mind seeing underneath his clothes before I get naked.

He crouches down, lowering his face until his eyes are level with mine and he's gripping my chin with his fingers and thumb. "Are you questioning me, Elise?"

The power with which he speaks has me replying, "No."

"Good. Then do as you're told and take your fucking bra off."

He lets go of my chin and stands back up, waiting, and there's something inside of me that desperately doesn't want to keep him waiting. I move my hands to the back of me, unhooking my bra and letting the straps fall down my arms, until I'm removing it completely and letting it drop in front of my knees.

My eyes meet his, and I bite on my bottom lip as I see the hunger in his eyes.

Fuck. I've never been looked at this way before. My husband used to just grunt and roughly grab my breasts before putting his dick inside of me and riding his way to the goalposts, leaving me unsatisfied and having to go to the bathroom on more than one occasion to finish myself off. So this is uncharted territory for me.

"Now stand up," Dorien commands, and I push up from my knees until I'm stood to my full height, my back arching a little to show off my breasts, which I know aren't the biggest, but fuck it. I'm here and I asked for this.

"Take off your knickers, Elise, and then get on the bed."

I hesitate momentarily, wondering what he thinks of my body, wondering if I'm good enough, if I'm sexy enough, but then I push back the comments Derrick used to make about me being too small on top and needing to have some work done, and I bend over, pushing the material down my legs and stepping out of them before I make my way to the bed. I have no idea how I even have the strength to do all of this, and I can only put it down to the adrenaline coursing through me.

I sit on the edge of the mattress and wait for his next instruction.

"Move back and spread those legs wide," he says, and I shimmy back on the bed, lying down so I'm looking at the ceiling as I spread myself before him.

"Fuck… already wet for me, Elise," he whispers. "Do you feel how wet you are?"

"Yes," I manage to reply, anticipating the moment he does what I asked and fucks me hard.

I jolt as I feel his finger brush up the middle of my pussy, and my head flies up to look at him as he brings his finger to his mouth and sucks the taste of me from him.

"Jesus…" he says on a breath, and I wonder if that's a good or a bad thing, but he quickly puts my doubts to sleep as he says, "Fucking delicious." And just those two words alone make me feel something akin to pride. Pride about my taste? Dear God, I have been suppressed for far too long.

I watch as he walks around the bed and goes to the side table, where he opens the drawer and pulls out a condom before he's back at the bottom of the bed, looking at me.

His hands go to his trousers, and he undoes them, pushing his boxers down with them until they free his cock. Oh my Christ, he's huge, and I find myself licking my lips in anticipation of how he tastes. He takes his dick his hand and starts to stroke, hardening even more in front of my eyes. I'm mesmerised as he works himself, not an ounce of shyness about his actions.

"Touch yourself, Elise," he says when his eyes connect with mine. "Show me how you get yourself off."

I should be shocked by where this is going, but I fail to give a shit as I move my hand and play with my clit, moving my finger in slow circles because I don't want this to be over too soon. I want to savour this night where I gave myself to a man who I may never see again. No attachment. No expectation.

I moan as watching him touch himself heightens everything I'm feeling, making it more intense, more intimate, more everything. I close my eyes and let my head roll back on the bed as I let out a groan. And then everything becomes more sensitive as I feel his mouth joining my fingers, his tongue connecting with my clit. I nearly jump off the bed from the sensations coursing through me.

"Oh my god," I moan out loud, and then I feel his finger pushing inside of me, moving in and out slowly as we work in sync. My orgasm quickly builds, and just as I am on the cusp of release, he pulls away and pushes my hand off my clit. I'm momentarily confused as I lift my head with wide eyes and look at him.

"No yet, buttercup. Sit up and move to the edge of the bed." He's no longer touching his cock as I move on trembling limbs to the edge, sitting before him, waiting expectantly. Does this make me look desperate? Does this encounter make me look weak because I'm doing everything he's asked of me?

I don't have time to process it as he moves between my legs and grabs his cock, running it along my lips before he says, "Open your mouth."

I think my mouth would have dropped open anyway at his command, and when I part my lips for him, he pushes inside of me and says, "Suck."

I can feel myself getting wetter as I pleasure him with my mouth, and when he moans, fuck, it makes me feel like a goddamn queen.

He grabs my hair, entangling it with his fingers at the back of my head as he fucks my mouth. There are all sorts of gargling noises coming from me as he does, but I don't care. He clearly wants this, and I'm just lost to the moment.

I swirl my tongue at his tip before he hits the back of my throat again and again and again. I breath heavily through my nose as I grab his balls with my hand and massage them. I feel tears pool in my eyes as his grip on my hair tightens to the point where I think he's going to rip it out. And I moan as he releases in my mouth, swallowing everything he gives.

Am I mad? Quite possibly. He could have slept with half of this city for all I know, and he told me he likes to fuck, but again, I'm allowing myself this one wild night to do what my heart and body wants.

He pulls out and quickly pushes me back, burying his face between my legs and using his fingers to pull me apart so he can taste every part of me. And when his tongue plunges inside, his fingers continue to work my clit. I'm panting, grabbing onto the bed sheets as I feel my orgasm take hold again. But just as before, when I am about to crash over that peak, he pulls away, stopping everything. I groan out loud as he lifts me, carrying me over to the floor-to-ceiling windows and opening the sliding door, before he takes me over to the side of the balcony, turning me around so I'm looking over the city below. It's busy, cars moving about, people walking along the pavement, but they have no idea we're up here—not unless they look, anyway.

He bends me, my arms hanging over the railing as he lifts me slightly and plunges his dick inside of me.

"You want me to fuck you like I hate you?" he questions, as he pulls my back flush against his chest, his lips by my ear. "Put your hands behind my neck and don't let go," he tells me, and I link my fingers behind his neck, exposing myself to the whole fucking world—or at least, that's what it feels like.

"Hold on, Elise," he growls as he pulls out and thrusts hard inside me. I bite my lip to stop myself from screaming as he fucks me without restraint, for anyone to witness if they choose to look up here. One of his hands finds my clit, while the other grabs my breast and he pinches my nipple roughly. His lips trace the skin on the side of my neck, and I can do nothing but lose myself to every second of what he is doing to my body.

I bite so hard on my lip that I taste blood. I link my fingers together so tight that I swear I'm cutting off the blood circulation. I move my face towards him, and he captures his lips with mine, plunging his tongue into my mouth at the same pace as he's impaling me on his dick.

And when I feel myself reaching release yet again, I clench around him, praying he doesn't stop it a third time.

He pulls his lips from mine and whispers against them, "Let go, buttercup. Let them hear what I do to you…" And fuck me, it's like a goddamn detonator has gone off as I scream loudly, my orgasm taking hold as his punishing rhythm doesn't let up. Every part of my body feels like it's alive, and right now, I couldn't give a damn if anyone can see me. All I can do is let myself be consumed by the man who releases inside of me seconds later, growling as he does. Not grunting. Growling. And it makes a shiver race across my body.

When he's taken everything from me, I collapse against him, and he carries me back inside until he's laying me on the bed.

And as my eyes begin to close, the sweat pouring off of me from the sheer exertion of what we just did, my mind suddenly reminds me that he never used a condom… but for some unknown reason, I fail to care.

Chapter Sixteen

DORIEN

Two a.m.

Elise has been asleep for the last three hours, and usually, I'd be pissed at a woman falling asleep in the bed I'm sleeping in, because I like them to leave once we've fucked. But Elise... I laid her in the bed and had no thought to try to wake her. And as I sit here, at the table by the window, in nothing but a pair of boxers, I think about how this broken woman came to me and asked me to give her one night. How she stood before me and opened herself up to me, that underlying determination running rampant inside of her.

I wonder what changed her mind, her morals, and the ideals that people have placed on her shoulders.

I wonder why she chose to come to me and help heal whatever plagues her mind.

The way she let me do what the fuck I wanted to her, no stipulations, no backing down, and how she let me fuck her in full view of anyone that looked at the balcony... I've never had an experience like it. The women I've fucked previously have all had reservations about being in open view of others. But her? She seemed to enjoy the thrill of it, her senses and emotions heightened by the experience.

And she's going to be my goddamn employee.

I've never crossed that line before, preferring to keep my business well away from my pleasure. So why the hell did I cross that line for her? And why the fuck didn't I wear a condom as I pounded into her ruthlessly?

I know exactly why. Because without even truly knowing her, I can see a broken form of myself in her. And my mind got caught up in the feel of her, the taste of her, and the fucking depths of her too much to consciously think about protection. Which could be a major fucking problem if she isn't on some kind of birth control. Not to mention the possibility of… I don't even want to think about it right now. I'll deal with it when I see my doctor, later today, because I keep myself checked regularly, despite her being the first woman I've ever forgotten to protect myself with.

Christ, Dorien, this could fuck you right up the bloody arse!

I guess all I can do is wait until she wakes to ask the questions that could possibly make her feel uncomfortable but are necessary.

Chapter Seventeen

ELISE

I groan at the feel of his hands moving my thighs apart. I writhe as his mouth sucks my clit, his teeth nipping gently and his fingers digging into my skin as he holds me in position. My hands move to his hair, gripping him and pulling him closer to me, needing him to give me everything. The growl that tears from him as he fucks me with his fingers and eats me like his favourite dessert makes me heady, delirious, and desperate.

"More," I whisper, pushing my pussy into his face harder and riding his fingers like I would ride his dick.

"More," I repeat, still not feeling like it's enough. And then I feel his finger graze up the middle of my arse, sliding against a spot that has never been touched before.

My eyes fly open and register the darkness. It's still night-time. And as his finger slips over the same spot again, I jerk in response but open my legs wider, lifting my head and looking down to see that Dorien is actually doing the things I believed were a dream.

He pushes his finger against my arse, and I fuck his face faster, needing more friction.

"Dorien…" My voice trails off as he continues to work me into a frenzy, making me want to beg him to just tip me over the edge already.

He doesn't let up as he sucks harder, swirling his tongue around my clit at the same time, adding another finger inside my pussy, and his finger pushing into my arse a little, making me scream his name as my body shudders from his touch. My pussy clenches his fingers, drawing it out, until I'm laid spent beneath him as he covers my body with his. Before I get a chance to catch my breath, he pushes his dick inside me, hooks one of my legs over his hip, and then he pounds into me relentlessly, the mattress sinking beneath us every time he plunges back in.

He moves his lips by my ear and says, "Are you on birth control?" And it shocks me for only a second as I tell him I am, and then he says, "Good," before he fucks me to another orgasm.

I lift my other leg and clamp it around him, opening myself up more, and he roars his release, nuzzling his face in the crook of my neck as my fingers bite into the skin on the tops of his arms, my nails probably leaving marks.

He bites my neck as he slows down, then licks the same spot before placing a gentle kiss there.

"Wow," I say on a breath as he stills on top of me, his dick still inside of me, the last pulses of our combined highs playing out. "That was…" I have no words, and he merely answers with a chuckle.

"You said one night, Elise, and the night isn't over yet," he says, lifting his face from my neck and stealing my breath with a kiss that leaves me needing this night to never end.

Reckless and stupid I might be, but having this man use my body in ways I never imagined is worth every reckless and stupid second.

I'm on all fours on the bed, with Dorien behind me, his dick pounding into me with a punishing rhythm as I grip the bed sheet in my hands.

He's taking everything from me as his one hand plays with my clit, and his other pinches my nipple. His mouth is on my back, his tongue darting out to lick along the tops of my shoulders. Every sensation is just incredible. I've never been fucked like this, ever. I've never had my body used in this way and felt like an absolute queen at the same time.

And when he reaches to the side, I hear him open something, before a cold sensation falls down the centre of my arse.

I jerk unexpectedly, but then his hand is there, rubbing the cold substance between my cheeks, warming it up as he does.

My heart is threatening to beat out of my chest. And it looks like this will be another first for me. I'm too lost in him to think clearly.

"Relax, Elise," he says, his voice surprisingly soothing. I take deep breaths as he slows his thrusts inside of me and I try to calm myself down. "If you want me to stop, then I will, but just remember, one night only… one night to forget everything and just live."

Just live.

I've been existing for so long that I've forgotten what living is like, and with a renewed sense of empowerment, I turn my head to look over my shoulder at him as I say, "Make me live, Dorien."

He smirks as he pushes his finger against my back passage, easing in slowly, and I turn my head back to the bed as I moan with an unexpected pleasure rushing through me.

Fuuuuuuuuck.

"Such a good girl," he says as he pushes in a little more and starts to thrust his dick a little deeper at the same time.

"Oh god," I say on a breath as his actions consume me, taking me far away from the shitty life I've been leading and showing me a whole new kind of world—one I never really thought about. Giving myself to this man has been the most exhilarating thing I've ever done, and when he pulls his finger back out and pushes in, I fucking sigh with satisfaction. He repeats his moves, his dick moving in and out of my pussy at the same time, and his other hand returns to my clit, rubbing in circles, taking me to my most intense orgasm yet.

I scream, I pant, I fucking cry from how good it all feels, before he finds his release and collapses on top of my trembling body.

I close my eyes, letting the tears fall down my cheeks. I'm feeling so much emotion that I barely realise he's moving me until I'm in his arms and being carried to the bathroom, where he starts to run the water, filling the bathtub as I sit on the vanity unit, focusing on keeping myself upright.

When the water has been run, he lifts me and lowers me in the tub, telling me to relax. He leaves me to sink into the water, the bubbles he added surrounding me and soothing my delicious aches.

And I sit back and smile, pushing thoughts out of my head about having to let this man go once the night is over.

Chapter Eighteen

DORIEN

I've tasted this woman several times over the course of the night. I've fucked her, I've licked her, I've done things she's clearly never done before, and I've given her the best fucking night of her life. And in the process, I've probably had the best night of mine too. I don't do feelings and shit, so this is as close to feelings as I get, but she is magnificent, stunning, beautiful.

As she sleeps, her hair fanning over the pillow, her lips swollen from my mouth being on hers, I think about how she did everything I asked and how she enjoyed every single thing I did to her. I may like to fuck, but I also like to make sure the woman I'm with is enjoying every second. I'm not here to make them feel uncomfortable, I'm here to give them a good fucking time, and when it comes to Elise Woods, I'm pretty sure I succeeded.

The way she said "more" the second time we fucked made me feel fucking feral for her. Everything about her is unique, and strangely, it intrigues me more. It shouldn't, but it does, and it's new territory for me.

My eyes roam over her face. She looks peaceful, serene… happy. It says something about her life when she looks happier asleep than she does awake. I wonder what brought her to my door? I wonder why she needed the release that being here gave her? If I were an emotional man, I might ask her, but I'm not, and she has to stay as just a one-night thing. It's what we agreed, and it's what she expects. I've already broken my own rules by drawing her a bath before I laid her in the bed so she could sleep some more, and I broke a fundamental one by kissing her on the mouth. I tend not to do that because it invokes emotion, but fuck, I couldn't resist her plump lips that have been calling to me all week long. I crossed my own lines, and as I sit here, watching her, I feel a sense of unease creep in.

Unease at how easily I could become infatuated by her.

Unease at how easily I could take her to my bed again, and again, and again.

Unease at how easily she could change me from the cold bastard that I am to someone who gives a shit about somebody else.

I've not done that before, and I'm not sure I want to allow it to happen, because my experience of watching others let someone in always seems to cause pain. The only exceptions are Gabriel and Chantel, my family, the ones I chose to let in and who got so fucking lucky to find each other, but their bond is a once in a lifetime thing, and I don't believe that path is for me.

So, when she wakes, I'll ask her to leave, because as the sun rises, it signals the night being over, and it signals the end of our one night together. It has to.

Chapter Nineteen

ELISE

I keep my eyes closed as I stretch my aching muscles, and I allow a smile to grace my face because of why they ache so much.

Last night was truly amazing, and as I open my eyes and blink a few times to adjust to the sunshine beaming through the windows, I feel like this is the start of a brand new me.

Someone who can put herself first for once.

I move my arm across the pillow, and I pause as it brushes against something… a piece of paper.

I quickly turn my head to look, and I see a single white rose placed by a small note. Intrigued, I sit up and look around the room, already knowing that I'm all alone. I gulp and look at the note, picking it up and bringing it in front of me, to read what it says.

Elise,

Last night is a night I will never forget. Truly.

Leaving like this was the last thing I wanted to do, but it was necessary.

Enjoy your life, buttercup. Let them see you smile.

We did say it was only one night, after all, but you may be the first person to make me regret my own rule.

The white rose... a sign of purity and innocence. But to me, a sign of peace, and the only way I can truly show you how it felt to be with you.

Peace. I hope you find yours.

Dorien.

My brows pull into a frown as I read his words over and over again.

Regret my own rule? Does that mean it was a bad thing that he gave me the most intense pleasure I have ever known? Was it so bad that he had to hightail it out of here without saying a proper goodbye?

I stop my thoughts abruptly.

No.

It's none of those things, because I know, deep down, that what happened between us last night was exquisite, amazing, unforgettable—just like he said.

I hold the note to my chest and pick up the single white rose, bringing it to my nose as I inhale.

I read the note again. His words hit me right at my core, over and over.

Peace. It's what I truly crave, what I yearn for, to have a life filled with experience, contentment, all the while being at peace with who I am.

Maybe Dorien was my stepping-stone towards that, and even as my heart sinks at the thought of never seeing him again, I know that he may just have come into my life at the right time. And maybe him leaving is meant to be, too.

Whatever the reason, I will always be able to look back on last night as the start of something new, something exciting, and something that will remain in my memories forever.

And if the next man I may fall in love with, date, or just simply fuck doesn't give me what he did, then I know it's not worth it.

He's shown me what it's like to be worshipped even as he made me kneel and called me a "good girl". It wasn't patronising, it was freeing. Pleasant. Needed.

Elise Woods is going to emerge from this room a less broken woman than she was before she got here.

Chapter Twenty

ELISE

"You did not..." Celeste says as she looks at me with wide eyes over our lunch break. I've just given her a brief rundown of the last twelve hours, and to say she's shocked would be an understatement. "What the fuck, Elise?"

I can't even find it in me to scowl at her, because the smile on my face won't allow me to.

"Damn," she remarks as I sip my coffee. "Well, it's about bloody time. I mean, I know I've been telling you to get some decent sex for years, but... shit, this is like the start of a dirty fucking fairy-tale."

I roll my eyes at her. "Stop it. It was just one night of sex."

"Please, this was not just sex. Look at you... it's like you slept with a fucking hanger in your mouth."

I can't help but laugh at her.

"It's good to see, Elise, and it's long overdue," she tells me, her voice a little softer.

"I know," I agree. "I can't tell you how alive I feel today, despite the way my body aches from what he did."

"I gotta meet this guy," she says, but I know that will never happen. He's gone, and a little part of me will probably forever wonder where he flew off to.

"He won't be back," I tell her.

"You don't know that."

"I do, and that's okay. He gave me an outlet, and for that I will always be grateful." I know deep in my heart that I'll never see his face again. Never get to stare into his eyes as they captivate me in ways I've only ever imagined.

"It's not over, you mark my words," Celeste says adamantly, forever the romantic at heart.

I bypass her comment, because there is no point in trying to convince her otherwise, not when she's as stubborn as they come and will argue that my mystery man will return in the not too distant future.

"I need to ask you a favour," I begin, but she holds her hand up in front of her face to stop me from saying anything else.

"Girl, you don't even need to ask. Of course you can stay with me. We can go pick up your things after work, and you can finally start the ball rolling with divorcing that wanker's arse."

"Wow, you've thought more about this than I have," I say, keeping my tone light.

"I highly doubt that." She gives me a pointed look before she continues. "The sooner you're out of his clutches, the better. And this has been a long time coming."

"It has," I agree. I checked my phone earlier to see if any messages were waiting for me, but there was nothing. Derrick probably thinks I'll stroll through the door later to make him food like nothing happened last night. "Come on," I say with a sigh as I push myself up from the table and grab my rubbish to put in the bin. "Let's get the rest of this shift over with."

The end of my shift came and went, and now I'm stood outside the house that was my home until last night—as much as it could be a home, anyway. I stare at the door, feeling a little of my determination seep away. Celeste is beside me, and she grabs my hand, reminding me that I'm not alone in doing this.

"Let's go," she says softly, and I simply nod at her.

I make my legs move towards the front door, and I push down on the handle as I open it slowly. I can hear the TV on inside as I walk in, with Celeste following me. She stops just inside the doorway, leaving it open and nodding to me. "You've got this," she encourages.

I take a deep breath and give her a small smile. I'm not nervous about this being over, I just can't be doing with the drama that he'll probably start when he realises I wasn't fucking around.

It's funny how by the time I get to the lounge doorway, I feel like a stranger in my own house. But then, I guess I never really thought of it as mine. It's never been a place of comfort. It's just been a place I rest my weary head at the end of the day as I pray my husband doesn't want to try and fuck me, to which I've made excuses for months anyway because I couldn't bear him touching me.

Derrick is in his usual position on the sofa, slouched, with empty food packets littering the place. When he registers me, he smiles. "Oh good, you're home. What's for dinner?"

Christ, he's like clockwork, and I know him far better than he probably knows himself.

"I'm just here to get my things," I tell him, my voice calm.

"Don't be ridiculous. Surely you've gotten your tantrum out of your system by now?" he asks, like he hasn't just belittled me and the way I felt yesterday.

"It's not a tantrum, Derrick, and I'm not here to argue with you. I'm just collecting my things and then I'll be gone," I tell him matter-of-factly.

"For fuck's sake, Elise, you're being unreasonable," he barks as he struggles to get himself sat upright.

"Like I said, I don't want to argue." It's all I say before I turn and walk from the room, making my way to the stairs and passing Celeste as she smiles at me. I quickly get to the bedroom and grab my suitcase from underneath the bed. I've packed two drawers before I hear Derrick shout, "What the fuck are you doing here?" He's never been a fan of Celeste, and that's probably because she's a true friend and wants the best for me, something he never has. I then hear his footsteps coming up the stairs and I empty another drawer before he walks in and watches me in action.

"Elise, this is preposterous, you can't fucking leave me, you don't have anywhere else to go," he barks, but I don't slow my actions. "Your parents will be disgusted with you, you know that as well as I do."

"I couldn't give a shit what they think about me," I tell him honestly, packing another pile of clothes into the case.

"They'll disown you," he continues, as if that would make me stop.

"I'm counting on it," I reply, refusing to show him that a small part of me feels any kind of pain at the thought that my only family will want nothing to do with me, even if they have screwed me over repeatedly.

"What the hell is the matter with you?" he shouts, and I throw another pile of clothes into the case before I turn to look at him, my hands on my hips and my temper climbing.

"I'll tell you what the matter is, Derrick," I say, spitting out his name like it leaves a bad taste in my mouth. "This whole marriage has been a fucking joke from the start. I know all about your little arrangement with my parents. I know all about how they guilted me into marrying you and staying with you to keep them secure financially. I know how you all manipulated me to serve your own purposes. And as if that wasn't enough, my mother then guilted me even more into giving up my dreams to become a fucking maid just so I could support your lazy arse when you got the sack. So, yeah, I know all about how little I mean to any of you, and I really couldn't give a fuck if I never see any of you ever again." I'm shouting by the time I finish, my chest heaving, years of hurt pouring out of me.

"You'll never be anything more than what you are now. A fucking scrubber with no prospects," he sneers, and I snap. I march a few steps towards him and I slap him clean across the face. The sound ricochets around us, echoing off the walls, as he looks at me with alarm.

"You don't know me, Derrick, and you never have. You have no idea what prospects await me."

"I told you before that you're nothing without me."

"I'm nothing *with* you," I shout, meaning every word. "I'd rather be down and out than spend another second living with you."

"You spiteful bitch," he barks, and I roll my eyes. I put a shield around me years ago when his insults first started. It's like water off a duck's back. "You won't get anything out of me. I'll keep the house."

"Clutching at fucking straws there, Derrick," I reply, zipping up my case and putting it on the floor, ready to get the hell out of here. A house is just bricks and mortar, and I have no doubt that in a divorce court, they will see that I have paid more than enough to be entitled to half. But ultimately, bricks and mortar mean nothing to me.

"You'll regret this," he says, his voice low as I walk past him and out into the hallway.

"No, I won't. The only regret I have is marrying you in the first place." And with those parting words, I make my way down the stairs with my suitcase, to see Celeste holding a couple of my coats that were hung up by the front door. I smile at her as we make our way out of the house and away from the toxic relationship I have lived for so long.

This is the end of my nightmare, and I'm ready to fight for my dreams.

Chapter Twenty-One

ELISE

"Okay, people, listen up," Hayley barks at us all as she enters the room with her hands clapping to get our attention—as if her voice alone didn't do that anyway. "We have exactly twelve hours to get this place looking its best. The owner is counting on all of you to have this place spotless, ready for the board members arrival tonight. I expect all hands on deck, no slacking, and no one is to leave until I'm satisfied that the floors sparkle. You will be paid a bonus for working past your shift time to compensate for the last-minute arrivals. Do I make myself clear?"

There are mutterings all around as the maids contemplate what she has said.

"Maybe I didn't make myself clear, but this is not up for debate. If you want to keep your jobs then you will stay and do what is required," Hayley adds on, making more than one of us look at her with a scowl on our faces.

"Is the owner coming too?" a girl at the back asks.

"And that is of your concern because?" Hayley replies, one eyebrow arched. I turn and see the girl shrink back, her face heating with embarrassment. She's new, and she has no idea how acidic Hayley's tongue is.

"Now, if there are no more musings, get to work," Hayley finishes before turning and leaving, the door closing loudly behind her. The room descends into chatter as we all get ready to work extra today, even though I'm pretty sure it's against the fucking law to tell us we have to stay and do extra, but then she dangled that bonus in front of us to make sure we were persuaded to stay without her even trying to convince us. We're all scraping to get by, and the more prestigious staff here know that and take full advantage of it.

"Has anyone ever seen the owner?" I ask Celeste as we make our way to the floor we're working on today, both of us sharing the top floor suites and the penthouse, which requires two people as opposed to one to make sure everything is immaculate.

"Hunter Ryley... I've seen him once. He's pretty easy on the eye for a silver fox. But from what I gather, he's more of a silent owner, preferring to let his board visit and make decisions," Celeste says as we get in the lift and make our way up.

I've only ever asked about the owner once, making the mistake of asking Hayley like the new girl just did, and I've never shown enough interest to ask again. Whenever anyone asks Hayley about the owner, she shuts it down. I have no idea why, and I've never really cared, because as long as I get paid, what business is it of mine?

We reach the designated floor and begin our shift, scouring every nook and cranny to make sure Hayley has no reason to deduct anything from the 'generous bonus' she mentioned. She'd take it away in a heartbeat because she has no soul.

Celeste and I work quickly and efficiently, the time flying by as we finish up the suites and head to the penthouse. We don't even break for lunch, and by the time we've finished, we're both starving and ready to go home and rest our weary feet.

But I guess Hayley has other ideas as she marches up to us just as we're about to enter the staff area. "You two," she says with a click of her fingers. "Come with me." She walks on by us without waiting for an answer, and we both groan quietly as we rush to catch up with her marching across the reception area. She leads us into the dining hall, which is bustling with activity, ready for tonight's guests who will be spending an extortionate amount of money on a plate that contains no more than three bites of food. I've never understood why people pay so much money for so little, but then, I guess being broke as fuck for most of my life means I can't comprehend spending so much money on meaningless shit.

Hayley stops abruptly, and I come to halt just before I smack into the back of her.

"Now," she says as she turns around to face us. "I'm short on staff again tonight, and after seeing how well you worked previously, Elise, I am expecting you to work to the same standard again."

"Um… it's been a really long day and I'm exhausted—" I begin to say, but Hayley cuts me off.

"I understand that, but as before, you'll be rewarded generously." She has a smug smile on her face because she knows she's just sealed the deal. Bitch. Another thing I hate is people who use money to get what they want, and they prey on those who desperately need it.

"And, of course, you will be allocated a room again for when you're done," she adds on, and even as I roll my eyes at her, I know I'll do it because it's too good to pass up. I received my paycheck this morning, and when I saw that I was compensated three-hundred pounds for working a few hours extra the other night, I was surprised and actually fucking grateful for her picking me. Another extra three-hundred pounds will go a long way, and it means I'll be able to put down a deposit on my own place sooner rather than later, until I've seen my divorce through, and then I can get the hell out of here. I know I could leave now, run away and never look back like I was going to do before, but actually, I want to get all my ducks in a row before I hightail it out of here. I want to know that I never have to deal with Derrick again, and make sure I get what I'm owed.

"Celeste," Hayley barks, turning to my best friend stood beside me. "Elise will fill you in on what is expected of you. You can both make your way to the staff room, where you will find extra uniforms for you to wear that arrived this morning, and I'll be there shortly."

"Are we working in here?" I ask, looking around the dining area.

"Of course not. I just didn't have time to waste by telling you this out there," she replies, nodding towards the direction we came from. And with that, her attention shifts, and she sees something over my shoulder and goes marching towards a waiter who is probably about to be ripped a new arsehole. I grab Celeste's hand and pull her along behind me, filling her in on what we'll be expected to do as I lead her to the staff room.

"What the hell is happening right now?" Celeste says as I push open the staff room door and spot the uniforms hanging on a portable rail in front of some lockers.

"I have no idea, but I know that the bonus of three-hundred pounds is totally worth it," I tell her as I shuffle through the uniforms, finding the sizes we'll need. "And wearing nicer clothes than a maid's outfit is another reason to just suck it up and do the job."

"But why is Hayley asking us to do it? Don't they have an agency for this kind of thing?" Celeste questions.

"Yes, but I'm guessing that they're running on too short notice, like the last time she asked me to do this." I'm not going to look a gift horse in the mouth, and neither is Celeste.

"Three-hundred pounds extra... wow... it takes me just over a week to earn that amount of money," Celeste says quietly, and I nod.

"Yep, so even though we're exhausted, take it as a win. And also, if this goes well again, maybe we'll get asked more and more. I guess it beats using an agency and having to give whoever shows up a rundown of what to do and what is expected of them. This way, we already know the standards set by the hotel, and she doesn't have to clue us up."

We quickly get changed, freshening up and using Celeste's minimal make-up to hide the bags under our eyes and give us a natural glow despite both being tired from a full day of work already. When we're done, we wait outside the staff room for Hayley to arrive and lead us up to the penthouse.

The lift pings at the end of the corridor, and my eyes drift to the doors opening, my heart racing as they connect with *his*. Dorien. He smirks as the lift closes, and I get that familiar feeling of my heart trying to beat out of my chest whenever he's around. He's here? But his note this morning was so final. A goodbye. So why the hell is he in the lift?

"Who was that?" Celeste asks, and I rip my eyes away from the lift to look at her.

"That was him," I whisper.

"Him?" she questions.

"*Him*," I reiterate, and her eyes widen.

"Oh, *him*, mystery guy."

"Bingo."

"Fuck, Elise, he's hot as hell," she comments.

"Yes he is." I have no time to say anything else as Hayley appears from around the corner and marches towards us. I suddenly feel empowered, like a new kind of energy is buzzing through me, and I have no doubt it's to do with the man I never thought I'd see again.

Chapter Twenty-Two

ELISE

I'm back in the penthouse, serving drinks to the board members and trying not to let my eyes roam the room for Dorien. I mean, I don't know why he would even be in here, he's clearly not a board member, so it's totally pointless. But still, I can't seem to stop myself from hoping to catch a glimpse of him.

"Champagne?" I ask as I stop by a group of four people, none of which I know the names of. Two of them take a glass each, while the other two ignore me, not even pausing their conversation.

"How much longer do we have to be here?" Celeste whispers as she comes to stand beside me, a fresh tray of hors d'oeuvres in her hand.

"Until the end, and then we get to clean everything after," I whisper back, keeping a smile on my face.

"The three-hundred pounds isn't feeling like it's worth it right now," Celeste mutters, and I can't help but chuckle.

"It totally is, and you know it," I reply before I move forward and offer out more champagne. Once my tray is empty, I make my way back to the kitchen area to grab some fresh glasses and pour some more.

The kitchen is less chaotic than the service one downstairs, with the head chef lovingly preparing the best food and the staff working with him seeming to be in complete sync. And they've all been pleasant, nothing but polite to me, and I wonder if this could somehow be a path to a better job than cleaning up after guests?

"If I could have your attention, please," is spoken through a microphone in the main room, and I quickly finish filling the glasses and carry the tray back out there, because if this is some kind of toast, then I need to be on hand for the snooty fuckers to grab a glass if they need one.

I stand near the back, off to the side but in direct view of anyone who wishes to take a glass from the tray. I watch as Hayley appears at the front of the room, thanking whoever the guy was that just spoke into the microphone as she takes it from him with a smile. God, she really can turn on the charm when she needs to—just not around us workers, obviously.

"Firstly, I'd like to welcome you all here tonight. I know how valuable your time is, and we appreciate you coming at such short notice," Hayley says, and the room seems to titter around me. "I'm sure you're all keen to know why you are here, but let me introduce the man who will be confirming the reason for tonight's impromptu get-together. Please welcome the owner of The Blue Diamond hotel chain, Mr Hunter Ryley."

Hayley claps, the room claps, and I stand here and wait to see what he's about to announce, suddenly having an interest in what is going on.

Hunter Ryley walks out and stands by Hayley, who he proceeds to air-kiss on either cheek before she hands him the microphone and takes a couple of steps back. Celeste was right, he sure is a silver fox. Not bad at all. I know he's in his late forties, he's not married, and he's got no kids... and now I can see that he rocks the peppered grey-haired look, his strong jaw clean-shaven and his light green eyes having a charm about them. His body looks to be in reasonable condition too, the dark blue shirt he's wearing seeming to hug his biceps. I take a quick glance at Hayley, who is stood on the opposite side of the room to me, and I can practically see her drooling from here. His voice is rather smooth too as he begins to talk about his reason for why he and the board members are here tonight, and I zone back in, listening as he explains about a merger that's been happening for a while. There's complete silence as he speaks, each person enraptured by what he has to say.

"I've had my time, and now, it's up to someone else to take these hotels to the next level. I have no doubt that it will continue to climb in status with this next man at the helm. Board members, please welcome, Mr Dorien Dukes, the new owner of The Blue Diamond Hotels." Hunter Ryley starts to clap, as does the rest of the room, as there are various gasps to accompany the clapping, but I stand here absolutely stunned as Dorien walks out and stands beside Hunter as he hands the microphone to him and shakes his hand.

My Dorien.

No, not mine. Christ, Elise, he was never yours.

Dorien Dukes. The man I had the most incredible night with. The one who made me feel free as he fucked me ruthlessly. The new fucking owner of this hotel. Of all the hotels in the chain. And ultimately, my goddamn boss.

Oh fucking hell.

Chapter Twenty-Three

DORIEN

I fucking hate these things. Board members kissing my arse and waiting for the next big cheque to come in. Unluckily for them, in due course, I'm going to give them news they've not been expecting. I'm sure their egos will allow them to think they'll be kept on as directors, but that's not how I work. I have a small team behind me that have been with me from the start and who earned my trust over the years. They do as I say and when I say, but they have no control over any final decisions. That's all on me.

"I'm not sure how many of you were aware of this deal taking place, but I'll keep it brief and say that we have been negotiating for the last few months on this merger with my own hotel chain, Classico Royale, and I am pleased to confirm that I signed on the dotted line this morning, so The Blue Diamond hotels and the Classico Royale hotels will become part of one powerhouse.

"This means that I will control fifty percent of the hotel revenue around the globe."

The claps come quickly, the smiles on the faces of the board members beaming. It also means I have a shit ton of extra responsibility added to my plate, but with work fuelling me since I can remember, I'm ready for the challenge. I built the Classico Royale hotels from the ground up, and I've worked towards this goal for what feels like forever. I don't need the money, I have more than enough to make sure I'm comfortable for the rest of my life, so this is about more than boosting my bank balance—not that the same can be said for the board members. They're all about the cash and status. It's a shame they have no idea that my next step will be to pull the rug out from underneath them and take back any shares they may have, because I don't fucking need them. Ruthless? Yes, but I fail to care. They've all served their purpose for Hunter Ryley, but I don't like to share, and I have already started the process of taking everything back from them. I don't want to consult them on my plans or have them trying to push me to make deals they see as profitable, when in actual fact, they can't see anything past the nose on the end of their face.

I've made my business what it is.

I sealed the merger, and in doing so, I've secured my place in the financial world, and I can damn well walk away from it whenever the fuck I please.

"Moving forward, I will be based here, in this hotel for the foreseeable." My eyes find Elise's, and hers are wide with surprise, and possibly shock. *Yes, baby, I'm staying put. First time for everything, I guess.*

"If you'd like to raise your glasses in a toast," I say as I raise my own glass in the air. "To the merger and growth of Blue Diamond."

The room repeats my words, and then we all drink, but my eyes never look away from Elise.

"Enjoy the rest of the evening," I finish, and then I start to walk, my legs moving in the direction of Elise. She's like a fucking magnet, and at some point since I left her in the bed in my room on the morning I disappeared, I decided I couldn't just let her be a one-night thing. I want another taste of her. I want her to scream my name as I eat her pussy and she urges me on. I want to consume her and take every-fucking-thing she has left to give.

I'm not a changed man by any means, but I know what I want, and I still want her.

One night wasn't enough.

"Dorien," I hear Hayley say from the side of me, and I curse her under my breath as I stop in my tracks and reluctantly turn to face her.

"What is it, Hayley?" I ask her, my tone showing that I can't be doing with any nonsense.

"Um, do you need me to set up room twenty-nine for you again? I mean, seeing as you'll be staying for a while, I thought that—"

"No, Hayley," I say, cutting her off. "I do not want my usual room. I will be staying here, in the penthouse, until further notice. And it's Mr Dukes, not Dorien."

"Noted." She nods her head when she speaks, her eyes looking at me with something akin to lust as her cheeks become flushed. Dear God, no. Never happening.

"Is that all?" I ask, because there is a delectable woman somewhere behind me who I would like to go and speak to.

"Uh, yes, sir." The way she says 'sir' does absolutely nothing for me, not in the way Elise saying it does.

"Good. And make sure this get-together is finished within the next thirty minutes. I want to be left alone," I demand.

"Oh… uh… of course," she stutters, and I turn away abruptly to find that Elise is no longer stood where she was. I guess I'll just have to go and find her.

Chapter Twenty-Four
ELISE

"He's my new fucking boss?" I say to myself in the mirror of the toilet. "Oh my god..." I have no idea what to do with that information. He owns this hotel... he owns half the fucking hotels globally now he's done whatever he's done with whatever merger he was talking about... he could sack me, send me on my way after I basically went and begged him to fuck me. Oh God, oh God, oh God.

A knock at the door has me jumping with a start. Bugger, I should have just gone somewhere else and not used the toilet in the penthouse, but I felt like I couldn't breathe in that fucking room, and my mind told me to just get somewhere I could lock myself away for a few moments. A few moments aren't enough, I need a whole chunk of time to process the fact that I have fucked my boss.

"Elise," I hear hissed from the other side of the door. Oh thank God, it's just Celeste. I open the door quickly and drag her in, shutting it and locking it behind her.

"Oh my Christ, Elise—" she starts, but I cut her off.

"Don't say it. Don't even think it," I warn her, but I already knew my words would be wasted because she's practically bristling on the spot.

"You've fucked our new boss.... No, no, you've fucked our new hot-as-hell boss." She squeals in delight, meanwhile I want the ground to swallow me whole and take me far away from here. If only I could teleport myself to somewhere unknown.

"Stop saying it," I tell her, my hands going into my hair as I grab chunks and hold them in despair. "What the hell am I going to do?"

"Nothing," she says, and I stare at her incredulously.

"Nothing? I can't do nothing," I state, keeping my voice as low as I can because I have no idea if anyone is outside the door.

"What exactly do you think is going to happen here, hmm?" Celeste asks.

"I... I don't know but I'm freaking out," I admit.

"He knew you were an employee here. He fucked you. He chose to fuck you whilst knowing this, yet you just thought he was a random guest," she points out.

"Yes, but what if he thinks I'm the resident slag that goes around humping guests here there and everywhere."

"Don't be so ridiculous, Elise. You need to calm down and think rationally."

"Rationally... right... so it doesn't matter that I've fucked Dorien Dukes, a guy who is so far out of my league he might as well be on another planet—"

"Except, he's not out of your league, is he? Because you've already had him. And I truly do not think he has any intention of sacking you, Elise. Did you not see the way he looked at you in there?" She points her finger in the direction of the main room, but I have no idea what she's talking about as I stare at her with a frown on my face. She rolls her eyes at me before saying, "He looked like he wanted to devour you right there."

"Stop it."

"It's true, but I don't expect you to see that, because all your life you've been put down, kicked around and used for other people's motives. He has no reason to have a motive with you, Elise, so stop bloody panicking and get your arse out there and face this head on. You have no need to hide."

"But he's my boss," I whisper, trying to stop the hope that is clawing at my chest, dying to break free and have me believe that

Dorien really isn't going to upend my life and send me on my way.

"Doesn't that make it even more exciting?" Celeste says with a cheeky smile on her face, and I can't help but feel a spark of excitement inside of me. "If nothing else happens, then fine, you got one amazing night with a handsome guy who gave you multiple orgasms. And if something else does come of this, then just go with it and enjoy it for what it is. There is no label here, Elise. Stop living in the dark and do exactly what you've always said you wanted to do… be free."

"Fuck, I hate it when you make sense," I say begrudgingly as she looks at me knowingly.

"Come on, let's go back out there, finish our work, and then we can go back to our room, and you can regale me about the fabulous sex you had with him, because my sex life is drier than the fucking Sahara right now."

So crass, and so uniquely Celeste. I love her, and I love how she can help ease some of my anxiety, even if it may only be short lived.

She grabs my hand and pulls me to the door, unlocking and opening it, only for us to come face to face with the man himself.

I gasp as his eyes hold mine, and at some point, I realise that Celeste is no longer holding my hand or standing in front of me, and then I'm stepping backwards as he steps forwards, until I'm hitting the countertop behind me. He stops inside the doorway and smirks before closing the door and locking it.

"Hello, Elise," he says in that smooth voice of his, sending fucking tingles through my body.

"What are you doing?" I ask as he takes a step forward and my hands grip onto the edge of the countertop behind me.

"What do you want me to do?" he asks, and I wonder what fucking universe I have found myself in.

"Stop that," I tell him, and he pauses his advances for a second.

"Stop what?"

"Answering my questions with another question."

"It was one question, not multiple, and it was a simple response," he states casually, stepping forwards again until he's inches away from me, his hands in his trouser pockets and his stance commanding me all over again.

"No, no, I need to get out of here." I can't be in here, Hayley would fire me on the spot if she found me in here with him.

"You're not going anywhere," he says, his arms going either side of me and caging me in. Fuck, he smells good.

"I'm working, Dorien."

"You work for me, and I say you're not leaving."

"Don't use the fact that you're my boss against me. Don't do that."

"I'm not using it against you. I'm saying it because no one can do anything about it if the owner requested you to be here himself," he states, and I suddenly realise that he's the reason I'm here tonight. He's the reason I'm working these extra hours. Is he the reason I got the bonus the last time I worked in this penthouse? Was it because of him that I got picked for that night in the first place, as well as this time, too? Oh my god… he's paying for me to be here… isn't that just wrong?

"I can see you're overthinking shit again, Elise," he says, and before I can stop myself, my hand leaves the counter and moves up as my palm connects with his cheek. His head turns to the side, and I feel the heat flood my face, my cheeks burning at the fact that I just slapped my boss, and I am so very, very fucked.

His face turns slowly back to me as I wish I could take back the last twenty seconds. He looks at me with an unreadable expression on his face, and then he stands tall, his arms moving from either side of me.

"Get on your knees," he demands, and I physically balk at his order.

"Pardon?"

"Don't make me repeat myself, Elise." He says no more, his eyes burning into me, and for reasons I cannot explain, I find myself dropping to my knees before him. Is there something wrong with me? I just got pissed off at the thought of him paying for my time, and yet, here I am, on my knees for him because he told me to?

"Good girl," he says as his hand caresses the back of my head, his words making my pussy fucking soaked. Yes, there is definitely something wrong with me. One hundred percent. His fingers thread through my hair and he pulls my head back, his fingers gripping my strands and pulling against my scalp. Shouldn't this make me feel vulnerable? Scared? Shouldn't I be on high alert and running from this room? Probably, but as my breathing becomes shallow and I wait for his next command, I know that I need more of him. More of whatever this is, despite the consequences I may face.

"Did you miss me, Elise?" he asks as he leans over me, his face so close to mine and my body begging for him to just give me what I want already.

"Yes," I answer pathetically, because I can't seem to find it in myself to lie to him.

He smirks at me, and all I want him to do is put his mouth on me, remind me of how he made me feel a few nights ago.

"Let's get a few things straight," he says as he crouches in front of me, his fingers still entangled in my hair and his other hand brushing the inside of my thigh. "I know that finding out I am essentially your boss is a surprise. I also know that you'll be thinking all kinds of fucked-up shit in your head, because you seem to have this need to see the bad in everything." He runs his fingers higher up my thigh, and I struggle to stop myself from moving to get his fingers where I want them.

"But when it comes to this thing between us, there is no bad. There is only good, and you need a reminder of how fucking good it can be…" His fingers brush against my knickers, swiping up and down. I need the fabric away from me, I need him to touch me properly, and it seems he hears my silent plea as he pushes my knickers to the side with his thumb and pushes two of his fingers inside of me—I'm that wet for him.

"Fuck, Elise, you feel that? You feel how fucking wet you are for me? You feel how your body responds to me, to us?"

"Yes," I manage to say breathlessly, his thumb rubbing my clit as he pushes his fingers in and out of me.

How can I feel this way? How can I feel like this after ending my marriage just days ago?

He pulls his fingers out and moves them up to his mouth, putting them between his lips and sucking my taste off of him. Good God…

"Fucking divine," he says, and then he's letting go of my hair and standing up. "Get up."

I rise on trembling legs and lean against the counter behind me, more so I don't fall back down again than anything. I bite my lip as he undoes his trousers, pushing them down with his boxers and freeing his cock. My eyes take him in as he grabs it and runs his hand up and down his dick slowly.

"Get on the counter and spread your legs," he orders, and I comply immediately. He nestles between my legs and uses his hands to push my thighs apart, as far as they will go. I have never been so aroused, ever, and that's saying something after what he did to me before.

He moves my knickers to the side again, and his dick nudges against my opening as he puts his face so close to mine that our noses are touching.

"I am still that stranger you met. I am still that guy that wanted to make you feel good." He pushes his dick inside of me a little bit at a time, and I struggle not to let my head flop back in relief as he does. "I may be the owner of this hotel, but I'm still just a guy who hasn't had his fill of you. So when we're doing this, I am not your boss. I'm a fucking man who wants to pleasure you and hear you moan his name." He pulls back out and plunges inside of me, and I feel like this orgasm is going to be quick and fast.

"I do not care what your job is. I do not look at you and see you as a maid. I look at you and see the fire in your eyes, the fucking keys to your soul, and I want it all for as long as you'll give it to me." He grunts out each word, taking me harshly and beautifully.

I look down as his dick impales me. I grab onto his shoulders as he shreds the lace material with his hands and rips my knickers off, so his hands can move under my arse, his fingers digging in hard enough to leave marks. I finally throw my head back as he buries his face in my neck and nips my skin lightly with his teeth. Such a contrast to how hard he's fucking me.

I try to keep quiet as my orgasm builds, clenching around him as he pushes me higher and higher.

"Let go, Elise. Let me hear you fucking scream," he says, and one of his hands finds my clit, pushing down and igniting me. I couldn't stop myself from screaming if I tried, and as I shout out his name, he follows me, his release hitting seconds after my own.

He doesn't let up until we're both spent and panting. He pulls out of me and reaches across to a basket on the sink with a fresh flannel in. He runs the warm water and wets it, before he puts it between my legs and cleans me, soothing me at the same time. His actions are so fucking sweet, and it adds another layer to this complex man who feels like he could be so much more than a fuck buddy… if that is what we are.

He places a kiss on the end of my nose and then moves away, leaving me feeling bereft even as he stands there.

"Until next time, Elise," he says before he's turning and walking away, leaving me speechless as he vacates the room. I have so many questions, so many thoughts running wild through my mind, but I know that I won't get any answers out of him now—and maybe I never will. But there is nothing that can wipe the smile off of my face as I make myself presentable and go back into the main room, wondering how on earth I managed to get on Dorien Dukes' radar.

Chapter Twenty-Five

ELISE

"You need to spill everything," Celeste says excitedly as we make our way back to the room we're sharing for the night.

"I don't even know where to start," I say with a sigh as I slide the key card Hayley gave me in the door and push it open. I'm more than ready to climb into bed, but Celeste has other ideas.

"Uh, from the beginning would be great. I need all the details."

"Celeste, I'm tired—"

"From all the sex?" she questions, her eyebrow arched.

"Stop it," I say, but the smug smile that I can't stop from appearing on my face totally gives me away.

"Girl, stop playing and fucking tell me," Celeste urges. I laugh at her as she sits down on the edge of the bed, her legs bouncing up and down expectantly.

"I don't know what to say, other than the fact he told me to get on my knees, called me a good girl, and then he sat me on the counter and fucked me so hard that I saw stars."

"Damn… that's… shit, Elise, that's hot," Celeste comments, seeming to be lost for words, which doesn't happen ever.

I kick off my shoes and flop back on the bed. "Honestly, Celeste, I don't know what's wrong with me. I mean, he is without a doubt the best sex I've ever had, but now I know he's my boss, it makes everything awkward," I admit.

"Why?"

"Because he's done things to me that make me blush profusely, and I don't want anyone to become aware of anything happening between us." I close my eyes as I try to block out the negative thoughts threatening to ruin my high.

"Elise, stop doing that," Celeste says, and I can hear the exasperation in her voice. "Live in the moment, and so what if anyone finds out? You're fucking the boss, so technically, if they're a dick, he can get rid of them."

"Oh my god, Celeste," I say through the laughter that bursts out of me.

"You gotta think of the perks, Elise."

"Come on, we need to get some sleep," I tell her. "We've got an early start and I'm beat."

We both strip our clothes off and put them ready to wash tomorrow. Luckily for us, there are complimentary pyjamas waiting in the bathroom for us to wear—thank God for the posh hotel we work in.

Once we've finished and climbed into bed, my eyes fall closed immediately, my body drained from the entire day, and my dreams filled with one man in particular.

My phone ringing wakes me up, and for a second, I think it's just my alarm, but then I register the ringtone and quickly jump out of bed, hoping not to wake Celeste, but it's too late as she grumbles whilst I go to my jacket which is hanging on the back of the door and has my phone in its pocket. I squint at the morning sun filtering through the windows, and then I feel my face pull into a frown as I take my phone out of the pocket and see that my mother has tried calling me, more than once. I guess I was so tired that I didn't hear it the other five times.

I check the time to see that it's only six in the morning, and I groan as I go back to the bed with my phone in my hand, because I could have had another hour of sleep before I needed to be awake. No chance of that now as the dread settles in the pit of my stomach as I stare at my phone. She hasn't bothered to contact me for days, and neither has Derrick, but I know I'm going to have to speak to her at some point. I know that she's going to tell me to go back to my husband and live the fake life I'd found myself walking around like a zombie in. She's going to be thinking of no one but herself, and possibly my father, but he's just as fucking bad as she is. I click the phone to silent and place it on the bedside table as I stare at the ceiling and sigh loudly.

"Who the fuck was that?" Celeste asks, her face buried in the pillow and her voice muffled.

"My mother," I say with another sigh, and Celeste's head pops up.

"Oh shit. And what time is it?"

"Just after six."

"Elise, nothing good ever came from a mother phoning this early in the morning."

"I know." Silence ensues for a few moments as Celeste turns to lie on her back, and I stay staring at the ceiling which has suddenly become rather interesting. "No one has tried to contact me since I left. No text, nothing. I know they think that I'll just be having a tantrum, but I guess they're done waiting."

"You don't have to speak to them, Elise. You don't owe them anything."

"I know that too, but I also know that I need to make it clear to them that I'm not going back. I don't know if this will give me closure or what, but there's still a small part of me that is praying that they take my side for once. The side of their daughter, and maybe it'll show me that I mean something more to them than just being a cash cow, even though that didn't exactly pan out the way they'd hoped." I'm still that girl that craves their approval, no matter what I try and tell myself.

"You've gotta do what's right for you, but I think you're setting yourself up to be disappointed all over again," Celeste admits, and the rational part of me knows without a doubt that she's right, but they're still my parents. They're still here, when millions of others have lost theirs and wish for one more chance to make things better. I have to try, don't I?

"Ugh, I can't deal with this before I've had coffee," I say as I push myself up from the bed and walk to the bathroom to get showered and dressed, leaving my phone on the bedside table, hoping and praying that when I call my mother back she's had some sort of epiphany when it comes to her only daughter.

I walk through reception, my feet aching already and my body still tired from yesterday, and I stifle a groan as I hear Hayley say loudly, "Elise, a word," from behind me. Oh fucking hell, what does she want now? I wearily turn and see that she looks really pissed off. She beckons me towards her with her finger and I fight the urge to roll my eyes as I move towards her.

"I've still got another two rooms to do before lunch," I tell her, hoping to put off whatever the hell this is about, but it seems I'm shit out of luck.

"I know, and you best make this quick otherwise you'll be working through your lunchbreak to make up for the lost time," she bites back before she whirls around and marches away, me following behind her, almost dragging my feet as I go. The reception staff give me a pitiful look and a soft smile as I walk past them, and I wonder what on earth is about to go down.

Surely, Hayley doesn't know about last night with Dorien? She couldn't know... could she? What if he's told her and now I'm about to lose my job? What if he's had second thoughts and realises he can't be around me because of protocol? What if... but the silent questions stop when Hayley opens the door to the staff room, and there, sat at the table in the middle, is my mother, looking all kinds of pissed off, and also Derrick.

"You have ten minutes, Elise," Hayley says as she walks around me and shuts the door.

"Elise, we need to talk," my mother says, and Derrick sits beside her with a smug grin on his face. Oh lord, this isn't going to end well.

"I'm busy, Mother," I bite back, because I'm already on the defensive and reacting to her tone.

"This is more important than cleaning rooms," she states, and I already know that she's got no thought for me. This is still all going to be about her and what she wants.

"It isn't, actually," I retort. "And I only have nine minutes left, so we need to make this quick."

"Don't speak to me like that. I'm your mother, and you will treat me with respect," she barks, and I can't help but scoff at her words. "This isn't a joke, Elise. You need to stop whatever the hell this is and get back home where you belong."

"Where I belong?" I repeat her words, the disgust in my tone apparent. "I don't need to answer to either of you. I left Derrick, and there is no going back."

"You stupid girl," my mother spits as she rises from her seat and bangs her hands down on the table. "You have to go back, you have to secure our future. Without you, he'll take everything, and then your father and I will be left with nothing. I won't be with nothing again, Elise, so you will go back to Derrick, and you will be a wife to him."

"What are you talking about? You don't need me anymore, you've got what you wanted from me, you have your house—"

"No, we don't," she says, cutting me off before I can ask anything further. "It's all in Derrick's name, every single asset, so if you divorce him, we'll be left with nothing," she reveals.

"So, me marrying him in the first place was for nothing," I say quietly, the tiny bit of respect I may have still had for my parents diminishing within seconds.

"It wasn't for nothing, Elise. It gave us security, but you need to go back to make sure it stays in place," she orders, like she isn't trying to give me a goddamn life sentence with the prick looking at me like he's going to win.

"No."

"You listen to me—"

"No, Mother, you listen to me for a change," I start, my tone firm. "I have been pushed around by all of you my whole life, but I'm done. You don't love me as a mother should. Hell, you don't even fucking care about me. I want nothing to do with any of you. And as for you, Derrick," I sneer, his name leaving a bad taste in my mouth. "You will be hearing from my solicitor soon." I could say so much more, but what's the point? It will only fall on deaf ears, they'll never change, not now, so I won't waste my breath. I turn on my heels and head back for the door, but as I'm about to reach for the handle, I'm quickly grabbed and pushed to the wall beside it, the breath being knocked out of me from the impact and the shock.

And as I look at Derrick with wide eyes, his hand connects with my face, sending pain shooting through my cheek and bringing tears to my eyes. I cry out in pain as he gets in my face, his hands bunched in the collar of my uniform, dangerously close to cutting off my air supply.

"You listen to me now, you bitch. You will fucking come home, because it is where you belong. And how dare you talk to your mother that way. She's your fucking mother—"

"GET OFF OF ME," I shout as loud as I can, which only makes him push his hands towards my throat more. The panic shoots through me at a rapid pace. Derrick has never laid a finger on me, so this is a whole new territory. I have no idea what to do, but I can feel despair mixed with rage swirling inside of me.

"You will leave here with us now, and you will forget all this nonsense about divorcing me. It's never going to happen, Elise. I fucking own you, and I will do whatever the fuck I want with you," Derrick says, his face so close to mine and making me want to gag.

"Fuck you," I say through gritted teeth before I shout at him to let me go. All he does is laugh in my face, but the laugh is soon wiped from his lips when the door flies open and he's pulled away from me, being thrown across the floor to land in a heap by my mother's feet at the table where she still stands.

My eyes fly to meet Dorien's, and he looks livid—fucking feral, even.

I gasp for breath as my body shakes with a mixture of relief, worry, shock, and adrenaline.

I watch as Derrick takes what feels like an age to get to his feet, puffing and panting as he does.

"I don't know who you are or why you're here, but get the fuck out of my hotel and never come back," Dorien barks, his tone leaving no room for negotiation. My mother stands tall, her head held high and her shoulders back as she walks towards the door. She doesn't say anything until she stops at the side of me and whispers, "This isn't over, Elise," before she disappears out of the door, a very dishevelled looking Derrick following behind her. He doesn't even try to look at me as he skulks away, clearly thinking better of trying to say anything to Dorien, who is stood there like an absolute powerhouse—which I guess he is.

He watches them until they're out of the door, and then he says, "Make sure they're never allowed back in here, or any of my hotels, for that matter." I presume he's talking to security, or maybe Hayley? I really don't care as the door closes and Dorien looks at me, his eyes landing on my cheek, which is no doubt red from Derrick hitting me, and then I feel my body give out as I slide down the wall, my legs no longer strong enough to hold me up. But I fail to hit the floor as Dorien's arms wrap around me, pulling me to him as he holds me against his chest and lets me weep into his shirt.

And even as hurt spreads through me from the very people who were meant to love me no matter what, I take a tiny bit of comfort as Dorien whispers, "I've got you, buttercup. Always."

Chapter Twenty-Six

DORIEN

I brought Elise up to my penthouse, and she's currently sat on the sofa, the red mark on her cheek looking like a fucking beacon and making my blood boil. I will never condone a man hitting a woman. It's one of the most cowardly things a man can do, and that guy sure as hell was no man. I'm not going to presume anything here. There is clearly a story, and Elise needs to be the one to tell it, if she chooses to.

I may have a heart carved of stone, because my past has made it that way, but for Elise… fuck, what am I thinking?

I shake my head and carry the tea I made her over to the coffee table in front of her, and I place it on a coaster. Her eyes are red-rimmed, and she hasn't so much as uttered a word since she composed herself just enough for me to get her up here without me carrying her like some kind of fucking caveman. I didn't fail to notice the deadpan expression Hayley gave me when she saw me whisking Elise away, but I also don't have to explain my actions to her, and she will quickly learn that if she is to stay working for me. At present, I have no plans to change the staffing arrangements around here, but if my hand is forced, I'll have no problem in putting certain people in their place.

"Drink," I say as I point to the cup and Elise finally looks at me, her eyes showing the broken parts inside of her. I thought those broken parts were on the way out, but whatever that little showdown was that I heard from the corridor, and then walked in on, have clearly set her back.

"Thank you," she whispers as she reaches for the cup and takes a sip. I put extra sugar in there for the shock she must have experienced. I don't know how it fucking helps, but it's the British way—drink a cup of tea and it'll ease all your problems. If only it were that fucking simple.

"I should get back to work," she says quietly as she sets the cup back down, only that one sip taken.

"You're not going anywhere," I tell her. "You're going to take all the time you need."

"I can't afford to," she admits, biting her bottom lip and blinking rapidly.

"You will still be paid, Elise, so there's no rush."

"I don't need you to make allowances for me, Dorien." Her tone is a little sharper, that flare igniting that holds me captive. It's still there, still simmering away. Good. She's going to need all the fucking flare to deal with me.

"I'm not making allowances. I'm merely making sure my employee is cared for."

"You do this for all of your employees?" she asks, stumping me. Bugger. "That's what I thought." She stands up and brushes down her uniform, probably just for something to do.

"Okay, fine, I might have a soft spot when it comes to you," I admit.

"But why?" she asks, as if it's an impossible thought that someone may actually give her some kindness, some compassion, some goddamn grace to fall apart.

"I'm still figuring that one out myself." It's true. I have no idea why she's so endearing to me, but I plan to keep on finding out. I haven't even thought about being with another woman since our first night together—another fucking first for me.

"I appreciate it, Dorien, I really do, but Hayley will have my arse if I don't go back out there."

"Hayley will do no such thing."

She scoffs. "You don't know her very well yet." And then her eyes widen as she admitted something I already knew. Hayley has seemed like some kind of shark since I first met her, which isn't a bad thing when it comes to business, but when it comes to actually dealing with the very staff that keep this place running, I'm going to need her to stop being so fucking callous.

I clench my jaw at the thought of her walking out of here still broken, but who am I to make her stay? Who am I to make her talk to me about what happened? Who the fuck am I to try and delve into any kind of feelings when I've had mine shut off for so long?

"If you need to talk, I'll be here," I tell her, giving her a nod to show I'm not going to stop her. Her lips are pursed as she nods back and then makes her way to the door, but she stops as her hand lands on the handle and turns her head back to look at me.

"Thank you for your kindness. You have no idea how much it means to me." A soft smile graces her face, and fuck me, why does she have to leave again? But I don't speak as she disappears, the door shutting quietly, leaving me with nothing but thoughts of how on earth she's making me feel something for someone other than myself.

Chapter Twenty-Seven

ELISE

My phone has been blowing up all evening, alternating between my parents and Derrick. I have nothing to say to any of them, and as I switch my phone off for the time being, I know that tomorrow I need to take the next step and contact a divorce solicitor. It'll take what pitiful savings I have, and it will probably cost me months of wages, but I need to start the ball rolling and be done with it all.

I'm sat on Celeste's sofa, and I've poured my heart out to her. She's let me cry and then rage, and now I'm throwing a little pity party for myself as I sip a vodka tonic and wonder how my life became so fucked-up to start with.

"Elise, you know you can stay here for as long as you need," Celeste tells me, for what feels like the millionth time. I hate imposing on anyone, which is probably why I stuck out my shitty marriage for as long as I did, if I'm being honest. I want to be able to stand on my own two feet and show the world what I'm made of, but I'm going to have to suck it up for the time being and graciously accept my best friend's offer of help.

"Thank you. I don't know what I'd do without you," I tell her honestly, thanking my lucky stars that we made friends all those years ago.

"Good thing you don't have to find out," she says as she throws a pillow at me and laughs. "Now, what are we watching? I'm going to say an action flick rather than a chick flick, you know, what with you having no tears left to cry."

"Sounds perfect," I say as I throw the pillow back at her and we curl up on the sofa, and I try to push all of my worries out of my mind, even if it's only for tonight.

I take a deep breath as I walk into the solicitor's office, which is just down the road from work. I figured my lunchbreak was a good time to bite the bullet, and there's no point in letting this drag on any longer than it needs to, especially not after yesterday.

"Hi," I say as I approach the desk and get the attention of the receptionist who smiles at me politely.

"Good morning, and how can I help you?" She's very over-the-top polite, but I guess she has to be, dealing with potential clients and all.

"Um, I was wondering if I could book an appointment because I need a divorce." Not quite how I wanted to word it, but it's too late to try and articulate the words now.

The receptionist looks at her computer screen and makes a humming noise. "I can get you an appointment for in two months' time," she tells me.

"Two months? Wow."

"Yes, we get booked up in advance."

"Yes, of course. Well, okay then, I'll take it," I tell her with a nod of my head.

"Excellent. Let me just get some details from you and then I can get it all booked in." I spend the next twenty minutes giving her the relevant information, which seems to be just about everything but my bra size. When I'm done, I only have ten minutes left of my lunchbreak, so I rush back to the hotel, shoving a breakfast bar down my throat as I go. I'll be bloody starving by tonight, but it'll have to do. I can't risk upsetting Hayley after what went down yesterday. Although, I'm yet to see her today, which is highly unusual. She's usually lording it about the place all day long, barking orders and scrutinising anyone for the slightest little thing. I'm surprised she doesn't bollock us all for breathing. The thought makes me chuckle quietly to myself as I walk into the staff room and put my things away in my locker. I make my way to the supply cupboard and start to fill my arms full of products, when the door opens behind me and closes again quickly. I don't take much notice as I continue to grab what I need—that is until I see that it's not another worker in here but the fucking boss himself. Dorien.

"You okay?" he asks, like it's perfectly normal for him to be in the supply cupboard with a maid.

"I'm okay, thank you. Are you turning into some kind of stalker now?" I ask playfully, really needing to keep conversation light, for my own sanity more than anything.

He smirks, and it makes me feel stupidly good. "Would it bother you if I was?"

I pretend to think about it for a moment. "Wouldn't that be classed as gross misconduct?"

"So is eating your employee's pussy, but it's not about to stop me," he says as he turns and locks the supply cupboard before pinning me with his gorgeous eyes.

"Dorien, don't..." But even I can hear how bloody unconvincing I sound.

"Don't what?" He quirks an eyebrow and begins to undo his shirt buttons. Oh lord have mercy, those abs are a thing of fucking beauty.

"We can't do this." I attempt to keep the lust out of my voice, but it's no use when he's walking towards me and letting his shirt fall to the floor.

"We can do anything we want."

"You can. I can't."

He stops in front of me, the scent of his aftershave making me stifle a moan. He smells so good.

"Think of the perks, Elise."

"The perks?"

He moves his hands to my waist, and I drop the products that were in my arms onto the floor.

"Fucking the boss is a pretty good perk," he says as he lifts me and sits me on the shelf behind before he nestles in-between my legs.

"It's the quickest way to get fired," I tell him, but he's clearly not about to stop, and I'm not about to end this either. He makes me feel good, and I desperately need good right now.

"Only if the boss is unhappy."

"So, if I keep fucking you, you'll be happy?" I ask, my head tilting to the side a little.

"Very," he replies before he leans down and licks my neck. "Tell me, Elise, are you already wet for me?"

There's no point in lying. I'm fucking soaked and he knows it. "Yes."

"Good fucking girl." His lips capture mine, and I moan into his mouth, my body coming alive from his hands running up the insides of my thighs and his tongue dancing with mine. My hands move to his trousers and undo them, my fingers greedy to touch his dick and ride the high that only he's ever given me. I push his boxers and trousers to just below his arse, and then I wrap my fingers around his cock, moving up and down oh-so-slowly as he continues to devour my mouth and run his fingers up and down my thighs.

I'm lost to anything other than him as he hardens in my hand and teases my pussy by running his fingers up and down my knickers.

"I need you to fuck me now, Dorien," I say against his lips, missing his tongue in my mouth already.

"So fucking needy," he says as he puts his hands underneath my arse and tilts me to the right position for his cock to claim me. He rips my knickers from me, tearing them from my body and holding them in his hand as I line his dick up with my entrance. If he keeps destroying my knickers like that, I'll have none left by the end of the week. He pushes inside of me slowly, and I let my head fall back to the wall behind as my eyes close.

"Look at me," he says when he's buried to the hilt. When my eyes connect with his, he brings his hand not holding my panties to my face and cups my cheek, the one that is still sore.

"Who was he, Elise?" he asks as he moves in and out of me at a deliciously slow pace.

"He was a nobody," I answer breathlessly, focusing on nothing but his eyes and how he feels sliding in and out.

"Your husband?" he asks, and I nod.

"Until I divorce him, of course." I have no idea why he's talking to me about this when he's putting his dick in me, but it doesn't feel weird… isn't that weird in itself?

"Has he hit you before?" he asks softly as he brushes his thumb over my cheek.

"No."

"Does it still hurt?"

"A little," I whisper, as his hand holding my knickers moves to my clit and he rotates his thumb in circles, applying slight pressure.

"Did he fuck you like this?"

"No."

"Did he make you wet like this?"

"God, no," I pant.

"Are you going to be thinking about him when I fuck you later?"

"No." Wait… what?

"Are you going to be thinking about him when I cook you dinner tonight?"

"Huh?"

"Answer the question, Elise," he demands, increasing the pressure on my clit.

I moan as I answer, "Fuck no."

"Now watch as I take what he gave away so freely. Watch as my cock replaces his, Elise."

Holy shit. I make my eyes move to watch his cock sliding in and out of me, a little faster than before. I watch as his thumb moves on my clit, more pressure being applied and it still not feeling like enough. I watch as he moves the hand that was on my cheek to my thigh, his fingers digging in as he ramps up his speed. I grit my teeth to stop myself from screaming out loud as my orgasm creeps up on me, pushing me over the edge.

Dorien doesn't let up until he's satisfied he's taken all of my pleasure, and then he lifts me and holds me against him as he fucks me against the wall and moans into my neck when his release hits.

We're both a sweaty mess by the time we're done, but he doesn't put me down. He keeps me caged in by his body, my legs wrapped around him, and I can't even find it in me to hate it. I love how he makes me feel. I love how he consumes me and eradicates my mind of anything but him. But I can't love it too much, because I can't give myself to a man who will never keep me.

"Dinner, tonight, seven-thirty, in the penthouse." He places his forehead against mine as he speaks, and there's something so fucking sweet about the way he's being that I find myself saying, "Okay."

His smile confirms that I need to take a step back, because the way it makes my heart flutter is not something I expected. But how can I take a step back when I'm already becoming addicted?

Chapter Twenty-Eight

DORIEN

I had one thing in mind when it came to her. Sex. One thing that has somehow turned into a whole host of other stuff that I can't even pretend to hate, or even try to ignore.

I'm not even thinking past each day, just seeing what happens, but it's quite apparent that I can't seem to stay away from her. She's running through my mind constantly, and I look forward to the moment when I can bury my dick in her. Is that all it is? Luckily, a knock at the door has my thoughts disappearing in a puff of smoke as I go to answer it. Seven-thirty on the dot.

Showtime, Dorien.

I answer the door to see her stood there in her maid's outfit, looking a little put out if I'm being honest.

"I'm sorry, I didn't have time to go and change," she apologises, but she has no need. I couldn't give a fuck what she's wearing.

"It doesn't matter," I say as I step aside and gesture for her to come in. "In fact, I'm glad you didn't, because I've got something waiting for you in the bathroom."

"Huh?" She looks as puzzled as I felt when I was setting it all up for her.

"Come on," I say as I shut the door and flick the lock before grabbing her hand and pulling her along behind me. When we get to the bathroom, I push the door open and hear her gasp behind me.

"Oh my goodness… is this for me?" she says, her eyes wide with surprise as they roam the room.

"Who else would it be for?"

"I don't know… maybe you have a bubble bath fetish?" she jokes, and it's good to see her smile—I mean really smile.

"I can assure you that I don't, so please, take your time. Dinner will be ready in thirty minutes."

I go to walk out and shut the door, to give her some privacy, but her hand comes to rest on my arm, stopping me. "Dorien, what is all of this? What are we doing here?"

I've asked myself the same question more than once, but I have no answer for her, because I don't fucking know myself.

"You're going to have a bath, and I am going to make sure dinner isn't burning."

"You cooked yourself?" she asks, astonished.

"Of course. I'm not totally fucking useless, you know?" I tease—fucking tease? Me?

"I would never think of you as useless, Dorien," she says softly, and fuck, the way she looks at me has my dick wanting to make an appearance already.

"Relax, and I'll be back to let you know when dinner is ready." With that, I leave her to it, pulling the door shut as I go, and as I walk to the kitchen to check on the food, I remind myself that I need to hold the fuck back. It's just sex. Really, really fucking good sex and nothing more.

Chapter Twenty-Nine

ELISE

I'm a little lost for words as I get myself dry and wonder if I'm having a dream which I'm about to wake up from any minute now. And if I am, I don't want to wake up, because this is so unexpected, and it's simply so fucking nice.

The bath was divine, the bubbles smelling like rose petals and soothing my aches away. The towel is the softest thing I have ever had wrapped around me, and the clothes… wait… where are there any clothes? Oh my god, am I going to have to put my sweaty maid uniform back on?

With a resigned sigh, I pick up my discarded uniform from the floor as there's a knock to the door, and then it opens slightly. "Elise," Dorien says, his head appearing around the door. "Dinner will be… what are you doing?" He pushes the door open fully and looks at me with his eyebrows pulled together in a frown.

"I'm getting dressed," I manage to say as I take in the fact that he is wearing grey joggers and a figure-hugging T-shirt that makes my mouth salivate. Fucking hell, he's hot in suits, but in casual dress… no competition. Joggers win, hands down.

"No, no," he mutters, coming towards me and taking the

uniform out of my hands and throwing it in the washing basket in the corner, by the door.

"Dorien, I can't just wear a towel," I tell him with a sigh.

"I think you absolutely could, but that isn't happening tonight." He reaches around me to some shelves behind and produces an over-sized shirt and a pair of sleep shorts. "This is what you'll be wearing."

I look at the clothes and look back at him. "Pyjamas?"

"Why not?"

"Um, isn't it a bit casual for dinner?" And also a bit weird that he's giving me sleepwear to put on when this is just a sex thing between us.

"That's the point, Elise. Casual and relaxed. Now, be a good girl and put them on. There's a hairbrush and toiletries in the drawers underneath the sink if you want to use them. Don't keep me waiting too long." And then he leaves, giving me a wink before he goes.

Umm… o-kay… what just happened? I quickly drop the towel and put the pyjamas on, and fuck, they are the comfiest pyjamas ever. I get that he has so much money he can have the best of everything, but why is he doing this for me? What have I done to earn his kindness? And does he do this for every woman he sleeps with? *No, stop it, I don't want to think about it. I'll remain in ignorant bliss, thinking that I am the first woman he's done this for. It makes it special, and these moments with him will be ones I will cherish forever, no part of them tainted.*

I pick the towel up and add it to the wash basket before quickly going to the sink unit and using the toiletries he said were available. I spritz some perfume on my neck and wrists, and I brush my hair to rid myself of the knots. I don't bother with anything else, because he sees me daily with no make-up on. I have nothing to hide when it comes to my body, he's seen it all.

I hurry out of the bathroom, double checking I've left it tidy, and I make my way to the main room. When I get there, I see a table has been set up by the window, with candles and a single rose in a vase in the middle, and place settings on opposite sides. It's so fucking romantic, but it shouldn't be, should it? This isn't about romance. It's about sex. Maybe this is how he does whatever he does, and maybe I should stop asking so many goddamn questions and just enjoy it all. I decide to go with the latter as he walks in from the kitchen carrying two plates, and smiling at me as he goes.

"Come and take a seat," he says, and I try to walk as casually as I possibly can, even though I want to squeal and run over there and pretend that this fairy-tale will last forever.

"This looks amazing," I say as I reach the table, and I feel his body behind me as his fingers brush my hair to one side, his lips placing a soft kiss on the side of my neck.

"Not as amazing as you, but food first," he whispers by my ear, and I shudder with delight. He taps my arse and tells me, "Sit."

He sits opposite, and I look at the food in front of me. It smells delicious, and I am absolutely starving.

"Hope you don't mind pasta, and help yourself to the tempura prawns," he says as he gestures to the sharing bowl in the middle of the table. "There's also fresh bread in the basket," he continues, as if I can't see it, and I wonder if he's a little out of his comfort zone with all of this.

"It looks delicious. Thank you." A genuine smile graces my face, and I feel my damn heart fluttering as I look at the man who has made this all seem so surreal. I take a slice of bread and butter it, dipping it in the sauce that the pasta has been cooked in before taking a bite. And when I do, flavour bursts in my mouth. "Oh my god, this is so good."

"You're welcome," he says smugly, but it's endearing.

"So, uh, how was your day?" I ask, wondering if I just made things really fucking awkward by having a conversation like a normal couple would have over dinner.

"We don't have to do small talk, Elise," he says, and I feel a pang of disappointment hit.

"Of course not, sorry." I look down at the food and feel like a bit of a twat if I'm being honest.

"No, that came out wrong. What I mean is that we've gone from nought to sixty in no time at all, so small talk seems…"

"Meaningless?" I say, filling in the blank for him. "I get it. This is something that I never saw coming, and I don't think you did either, so it's new ground for both of us." I have no idea where I'm getting the confidence from to say all of this, but I've been nothing but open with him since day one—to a certain point, anyway.

"You're right," he says as he leans back in his chair. "I never do this, Elise. I never invite women to dinner or run them a bath."

"And I didn't ask you to do any of that."

"I know, but…" His voice trails off as he runs a hand through his hair and blows out a breath. "I'm never like this with anyone, and I mean no-fucking-one."

"So, why are you doing this for me?" I ask quietly.

"Honestly?"

I nod at him.

"I don't know," he admits.

Well, it's not the answer a girl wants, but it's honest if nothing else.

"I am known for being a hard man to crack, and trust me, plenty of people have tried and failed. I don't trust easily, Elise, but from the moment I met you, I don't know, I felt something without you even trying to break me down."

"I get it." I truly do, because there's this 'thing' between us that neither one of us can seem to shake. It's been crazy from the word go, and it doesn't seem to want to stop.

Silence descends upon us, the food forgotten as our thoughts consume us. And then, out of nowhere, he pushes his chair back and says, "Come here," in the most seductive voice I've ever heard.

I gulp as I push myself up slowly from my chair, unable to resist his call. I walk around the table, feeling all kinds of vulnerable as I do, but also knowing that he came into my life at this moment for a reason. A reason I'm yet to truly understand.

I stop when I stand in front of him, and his legs part more as he reaches forward and pulls me between his thighs. He runs his hands up my bare legs and over the pyjama shorts I'm wearing, and when he reaches the waistband, he moves them down, until they're pooling at my feet. No need to remove any underwear, because I wasn't wearing any. He licks his lips as he sits back and frees his cock from his jogging bottoms—his very hard cock.

"Sit," he commands, and I bite my lip as I feel excitement race through me. As I move to straddle his lap, I lower myself down until he fills me completely and I'm adjusting to the feel of him.

"Fuck," I say on an exhale. His hands move to the buttons on my shirt, and he undoes them, one by one, oh-so-slowly, as I sit in his lap, waiting until he tells me to move.

He pushes my shirt apart and exposes my breasts, and my neediness takes over as I arch my back and push them towards him, needing something to take the fucking edge off.

He chuckles as his lips run over my nipples. He knows what I want, and yet, he's making me wait.

"So fucking eager, Elise," he whispers against my skin, placing light kisses between my breasts, and my body shudders with need and delight. "You want me to make you come, buttercup?"

"Yes," I say without hesitation. I mean, my wet pussy shows just how much I want him anyway.

He takes my nipple in his mouth, his teeth biting down lightly and eliciting a low moan from me.

"Ride me, Elise. Ride me hard on this fucking chair," he commands, and my hips start to move, grinding on him before I lift up and slam back down repeatedly.

"Jesus," he says at my relentless rhythm. I grip onto his shoulders, my nails digging into his skin. I feel fucking wild as I give him everything. I feel fucking free as all of my hang ups fall away. The way he does that is magical, and I know that a part of me will never want to let that feeling go.

I move my lips to his, needing a taste of him. His tongue dances with mine, his hands holding my hips as I swirl and grind on him. My body fits so perfectly with his, and I think he knows it as well. My hands move to his hair, gripping and tugging as I cry into his mouth, pleasure exploding through me.

"Dorien," I whisper, his name swallowed by his lips devouring mine as I tremble on top of him. His teeth nip my bottom lip as I groan loudly, my orgasm sweeping through me and clenching his cock until he's roaring his release.

I move my hips until we're done, and even when the orgasms are over, I stay where I am, my lips moulded to his and my hands now caressing his hair affectionately. His fingers are on my back, holding me close, his dick still inside me, his cum seeping out of me, and all I can think is how truly fucked I am, in more ways than one.

Chapter Thirty

DORIEN

She's still on top of me, on this chair, my cum leaking out of her, but I can't seem to break my lips from hers. She's addictive, like a drug that I never knew I craved. Fuck.

I'm in deep shit here.

She's just gotten out of a marriage—albeit a shitty one, but still, she was *married*.

I'm pretty sure I've turned into a randy fucking teenager since I met her, unable to get through my day without wanting her—needing her.

I haven't even asked her age. I don't know about her private life, other than the husband thing. I don't know fucking anything about her, and yet, I can't stop.

She's mine.

And as I pick her up with me and carry her to my bedroom, the one in the penthouse which I'm quickly regarding as my own, because she's here, the one I would never usually share with a woman because it's too personal, it seems my heart is fighting my mind. One wants to draw a line in the sand and move on, while the other doesn't want to let her go. Ever.

Chapter Thirty-One

ELISE

He's on top of me, his body caging me in, his tongue sweeping through my mouth, my legs wrapped around him, unable to let go.

This is different. So fucking different. And even as I feel the change happening between us, I know I won't be able to stop it.

My heart already knows that Dorien has taken up residence there, even as my head tries to throw some reason into the mix.

We've known each other a matter of weeks.

It's crazy to be so involved with someone and yet know so little about them.

I've just got out of a marriage that I am pretty sure will have scarred me in some way for life.

I'm too young to get in this deep so quickly.

I need to experience life on my own, to learn about myself and learn the world around me.

I know Dorien likes to fuck, he told me so.

Shouldn't he be a red flag?

But even as I ask the question in my mind, I know that red flag or not, I don't want to give this up. Not yet, anyway.

My fingers entwine at the back of his neck as he continues to kiss me and slowly inch his cock inside of me. We both groan in unison as he fills me completely, my legs being wrapped around him allowing him to hit me so deep. And then he moves out slowly and pushes back in, over and over again as pleasure wracks my body.

This doesn't just feel like fucking. Not anymore.

But my broken heart doesn't want to truly believe it, even as he starts to invade it. It's still damaged despite what I'm starting to feel for this man.

I know I don't want to let him go.

I know I want this elation from being with him like this to last forever.

But I also know that I need to find myself, too. I need to know who I am without a man clouding my judgement. I need to discover all the things I've missed out on. I need to take back so much, and I know if I give myself completely to Dorien right now, I'll regret it. And that's even if he wanted to take things to that level—I mean, he did tell me that he just wanted sex, so I could be overthinking all of this… and, oh dear God, he's moving down my body, interrupting my raging thoughts as he puts his tongue on my clit and gently moves it in circles. I fist the bed sheets as his tongue circles so seductively, teasing me but giving me intense pleasure at the same time.

I writhe when he softly nips my clit with his teeth. I groan when he runs his fingertips up the insides of my thighs at the same time. And I fucking combust when he pushes two fingers inside me and takes me to another high, only for me to come tumbling back down at a deliciously slow rate.

It seems that he's not done though, even as I lay exhausted beneath him, as he crawls back up my body and hooks one of my legs over his hip as he enters me slowly, bringing the fingers he just fucked my pussy with to my mouth and telling me to "suck" the taste off of him. I take it all like a good fucking girl as I taste myself on his fingers.

I didn't realise how much of a turn-on it was to be commanded a little in the bedroom until him. He's made me see things differently, even if it is in a really intimate way and totally at odds with what I should be doing post marriage break-up.

As I lie beneath him, moving in sync with him as his dick rocks into me, I can only wish that I had met him first, and maybe, just maybe, I would have been given a different outlook on how a man is supposed to treat a woman. Or maybe I'd have just been what I am right now, a fuck, even if it does feel like more than that.

Chapter Thirty-Two

DORIEN

It's the morning after the night before, and my thoughts are all over the fucking place. I don't have thoughts, not on any kind of emotional level. I'm a rock, solid fucking stone, and the hardest nut to crack.

Until her.

Because she's slowly giving me fucking feelings, and I don't know if I'm okay with that.

I watch her from the doorway as she sleeps, sipping my coffee and admiring her delicious curves that aren't covered by the sheet on the bed, having slipped off of her at some point in the night.

Her long hair is fanned out across the pillow, her lips slightly parted as she inhales and exhales so peacefully.

Fuck.

I force myself to turn and walk back into the main room, where I find my phone discarded on the coffee table. Another thing I never do is leave my phone unattended, because I am a businessman first and foremost, but last night, I didn't even question it. I pick it up with an angry swipe, looking for the one number that I can call and actually gain some sort of clarity from.

I find the name I'm looking for and hit dial, the phone only ringing twice before it's answered.

"This better be fucking urgent, Dorien," he barks into the phone, his voice gruff and telling me I have roused him from sleep. My eyes move to the clock on the wall, telling me it's just after six a.m. Okay, so maybe I could have waited longer, but I don't have time to fuck about.

"Is it classed as urgent when I have a recently separated married woman in my bed who I've fucked on more than one occasion and invited for dinner last night in my penthouse?" I don't pull any punches, and the silence on the end of the other line tells me that I've shocked the shit out of him. *Yeah, you and me both, buddy.*

I hear Gabriel sigh on the other end of the line before he says, "Fuck me, I need coffee for this kind of deep-rooted shit this early in the morning."

"Thought so," I muse as I take my coffee out onto the balcony, sliding the door closed behind me. I look out over the buildings and wonder if I'm being a total fucking pansy and reading far too much into this, but if I am, then Gabriel will tell me. He's the only one I'd trust to tell me the truth, and he's the only one I'd ever call to discuss anything of this nature. Although, it's never cropped up before, because I don't fucking do this.

"Right, I've got coffee, so hit me with it," he says a few moments later, but I don't even know what to say. He must sense my unease, because he says, "Is she hot?" to break the ice, and I blow a puff of air out of my mouth.

"Insanely hot."

"Wanna send me a pic?"

"Fuck off."

"Okay, okay," he says, laughing at my reaction. He's been tied down for years, but he still likes to fuck with me about being an over-aged playboy who doesn't know what to do with his dick. Wanker. "You said she's married?"

"Separated," I clarify.

"For how long?"

"A week or so."

"Jesus Christ, Dorien," he says with a sigh. "She's barely in the rebound zone, and you're catching feelings for her?"

"I'm not catching feelings, and I'm sure as shit not a rebound," I boom, offended by the insinuation.

"No? Then what the hell are you?"

"I… I don't fucking know."

"Might want to get clued up before you start calling me with woman drama," he taunts, and if he were in front of me, I'd be sticking my middle finger up and telling him to go and swivel.

"I do not have woman drama."

"Oh, you do, you just don't want to accept it."

"Fuck my life," I say on a breath as a car toots it's horn below, disrupting the peace of the morning.

"Want me to put Chantel on the phone?" he asks, referring to his wife.

"Christ, no." I adore Chantel, but I don't need her on my case about fucking a married woman and having no direction other than my hotel chains.

"Then pull your head out of your arse, Dorien, and figure out where your fuck boy life is really taking you." He pulls no punches, just like me, and I guess it's why our friendship has stayed the course.

I grit my teeth and wonder why I bloody called him in the first place. "I wanted clarity, not a goddamn lecture."

"Then you called the wrong person."

"Bastard."

"Always," he says, not even a little bit bothered by my response to him being perfectly reasonable.

"You're going to tell Chantel anyway, aren't you?" I ask, even though I don't really need to.

"Of course. And you can expect us to be at the hotel in the next twenty-four hours," he tells me. They know which hotel I'm staying in, because of course I told them about the merger and my impromptu plan to hang around here for a little while, missing out the fact that Elise is one of the maids, of course—they'll find out soon enough, anyway.

"Wonderful," I reply sarcastically.

"Looking forward to it," he says before he hangs up, but not before I hear the sound of his laughter ringing out. But even as I know I'll get an earful from both of them, I'm okay with that, because they are the family that I chose.

Chapter Thirty-Three

ELISE

"Shit," I say as I fly from the bed and across the hallway to the bathroom, where I find my maid's uniform… washed and dried and hanging up in front of the mirror. I frown, but I don't have time to waste, so I quickly move back into action and get dressed, hoping I can make it to the staff quarters in the next fifteen minutes. I guess being a billionaire hotel owner means that when you request your shit to be washed and dried, it gets done in double quick time. I quickly grab the brush I used last night from the drawer underneath the sink and spot a hair tie next to it. I don't have time to question how efficient Dorien is with seeming to have everything to hand as I throw my hair up and use an unopened toothbrush to clean my teeth. I'd like to lie in bed all day and relive every moment from last night, but sadly, real life always gets in the way of my fantasies.

I rush from the bathroom and make my way into the main room, my eyes landing on my shoes sitting by the front door, and my body instantly reacting to Dorien stood in the kitchen doorway, leaning on the door frame. Mother have mercy. He looks positively scrummy, but again, no time.

"Morning," I manage to say as I go to my shoes and slip my feet in them.

"Good morning, Elise," he rumbles. Christ, his voice alone is like a fucking sin.

"I'm going to be late if I don't get going," I say, shifting on the spot.

"Of course." He nods, and a feeling of disappointment hits me.

"I'll, uh, see you around?" I question, because this feels weird. Like there's been another shift between us that I'm unaware of.

He says nothing as I thank him for last night and then disappear out of the door, going to the lifts and pressing the call button.

I feel my face flush, embarrassment overwhelming me. But then my body goes on high alert as I feel him behind me. I pray for the lift to hurry up and get here, but the dial at the top tells me it's stuck on floor five. Of course it is.

"Elise," he whispers, his lips by my ear and his body heat making me want to fucking melt on the spot.

"Don't, Dorien," I say, albeit unconvincingly. Something isn't right, and I can't shake the feeling that I am going to end up being irreparably damaged by him.

The lift starts to move, slowly making its way to me, and when the doors open, I step forward, just needing to be away from him. Such a contrast to last night. Such a shame, too, because last night was everything I never knew I needed.

I move my hand to the side and press the button for the ground floor, and I don't turn back around until the doors close, but I know he was stood there, waiting, watching. I could feel his eyes boring into my back.

"You look like shit," Celeste remarks as she drops down in the seat across from me, her lunchbox landing with a thud on the table.

"Gee, thanks," I sarcastically respond while I roll my eyes and continue to try and eat the food in front of me. I'm not hungry in the slightest, but I need to keep my energy up for the rest of the day, not to mention the energy I probably burned off last night while I was fucking my boss. I stifle the groan that wants to escape me.

"What happened?" she asks, because she knows where I was last night—of course she does, seeing as I now crash at her place and all.

I drop my fork to the plate, letting it clatter, and I put my head in my hands. "I can't do this, Celeste. I never should have gone there last night."

"Did he hurt you?" She speaks quietly, because we work with some nosey fuckers who are milling around the place, and for that, I'm grateful. She would never want to air my private life, and vice versa.

"No, he did quite the opposite," I admit, and drop my hands from my face to look at her. "He made me feel like I was the only woman in the world. I've never known pleasure like it, and fuck me, I can't let myself…" I stop short of admitting what I've been trying to push out of my mind all day.

"Oh my god… you've fallen for him?" Celeste questions, her eyes a little wider than before.

"No, that's stupid."

"Is it?" she enquires, one eyebrow raised.

"Of course it is. No one can fall for someone that quickly."

"Can't they?"

"What is this? A bloody inquisition?"

Celeste chuckles, but I fail to see the humour. "You know I'm right." A smile tips one side of her mouth.

"No way, definitely not." She can't be right. I won't allow her to be right.

"You keep telling yourself that, Elise, but I can see right through you, and you've got it for our boss man real bad."

"Shut up," I scold her, which just makes her laugh a little harder. "This isn't funny, Celeste."

"If you don't laugh, you'll be eaten up by your goddamn feelings, so just let it be what it is."

"How do you make everything sound so simple?" I ask.

"It is a gift," she replies, holding her hands out either side of her, like the goddamn ray of sunshine she is.

"I hate you," I tell her, but I smile at the same time. I could never hate her, not in a million years.

"Love you too," she says, more laughter leaving her and making my lips twitch. "Come on, smile, you know you want to."

And I do, because she is a gift—at least, to me she is.

"I can't fall for him, Celeste. It's too soon, it's too much."

"Hate to tell you this, but there is no time limit on your heart, Elise. It wants what it wants, and sometimes, you need to see where it leads you."

"And what if it leads to a world of hurt? Because we both know a maid and a top businessman is a recipe for disaster."

"Or it could be the greatest love story."

"Ugh." I roll my eyes, wishing it could be the latter, but knowing that the real world doesn't work like that. "I have a messy divorce ahead of me, an uncertain road that I have no clue how to walk down—"

"And yet, you're walking down it anyway," she says, cutting me off, trying to keep me from my pessimistic self.

She's right. I continued walking down it even when I found out he was my new boss, because I can't resist the handsome, filthy bastard. He's alluring, his darkness inside of him calling to me like a sodding beacon. Because even though I don't know shit about his past, I can see the dark that lives inside of him. And as much as Celeste might want this to be a beautiful, unexpected love story, I still get the feeling that it's going to end up with me as the tragic heroine who couldn't resist the forbidden fruit in front of her.

"Come on," I say as I pick the plate up with uneaten food on and throw it in the bin. "Time to go scrub."

"Miss Elise," the doorman says as I reach the steps, ready to go back to Celeste's place and forget about the torment that has plagued my mind all day long.

"Yes, Noah?" Noah is new here, wanted a little part-time job to occupy him during retirement. But I guess he's no longer retired, seeing as he's working here.

"I have a request for you to go to the penthouse."

"Do you now?"

"Yes, Miss."

Noah is a kind man with a heart of gold, and I hate to have to burst his bubbly bubble with my next words. "Please inform the penthouse that I will not be attending whatever is happening up there tonight."

"But, Miss Elise, Mr Dukes—"

"Noah," I interrupt, feeling awful that I am about to put him in a predicament, but failing to work up the nerve to face Dorien again today. "It's been a long day, and I've been working extra hours the last couple of weeks. I need to go home." Home. I don't have my own place to call home yet, but Celeste has told me to treat her place as such, and for the foreseeable, I will. "I'm sorry." I give him a soft smile and link my arm through Celeste's as I lead us forward.

"I can feel your eyes burning into me," I say, not looking at her, keeping my head forward.

"Elise, you cannot leave that fine man waiting."

"I can, and I am. We're going home to watch a film and eat all the snacks," I inform her.

"He's going to be pissed."

"Then let him be pissed," I say, as if I don't care, when in actual fact, I do. More than I probably should.

Chapter Thirty-Four

DORIEN

I watch as she makes her way across the road. I know it's her, even from the penthouse, because she's like a fucking magnet.

She's ignored my request to come here tonight.

I don't even know what that means, but maybe I should take note.

Except... I feel rage burn inside of me that she's not here. I feel frustration that we can't just be two simple people who meet and fuck. I feel all kinds of pissed that I won't be able to unleash that frustration in one of the only ways I know how—buried deep inside of her, because for the life of me, I can't bring myself to go and sweet talk another woman into my bed. Even the thought of it feels wrong. And isn't that the problem?

She's fucking ruined me in a matter of weeks.

Do I just give in to the feeling of wanting her so fucking bad that my blood boils at the thought of another man touching her?

Or do I fight it with everything I have to get back to the soulless arsehole that I know I am?

"Hello," I hear shouted loudly from behind me, and I turn around with a stifled groan as I see Chantel bounding her way into my penthouse, with a smug looking Gabriel behind her. Usually, I'd be rolling my eyes right about now, which would cause her to punch me on my arm, but tonight, I'm actually fucking relieved at the interruption, despite my stifled groan. It stops the continuous thoughts of Elise from playing on a goddamn loop in my mind. Or it should do, anyway. I don't even question how they were able to walk in here without knocking, because like the dickhead I am, I'd left the door slightly ajar, hoping Elise was going to be the one walking in here tonight.

"Why are you hiding out here and looking all grumpy?" Chantel asks as she walks towards me and gives me a hug. She's one of the few people I'd let hug me.

"Looking as gorgeous as always, Chantel, and I am not grumpy," I tell her, to which she pulls back from me and gives me a knowing look. She's classy without being stuck up, her green eyes sparkling in the moonlight.

"You look pissed off," Gabriel says from behind her, and we clap hands in the way that guys do as he pats my shoulder in greeting.

"Not even through the door for two minutes and already on my case," I remark, which just makes Gabriel smile wider.

"Shut up whining," Chantel says as she walks back into the main room and shouts, "Come sit down and tell me all about this woman."

"Fucker," I say to Gabriel, and he laughs.

"She dragged it out of me," he insists, but I know that's just bullshit. They are the epitome of a hopelessly happy couple who love each other more now than they did when they first met. It's bloody sickening, and I am so bloody happy for them.

With a sigh, I walk past him and his smug face, and when I enter the main room, I see Chantel is already settled on the sofa, waiting for me to open up to them and try to explain what it is I'm feeling. Christ, I hate that word. Feelings. Emotions. It always ends up with someone being fucked over. It's just life, and I had made my own peace with that. But now it's all up in the air.

"Sit," Chantel says as she pats the other side of the sofa, and I reluctantly take a pew, knowing that the questions will come quick fire in the next few seconds.

"I'll grab us some drinks," Gabriel says, disappearing into the kitchen area.

"So, what's her name? What's she like?" Chantel starts, and I shout to Gabriel to hurry the fuck up, because suddenly, I need all the scotch. "Don't deviate, Dorien," Chantel says, knowing me all too well.

"Do we have to talk about this? Can't we just catch up and get pissed?"

"You're nearly forty, Dorien, getting pissed is child's play." Chantel tsks and watches Gabriel as he makes his way back into the room, a glass of wine poured for her in one hand, and two tumblers and the bottle of scotch in the other. Good man.

"Fuck, don't remind me," I say as I take the scotch Gabriel has just poured and down it in one. The burn in my throat feels good, and I put the glass down and nod for him to pour another one.

"Oh my, this is serious," Chantel comments, looking at Gabriel.

"Told you," he says with a smile that has her eyes twinkling.

Fucking hell. I don't need this shit.

"Will you two stop being so... well, whatever this is you do," I say, taking the newly refilled glass and sipping, if only to appease them both.

"It's called love, Dorien. You should give it a go, it's totally worth it," Chantel says with a grin, and Gabriel laughs as he takes a seat on the other side of his wife. They are the perfect picture of a healthy marriage, and I know they want the same thing for me, but we're not all born from the same cloth, and we can't all have the same outlook on love when we've been kicked in the balls and left in the dirt.

"So, she's married?" Chantel continues, like I knew she would.

With a sigh, I resign myself to this conversation happening. "Recently separated."

"So I gather. And when do I get to meet her?"

I nearly choke on the mouthful of scotch I was drinking. "You don't."

"Don't be such a spoil sport. I want to meet the woman that got more than one night with the fuckboy-for-life Dorien Dukes."

Gabriel pisses himself laughing, and I can't help but scowl at the pair of them.

"Remind me why I keep you two around?" I question.

"Because you'd never get rid of us even if you tried," Chantel says, a beaming smile on her face. She's right. They'd hound me like a dog if I ever tried to cut them loose, which I wouldn't, this is just our way.

"Come on, man, just give it up already. You know she won't stop until she's got it all out of you anyway," Gabriel chimes in, and doesn't he just speak the fucking truth.

And so, over another few tumblers of scotch, I give them as much as I can, which is basically keeping it minimal because talking is overrated.

"Huh. So, she didn't love the husband, but you don't know the backstory. Then he shows up here, where you find them in a room with him putting his hands on her in a way that he never should have, and you let him walk out of here on two legs?" Chantel questions when I'm done.

"And your point is?"

"Well, I've seen you lose your shit for less, Dorien, so what gives?"

She's right. In the past, I've thought nothing of punching some fucker on the nose who thinks he can have his way with her when Gabriel has left her side for more than five minutes. I'd certainly do the same thing even now.

"I didn't want to upset her further, and I didn't know if she'd want me to do that, so I put her before my rage," I admit, and I know my mistake the moment the words have left my lips. Chantel gasps, one of her hands flying to her mouth in shock.

"Oh," is all that comes out of Gabriel's mouth, as they both look at me like I'm someone they don't recognise. I guess they don't, because I barely recognise myself anymore.

"Dorien, she's your—"

"Nope, don't want to hear it," I say as I neck the rest of my scotch and stand up, quickly making my way to my bedroom. "Help yourself to anything, and the guest room is yours. First door on the left," I shout, pointing to it as I pass.

And I don't fail to hear Chantel's words as I round the corner. "She better not break him, Gabriel, because if she does, I don't think he'll ever come back from it."

Chapter Thirty-Five

ELISE

It's been three days since that night with Dorien. Two since I turned down his invitation to the penthouse, and I've never been so glad to have gotten sick before. I mean, being sick sucks, but at least I haven't had to try and avoid the awkwardness. Sure, it'll be waiting for me when I go back, but I'll deal with that when the time comes. Right now, I need to focus on getting better, because for two days I've been praying to the toilet almost hourly.

I also know that Hayley was unimpressed when I phoned in sick, so I'm sure I'll go back to her wrath and be cleaning the shittiest of rooms as punishment. Luckily for me, the hotel chain pays a little for sickness leave, and even if it isn't the usual hourly amount, it's better than nothing.

I groan as I sit up, feeling weak and shaky as I do, but I force myself to get out of bed to grab a fresh glass of water.

Celeste has been a godsend, but she's still got to work, and it does me good to try and get out of my pit… I think, even if it doesn't feel like it right now.

I slowly make my way down the stairs and to the kitchen, where I fill a bottle with water and click the kettle on to make a hot drink. It's all I can stomach really. I'm hoping it's just a forty-eight-hour bug, but with day two almost done and me still feeling like death, I think I'm just being a bit too hopeful.

If I was sick when I lived with Derrick, he'd have just moaned at me for losing pay and for not pushing through. And speaking of, he's been phoning me for the last three hours. I've ignored every call, even as my inquiring mind wants to know why he's suddenly blowing up my phone. I haven't seen or heard from him since he slapped me around the face, and I haven't heard a peep from my mother. Not that I expected to. She will still be wallowing in her hatred of me for fucking up her plans. I know that won't be the end of it, she's just biding her time, because she won't let this go. She'll try to bully me back there eventually, but it will just be a wasted effort on her part. I'll never go back.

The kettle finishes boiling, and I make a cup of tea, adding a little extra sugar than usual. Taking my drinks back to bed, I'm stopped by someone knocking on the door. I'm not in the mood to be bothered with a door-to-door salesman, so I continue to make my way to the bedroom, but the knocking is relentless, making me question who the hell is out there. I momentarily panic that it's Derrick or my mother, but neither of them know where Celeste lives, so it can't be them, which puts me back at ease a little.

The knocking continues, and with the little energy I have left, I place the drinks down on bedside table in my room, and I go back to the door. There's no peephole to see who it is, but I leave the chain across the door as I open it a sliver to see who could possibly want my attention so badly.

My eyes widen when I see a burly man stood there, shades covering his eyes and his mouth pulled into a straight line. He's massive, like a giant as he towers above me.

"Elise Woods?" he questions, and I nod. "I have a package for you." He bends to pick up said package, which is a large paper bag that has pink tissue paper spilling out of the top of it, covering whatever may be inside.

"Oh." A package for me? Here? But no one knows I'm here. "Are you sure it's for me?" I ask, even though he said my full name when I opened the door.

"Yes. You wanna open the door, or shall I leave it on the floor so you can get it once I've gone?"

"Um..."

"Tell you what, I'll just leave it," he decides, placing the bag back down and giving me a firm nod. "Good day, Elise Woods."

Woods... I hate that name. I should go back to my maiden name, but I fucking hate that too. I would rather not be tied to any of the people who have brought so much misery to my life.

My eyes flit down to the bag, and I push the door closed a little, sliding the chain across and opening the door just enough to slide the bag through. I shut the door and pull the chain back across, my eyes fixed on the bag like it's going to bite me.

Who would be sending me whatever is inside there?

Open the fucking bag and find out, for goodness' sake. I roll my eyes at how ridiculous I'm being, and I pull off the tissue paper on top, my eyes nearly bugging out of my head when I see an array of items that have been sent to try and cure me of this bug. Fresh soup, fresh bread, tissues, medicine, soothing headache strips, vitamins, you name it and it's in here.

"What the hell?" I say out loud as I pull each of the contents out and marvel at the thoughtfulness of whoever sent it.

I don't have to wonder for long when I see a small card at the bottom, and I eagerly swipe it up.

DON'T KEEP ME WAITING TOO LONG.
DORIEN.

My nose scrunches up at the short message, even as my heart melts a little at the kindness of him sending me anything.

Don't keep me waiting... I have no idea what to do with that as I repack everything in the bag and use the last of my energy to put it in the kitchen, popping the fresh soup in the fridge before going back to bed. The exhaustion hits me, and as soon as my head hits the pillow, I forget all about the drinks I made and let sleep take me, to dreams about a tall, handsome guy who puzzles me more by the day.

"Elise…" I hear shouted from the hallway, rousing me from my sleep.

"Yeah," I croak out, reaching for the water I refilled earlier but haven't touched. I gulp down a load, ignoring the swirling of my stomach as I do. I haven't thrown up all day, which is a start, and I'm hoping to keep it that way.

"Did you get it?" Celeste asks as she appears in my doorway, looking like she's been through a whirlwind with her hair coming out of her ponytail and her cheeks flushed. She drops on the edge of the bed and bounces a couple of times, making my stomach swirl a little bit faster.

"Celeste, stop," I say quietly as I close my eyes and take a few deep breaths, my hand going to my mouth in a feeble attempt to stop anything coming up. If it's going to then it's going to, so it's totally redundant, but still.

"Shit, sorry," she apologises, but I can feel her excitable energy buzzing away, even with my eyes closed and my mind on not throwing up again.

"Give me a minute." I wait until the swirling has subsided a little, before I sluggishly sit up and rest my head against the headboard.

"Not feeling any better?" Celeste asks, and I squint as I open my eyes.

"I was earlier."

"I'm sorry… want me to go?" she says sheepishly.

"No, no, I'm fine."

"Even when you look like shit, you're still gorgeous," she tells me, and I manage to pull my lips into a small smile.

"Thanks."

"So, did you get it?" She repeats her earlier question, and I know she is clearly aware of Dorien sending me the 'get well' bag.

"If you're talking about the bag, yes, I got it."

"Of course I'm talking about the bag." She rolls her eyes in a comical way, and I chuckle as I hold my stomach. "So, what was in it?"

"A few bits…" I toy with her.

"Don't get smart, Elise," she says, but there isn't a pissed off bone in her body, she's merely being curious, as I would be if it were the other way around.

"I'm guessing Dorien came and informed you?" Because who else would it have been?

"He didn't, actually, but Hayley did with a disgusted look on her face."

"What? Hayley did?" My eyes widen as she tells me that Hayley was under strict instructions to make sure everything was in there that would help you get back to work quickly.

"Pfft, work my arse, he just wants to bang you again. Your pussy must be magical, Elise, because I know I wouldn't get a damn 'get well' package from him."

"Fuck, does Hayley know about me and Dorien?" I ask.

"I don't think so… she mentioned it was part of the new policies in regards to staff absence. But, between me and you, I think he's just covering his arse so she doesn't suspect anything."

"She probably already does suspect. Oh great, can't wait to get back there," I say sarcastically.

"She doesn't know anything, so don't overthink it."

Silence ensues for a few moments before I speak. "Derrick never got me anything when I was unwell, even when he was working and seemed to have his life together, he never did anything like this…" My voice fades off, unsure of how to process that. A man I've been sleeping with has shown more kindness than my husband ever did.

"Derrick is a dick," Celeste remarks, but we already know this.

"He's been blowing up my phone most of the day," I tell her, and speak of the devil… my phone starts to flash on the side, the ringer set to silent but his name like a fucking beacon on the screen.

"So that's why you didn't answer my calls at lunch," Celeste says.

"I didn't even know you'd tried to phone, sorry."

"Don't be daft, you're unwell, so I thought you were just asleep."

"I was, but even when I noticed the phone flashing, I ignored it, because I presumed it was him every time."

"Want me to rip him a new one?" she offers, but with a soft laugh, I shake my head.

"Thank you for the offer but I'll deal with it when I feel more like myself."

"Okay. So are you going to tell me exactly what was in that bag or am I going to go and have to hunt for it myself?" she says, and just like that, my best friend makes me feel a whole lot better with her easy going nature.

Chapter Thirty-Six

ELISE

It took me six days in total to return to work, and now I'm waiting outside of Hayley's office for my back to work interview. As if being ill wasn't bad enough, now I have to justify why I wasn't in work and make the ice queen believe me.

I blow a strand of hair off my face as I watch the clock ticking by. I came in a little bit earlier to get this over and done with, but of course, Hayley only works to her time, and she will give no fucks about me having to rush around and make up for the time I'm losing here to get the rooms designated to me ready for the next guest's arrival.

I've got a shitty evening ahead of me too, because I never called Derrick back and he's been trying to reach me every day since the phone calls started. I'm dreading it, but I need to deal with whatever he has to say, until I have my meeting with the solicitor, and then they can deal with whatever he has to say.

"You can come in," Hayley says from her doorway, disturbing my thoughts. I didn't even realise she'd opened the door, I was so deep inside my own head.

With a fake smile, I stand, walking into her office and closing the door behind me, and I nearly fucking faint when I see that she isn't alone. Dorien is sat in a seat behind hers, and as she resumes her position at her desk, I wonder why he's here too. It's the first time I've laid eyes on him in over a week, and fuck, he looks good. I haven't yet had a chance to thank him for the 'get well' bag, but I will, when Hayley isn't around, because I won't be able to hide how much I have the hots for our boss.

"Sit down, Elise," Hayley barks, and I see Dorien's eyebrows pull together briefly before he schools his face, his eyes feeling like they're burning into me.

I sit down and blow out a breath, ready to get this over with and get back to work.

"So, records show you've been off sick for the last six days," Hayley starts, her eyes glued to a piece of paper in front of her.

"I apologise for being ill, but I couldn't come to work whilst I was… um… being sick." I want to face palm myself. I was going to say throwing up, but I didn't want Dorien to have the image of me with my head down the toilet—I don't even know why that matters, but when you've had his head between your legs and his dick inside of you, the last thing you want is for him to be picturing you chucking up. Which I'm sure he probably is now, anyway. I try to stop the flush from creeping up my neck and cheeks, but it's useless, I can feel it happening, and when I chance a quick look at him, I don't fail to notice the side of his mouth twitching into a smile.

"Did I ask you to speak?" Hayley chimes in, giving me a pointed look, her tone sounding more than a little pissed off.

"Sorry," I say as I drop my head and wish that this was over already.

"Hayley," Dorien barks, my head whipping back up as my eyes land on his furious face. "You can leave," he tells her, and her mouth drops open as she stares at him aghast.

"What?" she asks, but even I can sense that there is no room for debate here.

"Leave." One word, nothing else. I hold my breath as she rises and walks around the desk, giving me the side-eye as she goes past me.

The door opens and shuts, leaving the room in what feels like deafening silence. I have no idea what to say or do, but I guess I don't have to think about it for long as Dorien says, "Are you feeling better?"

"Um… yes, thank you," I reply quietly, my mind already on how much Hayley is going to make me suffer for witnessing her being kicked out of this room.

"Good." He stands from his seat and walks around the desk, until he's in front of me, his arse perched on the edge of the desk. His bulge is in line with my face, and flashes of us together flit through my mind. "Are you sure you're well enough to return to work?"

I nod my head as my eyes connect with his, and once again, the heat pools between my legs. Does this guy have some kind of secret tactic to turn me to putty? *Yes, Elise, it's his dick and his… charm.* I almost laugh at Dorien having charm, but I guess, in his own way, he does.

He sure as hell charmed the fucking knickers off of me in the most dominant way… "Elise?"

"What?" I blink a few times, realising he's been speaking and I totally zoned out.

"Did you get your package?" he reiterates, although I have no idea if that is what he actually asked previously.

"Yes, thank you."

"I wasn't sure because I never heard from you," he says, looking at me curiously.

"Well, I don't have any way of contacting you," I say with a shrug of my shoulders.

"We better remedy that. Give me your phone," he demands, holding his hand out ready. I'm yet to put it in my work locker, because I was going to do it after this back to work meeting, so he can clearly see the outline of it in the front pocket of my apron.

"I don't think that's a good idea," I admit.

"Give it to me."

"Are you always this bossy?" I enquire.

"Not always."

"Then why are you always bossing me around? Aside from work, of course."

"I thought you liked it when I did that," he says quietly, his eyes blazing with heat. My pussy clenches at the thought of him being dominant in the bedroom, or anywhere where we're naked, really.

To save myself from answering the question, I take my phone out of my pocket and go to pass it to him, but he reminds me to unlock the screen first, and of course, I do, because even though I said this was a bad idea, I'm not totally against having his number. I watch as he taps the screen and then declares, "Problem solved. Now you can get hold of me whenever you need to."

"And why would I need to get hold of you?" I question, fighting the smile from forming on my lips.

He leans down, my phone still in his hand, and he rests his hands on either side of the chair, until he's low enough that his face is level with mine. "Don't fucking toy with me, Elise."

"I'm not. I'm just asking why I would need it when we're just fucking on the side." I almost let my jaw drop open at how frank I just spoke, but sod it, I'm confused about what this is between us and, damn it, I need some goddamn clarity in my life about something—anything.

"Is that what you think this is? A quick fuck here and there?" he questions.

"Well, you told me you like to fuck, so you tell me." I'm not backing down, I'm fed up of wondering what the fuck is going on and if I'm going to be fired at any moment because I have crossed the line and someone has found out, or he no longer wants me around.

He quickly gets up and goes to the door, clicking the lock into place before he's back in front of me, resuming his position.

"I also told you I only fuck a woman for one night, but here I am, Elise, breaking all the rules for you," he confesses.

He's breaking the rules for me. His own rules. Stupid rules he's lived by for years.

"But why?" I ask, suddenly finding that I need the answer to that more than I realised.

"Because I like you."

I let out a snort of laughter, unable to stop myself. "You like me?"

He lifts one hand and runs it through his hair before putting it back on the arm of the chair I'm sitting in. "Yes, Elise, I fucking like you." It's the first time I've seen him look so unsure of himself, and honestly, it's so endearing.

I become a little braver and reach one hand up, letting it rest on his cheek as I tell him, "I like you too," and place a quick kiss on his lips. It's the first time I've initiated things between us, because it's always been his call and I've gone to him, and it seems to spark something inside of him as he lifts me from the seat and turns me around, sitting me back down on the desk and nestling himself between my thighs. His lips devour mine, making my head spin. And then, my phone starts ringing in his hand, abruptly stopping all kissing.

He holds it up as we both look at the screen, and I see that it's Derrick calling. "He always did know how to kill a beautiful moment," I comment without thinking, and Dorien barks out a laugh.

"He's not going to kill this moment," he tells me as he passes me the phone and says, "Answer it."

"What? No."

"Be a good girl, Elise, and answer the fucking phone and put it on speaker," he demands, and as I gulp, my finger accepts the call and clicks the speaker on.

"Elise?" Derrick's voice comes through the line, and I grimace, but Dorien indicates for me to keep my eyes on him, and I find the strength to speak.

"Yes, Derrick?" I reply, as Dorien moves his fingers to the insides of my thighs and runs them up and down slowly, softly.

"Why the fuck haven't you been answering my calls?" I see Dorien's jaw clench at how Derrick speaks to me, and I quickly answer.

"I've been ill."

"What do you mean you've been ill?"

"Well, what do you think it means when someone says they've been ill, Derrick?" I can't help the sark in my voice, and it earns me a smirk from Dorien, who start to move his fingers over my knickers, feeling how wet I am for him already.

"Don't get fucking smart with me, Elise. You need to stop being a baby and come home," he barks down the phone, but I'm too focused on Dorien crouching before me to really give a damn. I watch as he pushes my legs apart further and pulls my knickers to the side, giving me a wicked smile as he does, before his tongue flicks out and connects with my clit. I stifle the moan that wants to rip free from my throat when he repeats the action over and over.

"Elsie, do you hear me? You're my wife, for fuck's sake," Derrick says, but I can't form any words as Dorien sucks my clit into his mouth, one of his fingers entering me at the same time.

"Oh shit," I say on a breath before I can stop myself.

"Elise? What's going on?" Derrick says through the phone, but I drop it on the desk and throw my head back as Dorien adds another finger. "ELISE! ANSWER ME!"

"Yesssss," I whisper, my breaths coming more rapidly as my orgasm gains speed.

"Yes? Yes what? Yes you're coming home?" Derrick questions as Dorien sucks my clit harder, swirling his tongue around at the same time.

"Oh god…" One of my hands flies up to cover my mouth as I combust on the desk, using all of my self-control to not fucking scream.

"Elise, this isn't funny… what the fuck?" Derrick rages, and I reach for the phone, ready to cut him off and compose myself before starting work, but before I can do anything, Dorien grabs it and starts to speak.

"I would appreciate if you didn't bother my staff when they're at work," he says, not even introducing himself.

"Who the fuck are you?" Derrick spits, and I can imagine he's red in the face right about now.

"It doesn't matter who I am, just watch your step." And then he ends the call, leaving me open-mouthed. "Problem?" he asks, quirking an eyebrow. My phone starts to ring again, but he abandons it on the desk, his attention solely on me.

"You have no idea what kind of grief I'm going to get now you've done that," I admit, biting my bottom lip.

"You're not going to get any grief."

"You don't know Derrick," I say with a roll of my eyes. He's made my life difficult from day one, he's not about to stop now.

"He's nothing but a fucking weasel, Elise, and I won't have him bothering you at work."

"Just at work?" I ask shyly, keen to see what he says.

"Dinner, tonight, my penthouse, seven o'clock, no excuses," he says, and then he leans down and kisses my neck, leaving a trail as he comes back to my mouth and places a soft kiss before saying, "Deal?"

And it must be the post orgasmic high that has me forgetting all of my problems and saying "deal." Either that or I really have lost my fucking mind.

Chapter Thirty-Seven

DORIEN

"You two need to fuck off," I bark, looking at Gabriel and Chantel as they smile at me like I'm having some kind of revelation about life. I mean, I might be when it comes to Elise, but other than that, I'm still just me, plain old Dorien who likes to be in charge.

"Can we really not stay and meet her?" Chantel asks, for what feels like the millionth time.

"No," I reiterate, having already made my feelings on them staying here perfectly clear. "And don't forget your key card for your room."

"Yes, yes, we've got it," Gabriel chimes in, placing his hands on Chantel's shoulders and steering her towards the door.

"You know we'll have to meet her soon though, right?" she says as they reach the door and Gabriel opens it, guiding her through and giving me a smirk as he shuts the door behind them. I blow out a relieved breath and run my hands through my hair, but that relief is short lived when my phone starts to ring and I pull it from my pocket to see Elise's name flashing on the screen.

"Elise," I answer, wondering why she's calling me when she should be here in the next few minutes. She better not be calling to cancel, because despite what she might think, I really do want to talk to her, as well as fuck her.

"Dorien," she breathes down the line, and my face pulls into a frown.

"What's wrong?" My body immediately goes on high alert from the tone in her voice and the way she spoke so breathlessly.

"I need you… help…" She lets out a groan as if she's in pain, and I'm instantly tearing towards the door and ripping it open, my heart suddenly kicking up a notch at my urgency to get to her.

"Where are you?" I bark as I march to the lifts and press the call button.

"Out back… staff entrance… please, hurry…" Another groan has me cursing the fucking lift for not being here and opting to use the stairwell instead. I march forwards and try to tell myself that I would get this worked up over another employee being involved in whatever the hell has gone on, but really, I'm just kidding myself. Sure, I'd be pissed, because employees are the ones who make everything run like clockwork, and I look after my staff, just ask any one of them that works for me at any of my hotels and they will tell you that I am a decent fucking boss. But Elise… I strain my ears as I continue to listen to her on the other end of the phone, her breathing raspy, as I haul open the door for the stairs and I charge down them like a raging bull—and to be fair, I probably look like one right now.

As my feet fly down the ridiculous amount of stairs it takes to get to her, my heart pounds that much harder. If she's badly hurt, I don't know what I'll fucking do. It's like I'm having an out of body experience. I never do this. Or I never used to do this. She's come into my life and flipped everything I thought I ever knew on its head, and when I finally reach the bottom of the stairs and yank the door open to enter the corridor where the staff entrance is located, I see her, hunched over on the floor, the bottom of her back resting against the wall and a look of agony on her face…

Her face… I see blood trickling down her chin, and I dart like a bat out of hell to get to her.

That dread multiplies inside of me, and I quicken my pace as her head turns in my direction, her eyes puffy and red-rimmed as she lets the phone drop to the floor. I cut the call and drop my phone beside me as I crouch down and take her face in my hands.

"Fuck... Elise, what happened?" I question, concern taking over the rage for a moment. I inspect every part of her, but with clothes on, it's hard to tell if there's anything else I should be looking for. And then my eyes land on her neck. There are angry red marks on her skin that make my blood boil.

She gathers her breath and inhales deeply before telling me, "Attacked, out back," as she lifts her arm and points to the door. I can see she looks exhausted, the top part of her uniform splattered in blood from her nose and a split lip.

"We need to get you cleaned up. Are you okay to move?" I ask her, because my urgency to see the resulting damage from whatever attack she's talking about is rising. And so is my need to find the fucker that did this to her.

"I can move," she rasps, and I pocket both of our phones before helping her to her feet, only for her to sway from side to side. I don't waste any time as I take her in my arms and carry her, letting her head rest against my chest as we go. Her hand clutches my shirt too, fisting gently in the material.

I'm focused as I take the stairwell back up to the penthouse, Elise's body shaking as I do. I hold her closer, a little tighter without hurting her, and I gulp down a lump that has suddenly appeared in my throat.

By the time we get to the penthouse, she's shaking a little less, but that does nothing to ease my state of mind. I'm worried, raging, fucking furious, and just plain frustrated that I don't have all of the answers and that someone has done this to her.

I open the door and kick it shut behind me, carrying her straight into the bathroom and sitting her down on the sink unit. The first thing I do is start running some warm water, so the blood can be washed away. She sits quietly, her head bowed and tears running silently down her cheeks. Tears that have soaked into my shirt, and that I wish she'd never had to cry.

I grab a fresh cloth from a cabinet to the right of the sink unit, and I let my fingers fall under the water as it runs, making sure it's the right temperature. I move in silence as I put my hand under her chin and tilt her head up, my eyes seeing the pain in hers and fucking hating that it's there.

I gently use the fresh cloth and wipe away the blood, clenching my jaw as I do, needing to know what happened.

"I know that you won't want to relive this, but I need to know what happened," I say gently, keeping my eyes on her face to make sure I clean all of the blood off of her.

Her eyes flutter closed for a second before she opens them again, her voice thick with emotion when she says, "Derrick did this."

I pause my movements. Her husband did this to her?

I resume my movements as she continues to speak. "I've never seen him like that before. He was so out of it, like he'd lost complete control. I don't even know where he came from, he just appeared, and then..." She stops for a second and takes a few breaths before carrying on. "He wanted me to go back, but I refused, and then he just lost control. He grabbed me by the arm, and I shrugged him off, but that made him shove me against the wall as he got in my face and said that if I couldn't be his then I would be no one's.

"I fought him as best as I could, but his hands squeezed my neck... and then he punched me." Her voice trembles, and I hate that she has to tell me this. Hate that someone who was meant to love her hurt her. Hate that she wasn't mine first, because then this would never have happened.

I find myself leaning forward and placing a kiss on her forehead, my hand going to the back of her head as she nuzzles against my chest and her hands wrap around me. I feel protective of her, a primal instinct being awoken by this incredible woman.

"Thank you, Dorien," she says, her voice quiet but packed with emotion. "Thank you for coming when I needed you to."

Fuck.

I don't know how long we stay like that for, but I don't even entertain moving until I feel her arms loosen around me, and only then do I pull back to look at her and say, "I'll always be here when you need me."

The soft smile she gives me is one of the most beautiful smiles I've ever seen, even with her split lip.

"I bet I look hideous," she comments shyly, but she's so far off the mark. She's never hideous.

"Not even close, buttercup," I tell her, and it earns me a wider smile that makes her wince slightly as it stretches the skin where it's split. "I'm going to call my doctor to come out and check you over."

"There's no need to—"

"It's not up for debate, Elise," I interrupt.

"I don't want you to go to any trouble, I'm fine."

"It's no trouble, and it's happening," I state, unwilling to waver on this for even a second. I hold her gaze, and eventually, she nods, as if I was waiting for her permission. I wasn't. I pull my phone from my pocket and scroll to the number for my doctor, the one I pay a handsome retainer to, to be at my beck and call whenever I need, not that he's needed to do that much since I tripled his wage three years ago and made him a lifelong offer he couldn't refuse. I mean, he gets to do fuck all most of the time, and I've never been more thankful for my foresight to have him on call no matter what. It's worth it, because he is the best doctor for miles, and what I need now is the very best.

The phone rings as I look at her neck, my fingers reaching out and running over the red marks that shouldn't fucking be there. The doctor answers on the third ring.

"Dorien," he greets.

"I need you to come to The Blue Diamond hotel, doc. It's urgent."

"On my way," the doc says, no questions asked. He'll bring whatever medical shit he deems necessary, and if he doesn't have everything he needs, I'll have it shipped here from the private hospital a couple of streets over.

"Let's get you changed and settled in bed for when the doctor comes," I say, lifting her off the unit and carrying her out of the bathroom and to my bedroom. She feels so small in my arms, and my inner caveman just wants to wrap her up in a cocoon and keep her that way. It's quite a turnaround for a guy who, until recently, refused to feel emotions about anything.

I enter my bedroom and place her on the edge of the bed, where she waits whilst I get a pyjama shirt for her to change into. It's one of mine, because I don't have the time right now to look for the one she wore not so long ago, when she came to dinner and life was a little less complicated. I place it on the bed beside her and say, "I know it will be a bit big on you, but I'll have something sent in your size as soon as the doctor has been."

"No, there's no need to do that, I'll be okay in this," she says as she picks up the shirt which will most definitely engulf her.

"I'll just go and wait for the doctor and make us some tea," I say with a smile as I leave the room and close the door to give her some privacy while she gets changed. I didn't have any bottoms for her, but I hope she'll cover herself with the duvet for when the doctor's here.

I enter the kitchen and fill the kettle, not even tempted to grab an alcoholic drink. I need my wits about me. I need to focus. And I need to watch the footage of when she went outside so I can hunt her fucking husband down and show him why he shouldn't put his hands on any woman, ever.

Leaning on the counter, my hands bracing me, I watch as it starts to boil, and it's not too dissimilar to the way my blood boils beneath the surface. The door knocks as the kettle clicks off, and I go to it, opening it to greet Doctor Ron.

"Thanks for coming," I say as I close the door.

"Of course. Where is the patient?" he enquires, and this is another reason I actually like Doctor Ron, because he doesn't fuck about.

"In my bedroom," I say, already leading him to where she is. "She was attacked outside the back of the hotel. She managed to phone me and I got her up here."

"Is she lucid?" he asks.

"Yes, appears to be. I cleaned the blood off her face but I want her fully checked."

"There is only so much I can do in a hotel room, Dorien."

"Then if you need more equipment, I will get it sent here," I state.

"I have no doubt." He chuckles, because he knows I don't do things by halves, the contract he signed five years ago shows just how serious I am. It's watertight but will set him up nicely for his retirement in ten years' time.

I open the bedroom door to see Elise sat resting against the headboard, with the quilt covering her bottom half. Good girl.

"Elise, this is Doctor Ron," I begin, starting the introductions. "Doctor Ron, this is Elise."

"Nice to meet you, Elise," Doctor Ron says as he walks to the side of the bed and places his medical bag down.

"Wish I could say the same," Elise says, earning a chuckle from the doctor. "I mean, under the circumstances…" She waves a hand around, and I find myself grinning at her sarcasm. Even in a dark moment, she's managed to find some light.

"Why don't you tell me what happened while I check your vitals," Doctor Ron says, and I excuse myself to go and make the drinks and give them some privacy. I don't want to leave, because I want to know everything, but I trust Doctor Ron with my life, and in turn, I trust him with Elise's.

I make the drinks and take them into the lounge area, placing them on the coffee table, ready for when Doctor Ron emerges. If Elise wants her drink in bed, then I'll make her a fresh one and take it to her. She better stay in bed, actually, because she's not wearing any fucking trousers or shorts. Reminds me, I must make that phone call to have some complimentary night clothes sent up here.

I pick up the room phone and call the front desk, requesting what I need and telling them I expect it as soon as possible, and within five minutes, there's a knock on the door. Christ, even for them that was quick. I make my way to the door and open it to see Hayley stood there, with the items I requested in her hands.

"I didn't realise the hotel manager had time to deliver requested items." It's the best greeting she'll get right now.

"Oh, I was on my way here anyway to check that you had everything you needed." Her eyes are darting behind me, raising my suspicions of why she's truly here.

"Well, I have everything I need now, so go do your job, Hayley," I bark before I shut the door and make a mental note to look into her weird behaviour just now. So many mental notes and so little time, but there is one that tops the list after I'm assured Elise is okay, and that is finding her fucking husband and making him pay.

Chapter Thirty-Eight

ELISE

Doctor Ron finishes checking everything he needs to, and by the time he's done, I feel even more exhausted than I did before. The bruising to my face will come out in the next couple of days, and he informed me that the injuries are superficial but that I need to take it easy for a few days. I don't have the time to take it easy, but I have a feeling that Dorien won't let me do a damn thing until he's satisfied that I am all right.

As I lay here, wrapped up in Dorien's pyjama shirt, I replay the moment my husband lost his mind.

"*Elise,*" *his gruff voice says as I lift the top of the skip to chuck the rubbish bag in.*

"*Derrick?*" *I question as he emerges from the shadows at the back of the hotel, his eyes wide and wild as he comes into the light that shines from above the door of the staff entrance.* "*What are you doing here?*"

"*I came to take you home,*" *he says, walking closer. I drop the rubbish bag and let the bin lid clatter back down as I take a few steps back, just wanting to go back inside and forget I ever saw him here.*

"*You shouldn't be here.*"

"*I know, because of that dickhead that banned me from coming into the hotel. But you are still my wife, Elise, and you need to come home.*"

"I don't have a home with you, Derrick. I never did." I keep my head held high. I won't back down from him, not anymore. He doesn't have the right to talk down to me or tell me what to do, it's just a shame I didn't have the backbone to walk away before I ever married the wanker.

"Don't play these fucking games with me, Elise. You're coming with me." He reaches for my arm and grabs it, but I shrug him off and move towards the door. It's a mistake on my part as he pushes me and shoves me against the wall, getting in my face, pinning me there with his body.

"Stop it, Derrick."

"Never." His hands go around my neck and he starts to squeeze, and I do the only thing I can think of in my panic and I claw his face, scraping my nails over his skin and making him roar out loud.

"If I can't have you, no one fucking will," he shouts, and then his fist connects with my lip, catching the bottom of my nose in the process. My eyes screw shut from the pain, my head swimming from the impact, and I desperately try to get him off of me, letting my adrenaline fuel me as I fight against his hold.

I start to feel dizzy, the lack of oxygen taking effect, but I refuse to give up. I left him, I got away, but it seems he's determined to haunt me.

I keep clawing until my arms feel tired, and just when I think I have nothing left in me, there's a noise, a loud clanging coming from the side of hotel, and Derrick drops me like a sack of shit as he steps back, his eyes wider than before as he starts to panic.

"This isn't over," he warns, and then he turns and jogs away, because let's face it, he's so fucking unfit he can't break into a sprint.

I manage to push myself up enough to open the back entrance, and I stumble through, sliding the lock across before I give up and plummet to the floor, my mind only on one man... Dorien.

The bedroom door pushes open, and Dorien appears, looking as handsome as ever.

"How are you feeling?" he asks, carrying a cup, which he puts down on the bedside table.

"Okay. Doctor Ron gave me some strong pain relief." I can feel it starting to kick in, making me feel like I'm starting to float.

"I know, he told me before he left."

"You always know everything," I say sleepily, my lips pulling into a smile.

He barks a laugh and sits on the edge of the bed, facing me. "I try to."

I lift my hand to his face, feeling the painkillers kicking in a little more as I clumsily stroke his cheek, the scruff of his jaw tickling my palm. "You're such a kind man, Dorien."

"And you're high as a kite right now," he says playfully. I like this side of him, a lot.

"It's still true whether I'm high or not."

"If you say so."

"I do," I affirm, and I drop my arm, it suddenly being too heavy to lift anymore. "You're the light I never expected."

He looks at me as my eyes droop, and I register him saying, "And you're mine too," before I give in and let sleep claim me.

Agony overwhelms me as I move and my body aches, the darkness lifting.

A cry of frustration leaves me as my side throbs and I struggle to try and sit up, the pain becoming too much.

"Shhh…" I hear as my hair is pushed away from my face. A hand cups my cheek. The feel of lips beside my ear. A low voice telling me to "calm down," and that "it's okay, I've got you."

My eyes don't want to open, but I quickly find myself less panicked as I feel something brushing against my cheek. A thumb? A finger? It doesn't matter what it is as I focus on that and not the throbbing threatening to cripple me.

I know the pain meds are wearing off, but I suddenly don't want to move, I want to stay right where I am and block the pain out as best as I can, because whatever is happening is luring me to accept the comfort I can feel wrapped around me.

I feel a hand on mine, and that soothing voice is back by my ear. "Good girl." And even as I fight the pain, I know that nothing could stop the movement of my lips, a smile, before I'm lost to the dark once more.

When I open my eyes, the room is dark, a small lamp in the corner the only light in here. I blink a few times and swallow, my throat burning as I do. I need a drink, some water, anything to ease the burn and the dryness of my mouth. I'm disorientated for a moment, but I can feel something on my hand as I try to move my fingers, and when I look to the side of me, I see a dark figure laying next to me, their head resting by mine, their fingers entwined with mine.

Dorien.

I allow myself a few minutes to admire him. His frame, his touch, his hair that is slightly trussed from sleep. He's facing me, his eyes closed, his breathing quiet, and I smile at just how peaceful he looks right now. I'm yet to see a peaceful Dorien. It's nice, calming, a look I want to see on him more often.

"Dorien," I croak, expecting to have to try and raise my voice a little higher, but his head shoots up straight away, making me flinch slightly. Not because I'm scared of him or anything, but because his rapid response shocked me.

"Elise," he says quietly, his hand squeezing mine a little as his other one comes to my face and cups my cheek. "What's wrong? What do you need?"

"A drink," I say, my voice raspy, and his hand immediately goes to a glass of water on a table at the side of him. He picks up a straw and puts it in the glass before bringing it to my lips so I can drink. The thoughtfulness of his actions doesn't go unnoticed as I sip greedily.

"Thank you," I say when I'm done, grateful for my mouth feeling refreshed even if the rest of me doesn't feel so good.

"Better?" he asks, placing the glass back on the table and taking my hand gently in his.

"Much." The way he's holding my hand and looking at me like I'm the only person in the world makes me feel… uneasy? No, that's not right. But it makes me feel like the shift between us is even bigger than it was before.

"You're due more pain meds, let me go and get them," he says, his hand leaving mine and the space on the bed feeling instantly cold. He's back a minute or two later, and I shuffle to a sitting position so I can take the tablets. The pain in my face is like nothing I've ever felt before, and I silently curse Derrick for doing this to me.

I swallow the tablets with more water, and then I ease back down, willing the meds to kick in quickly. Dorien returns to his space on the bed, his hand coming up and stroking my hair as I close my eyes.

"I promise you that he won't get away with this, Elise," I hear him whisper, and I know that he'll keep that promise, even if we did only start out as a meaningless fuck with no expectations. That's all changed. I feel it. I'm living it. And I have no idea what comes next, because even the thought of leaving Dorien hurts.

Chapter Thirty-Nine

DORIEN

I didn't go back to sleep after Elise woke up in pain. I just lay there, listening to her breathing peacefully, finding myself wanting her to have the same peace in life that she does in sleep.

I'll give her that peace, even if it doesn't include me. I'm hoping it does, something I never thought I'd hope for, but if it doesn't, then I want to know she's going to live her life with no worries of an out-of-control soon-to-be ex-husband to worry about. The ex-husband part will come quicker than expected for her, because I've already been in touch with my solicitor, and she will have full access to my legal team to divorce his arse the minute she says the word.

I've also hired a private investigator to get every single bit of dirt on him that I can, so she can use it in the court room, if it comes to that. I don't expect it to because my team will wipe the floor with him before he gets the chance to step one foot in front of a judge. And then, only then, when she's well out of the equation, will I go after the bastard and show him exactly why he should never have touched her.

It's going to pain me to no end to bide my time, but I can exert patience for her. She doesn't need any comebacks from the cunt that made her life miserable.

I've got two guys on the way to the house she used to share with him, to get any belongings she may have there, and another two that will watch the weedy fucker until I'm ready to pounce. This is when having an obnoxious amount of money pays off, because without it, I wouldn't be able to do half the shit I've put in place already today, and it's not even nine in the morning.

My phone vibrates to the side of my laptop, and I see Gabriel's name flashing on the screen.

"Morning," I say as I pick up the call and stand from the couch, needing more caffeine.

"Dude, tell me when I can let Chantel loose, because she's dying to get all the details of how your date went last night," he says, not bothering with any formalities first.

"This is why you don't tell your woman anything, Gabe, because she's like a dog with a bone."

"Did you just call my wife a dog?"

I roll my eyes. "Not in the way you're implying, you twat."

"He called me a what?" I hear Chantel screech in the background, and then Gabe's laughter rings out.

"Fuck my life, are you trying to make my life more difficult?" I question, but he just laughs harder.

"It amuses me," he replies, and then he stops laughing. "Wait, why *more difficult?* Is something wrong? Did last night not go to plan?"

"Not exactly," I admit. "And you spend far too much time with your wife. You ask just as many questions as she does."

"Not quite, I'm sure she'll have plenty more than me when you've let us in on what has made things more difficult in the space of fourteen hours."

With a sigh, I resign myself to the fact that they will be knocking on my door imminently. "I've got the coffee ready. You better come up."

"As if we weren't already. See you in a few." He hangs up the phone and I take some extra mugs out of the cupboard, ready to regale them with what went down last night. It might do me some good to offload a little. I tend to be a closed book most of the time, but they're the family I chose and they're the only ones I've ever opened up to, when the need has called for it.

Two minutes later, the knock comes at the door, and I let them both in.

"Is everything okay?" Chantel asks, concern her first response.

"Sit down, I'll get the coffees," I say, and they make their way to the couch while I get the caffeine. Pretty sure I'm going to need a shit ton of it for the rest of the day.

"Something's different," Chantel muses when I set the coffee down and park my arse on the oversized chair.

"Can't wait to hear what," I mutter sarcastically as I pick up my coffee and settle back.

"Wait… is she here? Because even as you radiate some kind of tension, I sense that you haven't just been dumped."

"Has she got a fucking camera in here?" I say as I make a point of looking around and scouring the corners of the room for surveillance.

"It's a gift, apparently," Gabriel says, earning a dig in the ribs from his wife's elbow.

"So, is she here?" she asks excitedly.

"See? Dog with a bone." I smirk, and it earns me a scowl from her.

"We'll talk about this dog and bone shit later, Dukes, but right now, just answer my bloody question," Chantel says, not sounding the least bit threatening but trying to.

"Yes, she's here, but it isn't because of what you're thinking."

"Well, fill us in before I meet her," Chantel says, eagle eyed and ready. I get that she's excited to maybe forge a friendship from all of this, but I haven't even talked to Elise about us, so she may end up disappointed.

I tell them about what happened, and why Elise is in my bed resting, both of them looking shocked by the time I'm done.

"Her husband beat her up?" Gabriel says, eyebrows raised, and I nod to confirm what I've just said in brief detail. "Fuck."

"Yeah, fuck," I echo.

"Oh God, I feel awful for her," Chantel says, her excitement on pause.

"Well don't, because she wouldn't want that," I tell her, and she goes from shocked to smiling. "What?"

"Look at you, getting all protective and shit," she comments. "I like this chick already."

My phone rings, saving me from having to try and respond, because she's right, I am protective of her, brutally so.

"What?" I bark down the phone, seeing it's one of the guys who has gone to pick up Elise's personal items.

"Boss, there was no answer at the house," he tells me, like he can't figure out the solution to that.

"So break the fucking door down."

"We did that, and we've got anything we think is relevant, but there is no sign of the husband being here." I gave the guys a quick rundown on who he was, but didn't go into detail as such, just mentioned he was the husband of a woman that needed protecting from him. "The place is a shithole though."

"I couldn't give a toss about the place, just get her stuff back here and get the other guys to find him."

"Will do." I hang up the phone, confident that they'll locate him in no time at all. Again, I only use the best, and these guys have never let me down, even if they are dodgy as fuck. I'm met with silence as I throw my phone on the coffee table.

"Dorien, you're not doing anything stupid, are you?" Gabriel asks, and Chantel tilts her head as he studies me.

"No more than usual," I respond, but I refrain from adding, 'not yet, anyway.'

Chapter Forty

ELISE

I wake up groggy and slowly make my way to the bathroom in the hallway. I don't pay much attention to anything other than needing to use the toilet and splash my aching face with some cold water, so once I'm done and I make my way to the main room, I'm stumped to see two people sat on the couch, with Dorien in the armchair. His head turns as he clocks me in his peripheral vision, and then the heads of the two on the sofa turn to see what's got his attention. And I'm stood here in nothing but a pair of panties and his pyjama shirt—luckily it falls to mid-thigh but it's still not ideal.

"I'm sorry, I didn't realise you had company," I say as I fidget on the spot. "I'll just go and um…" I let my voice trail off as I turn and start to go back to the bedroom, but seconds later, I feel him behind me, his body shielding mine and his hands resting on my shoulders.

"It's okay, Elise, they're friends—more family than anything," he tells me quietly, his lips by my ear.

"And I've just walked out here looking like I've not groomed myself in a week, and in just a pyjama shirt." My response earns a chuckle from him, and I find myself leaning back slightly to rest against his chest.

"They won't judge you for the way you look, and trust me, you look beautiful."

"Pfft. I look horrendous with the split lip, the red marks on my skin, and the bruising starting to show. Not to mention my hair is all over the place."

"I never had you down as caring too much about appearance," he comments, and I bite my bottom lip, quickly hissing as my teeth connect with the split there.

Dorien turns me around and glares at me. "Will you be fucking careful."

"Sorry," I mutter.

"I've got your things on the way here as we speak, so as soon as your clothes arrive, I'll bring them in and you can change into whatever feels comfortable."

"Wait, my stuff is coming here?" I question.

"Yes."

"Um, why?"

"Because you're staying with me," he confirms, like we've had this conversation and duked it out already.

"What? No, I'm not."

"Yes, you are."

"Dorien, I'm very grateful for what you've done for me, but I live with Celeste, and she'll wonder where I am," I tell him, hoping he'll see reason.

"You have a phone, so text her to tell her to come up here later, so you can inform her."

My mouth literally drops open.

"Dorien, I need to go home," I say, and he looks at me like I've said the dumbest thing ever.

"*You are home*," he tells me, and I look at him perplexed. And then I snort a laugh, which I'm hoping he finds kind of endearing rather than cringe.

"Dorien, you can't be serious about me staying in your penthouse," I say, not even forming it as a question because it's too crazy to even contemplate.

"I absolutely fucking am," he reiterates, his face deadpan.

"Dorien, listen to yourself," I begin, and he keeps his mouth shut to hear exactly where I'm going with this. "This is nuts. I can't stay in the penthouse… I work at the hotel, for goodness' sake. What would the other staff think?"

"I couldn't give a fuck what they think."

"Yes, I'm well aware, but… I work here, Dorien, and not to mention we're just fucking—"

"Excuse me?" he interrupts, unable to keep the irritation out of his tone. "Just fucking?" he questions as he bends, getting down so our eyes are level.

"Well, yeah…" I sound unsure, and I know he can see it as much as I can hear it in my voice.

"We are not just fucking," he states. "We went past the 'just fucking' stage before last night." I go to bite my lip again but quickly stop myself as he stares at me with a new kind of fire in his eyes. "Are we clear?"

I wonder if he can see the tug of war going on in my mind, and I wonder if he understands it.

"But… we've gone from one extreme to the other," I say quietly, still unsure of myself. "Shouldn't we have dated first? Got to know one another? Learnt about our likes and dislikes, that sort of thing?"

"I know you dislike putting yourself out there, especially now, and I know you like being called a good girl in the bedroom," he responds, which earns him a light smack on the top of his arm.

"Be serious, Dorien."

"I am being serious, buttercup."

"Buttercup… why do you call me that?" I enquire.

"Because the first time I met you, I knew you had a light inside of you that needed to be coaxed out—I saw it, I still see it, and buttercup was born."

I frown. "And you got buttercup from that?"

"Would you prefer good girl in public?" he teases, and I roll my eyes.

"Okay, okay, but, Dorien, shouldn't we just hold off on the moving me in part?"

"No." And with that, he gently guides me back to the bedroom, covering my modesty as I go, and I resign myself to the fact that Dorien Dukes just moved me in.

Chapter Forty-One

ELISE

"Hi," I say shyly, once I emerge from the bedroom, feeling a little better in the clothes Dorien brought to the room not long ago. I'm only dressed in some loose joggers and an over-sized jumper, so his guests will have to excuse my shabby appearance in my preference for comfortable clothes. I'm due another dose of painkillers in about an hour, but I guess the dull throbbing is going to be something I have to get used to for the next few days while my body tries to heal.

Dorien stands and comes over to me, taking my arm and helping me to the chair that he was just sat in. "You okay?" he asks as I get settled.

"I am, thank you." I smile and feel a blush creep across my cheeks, because I am very aware of the two pairs of eyes staring at us from the couch. "I'm sorry about, well, this," I say as I point to my face and laugh to try and lighten the moment. Out of the corner of my eye, I see Dorien fighting a smirk, and then the two on the couch begin to laugh.

"Elise, meet Chantel and Gabriel," Dorien says, and I smile at them both. "Chantel and Gabriel, this is Elise."

"Nice to meet you," Gabriel says with a head tilt, while Chantel is beaming at me, her eyes lighting up like Christmas morning.

"It's so nice to finally meet you," she says, and I can't ignore how stunning she is with her long, silky hair, bright blue eyes, and casual dress of skinny jeans and an off-the-shoulder tee.

"Finally?" I question, turning my gaze on Dorien. "Been talking about me, have we?"

"To tell them you were here, yes," he says, but I see his eyes dart to them in warning, which just makes them crack up laughing again.

"Oh, we are going to have so much fun winding him up," Chantel says, goading him, and I can't help but instantly like her cheeky nature.

"For fuck's sake," Dorien mutters, and this time, I burst out laughing, holding my stomach as it hurts. "Will you stop hurting yourself?" he scolds me, but the laughter is freeing, delightful, and something I truly needed after a dark twenty-four hours.

"I'm fine," I assure him, tears springing to my eyes. "Stop fussing." Although, I kind of like it when he fusses, but I'll keep that to myself.

"So, how did you two meet?" Gabriel asks, earning another scowl from Dorien. He knows full well how we met, I can tell from the glint in his eye that he's goading Dorien further, and I see in these few moments that these people really aren't just his friends, they're absolutely his family, just like he said. Dorien doesn't take shit from anyone, so this is the first time I'm seeing his dominant, intimidating self be put to the test, and as much as he scowls at them and curses, it's easy to see they all have a bond that has been there for a long time. Unbreakable. Fierce. It humbles me that he has people in his life like this, just like I have Celeste. Speaking of, I need to contact her and let her know what's going on.

I go to get up from the chair, but Dorien stops me. "What do you need?"

"I was just going to go and grab my phone to send Celeste a text," I inform him, but he simply waves his hand at me.

"No need, she'll be here when her shift ends."

My eyebrows raise in surprise, because although he said earlier about me telling her, I didn't expect him to arrange it.

"Oh, Elise, you have so much to learn when it comes to this

terror of a man," Chantel teases, but I know she's not wrong. There's so much I don't know, and so much I want to find out.

I spent the next hour chatting with Chantel and Gabriel, Dorien chipping in every now and again, and by the time my meds had kicked in and made me feel sleepy, it was like I'd known them for years. They didn't treat me like broken glass because of what my husband did, and they didn't show any judgement for the fact that I am a maid and Dorien is, well, a powerful business with millions at his disposal. I can only assume they got a good vibe from me, even with me being visibly younger than him—not that our ages were mentioned at all. It hits me then that I don't know his exact age, and fuck me for not asking that question sooner. The drama surrounding me has just been ongoing, not to mention that we weren't going to delve into anything other than sex back when this first started. *That worked out so well for us*, I think to myself with a chuckle.

I'm lying in bed, waiting for Celeste to arrive, but I feel like I should go out into the main room, because having her come in here would be a bit too personal, what with Dorien being her boss too.

Christ, the hot mess that is my life right now is exhausting.

But even as I wonder how this is all going to work, I know that I wouldn't have gotten through the last few weeks without Dorien being the only one to give me that high that only he can give, regardless of if it's while he's fucking me or not. Seeing him being so attentive for the last few hours has been eye-opening, and it's shown me what a real man does for a woman they… care about? Does he care about me like I'm starting to care about him? Does he feel more for me than just a bond created by the need to escape? My heart hopes so, seeing as he's not letting me leave his sight and all, but my head is wary, permanently scarred from being used for so long by those who were meant to do nothing but love me.

As I wander out into the hallway, I can see Dorien in the

kitchen, a towel over his shoulder as he chops some vegetables, looking like domesticated bliss. Except, that's not what we are. I don't know if we'll ever be domesticated bliss, but for a moment, it's heart-warming to witness.

And as if he senses me, he looks up, his eyes raking up and down me as I lean against the wall, that fire that burns for him deep in my stomach igniting, despite the aches. Even with my face bruised, my lips still swollen, and the bags under my eyes regardless of the amount of sleep I've gotten today, he still looks like he wants to eat me.

I push off the wall and walk towards him, needing to be close to him for reasons I'm yet to acknowledge. I'm just going with it for now.

When I make it into the kitchen, I sidle up to him and push up on tiptoes, placing a light kiss on the bottom of his jaw.

"What was that for?" he asks, the knife still paused in his hand as his focus is solely on me.

"Just because," I say with a shrug. *Because this may not last forever. Because while the opportunity is there, I'm taking it. Because even if I never feel like this again in my life, I want to regret nothing.*

"If you weren't in pain, I'd be fucking you over this island," he informs me, and my pussy tingles at the thought.

"We could just—"

"Absolutely not, Elise," he interrupts, and I pout at him and then hiss as it stretches my lip.

"For fuck's sake, I told you to stop doing that," he barks, but I just find it so fucking hot that he's concerned about me. A knock at the door interrupts us, and he tells me to go and answer it and then sit my fine arse down. I roll my eyes and move, feeling more relaxed than ever before, because he makes me feel safe, secure… wanted. I don't feel like a burden here, because he hasn't made me feel like one.

I open the door and am met with Celeste standing there, looking partly worried and partly relieved.

"Fucking hell, Elise," she says as she takes in the bruises on my face and wraps her arms around me. I can't stop the yelp that leaves me as her arm pushes against the bruising on my side. "Oh shit," she exclaims, stepping back from me like I just electrocuted her. "I'm sorry, I didn't mean to hurt you."

"It's fine," I tell her with a wave of my hand as I feel Dorien at my back.

"Christ, go and sit down," he demands, turning me and guiding me to the chair that he likes to plonk me in.

"I'm fine, Dorien, stop fussing." I bat his hands away, but he leans down on the arm of the chair and whispers, "You're mine to fuss over."

Well, doesn't that just make me bloody wet for him.

"Take a seat, Celeste," he says sternly, and I frown at him as he walks back into the kitchen area, leaving tension hanging in the air.

"He's pissed at me," Celeste whispers, and I try to placate her with a smile, but it doesn't work as I see her fiddling with her hands in her lap.

"He's just being… oddly weird." I can't even begin to get into what Dorien and I are right now. I'm still figuring it out myself.

"It's not weird, Elise. It's what happen when a guy cares about you."

"Of course it's weird, he's still my boss," I hiss, because what the fuck is going to happen when I go back to work? Is he still going to want me to stay here? Are we going to have the chat about what the hell we're doing? Because he's made it pretty clear that we've gone past the fucking stage, he even said so himself, so where does that leave me with everything?

"I don't think you'll be working as a maid again," Celeste admits, and I feel uncomfortable talking about this with Dorien a few feet away.

"Can we talk about it tomorrow, over coffee, maybe? I could meet you on your lunchbreak," I suggest.

"Yes!" Celeste replies excitedly, and I chuckle. "But I'll come here, so you don't have to…"

"Walk around with a busted face and have the other staff question what happened?" I finish for her, and she grimaces slightly.

"I didn't mean it to sound like that."

"It's the truth… I look a bloody mess."

"Stop it," she tells me with an eye roll. "And anyway," she continues, with a flick of her hand to brush over having to placate my insecurity of how bad I look. "It's so fucking boring at lunch without you there."

"It's been, like, a day, Celeste."

"Not to mention that since Dorien contacted me earlier, I've been worried sick about you," she admits.

"Dorien was the one who contacted you?" I ask, because I assumed he probably had a message sent to her by someone else.

"Yeah, he said there had been an incident and that I was to come here after work. Of course I questioned him, because even if he is my boss, you're my best friend, and you know what I'm like," she says, and I nod. I do know what she's like, and I love her more for it. "So, he told me that something had happened and you wouldn't be at work for a while because you need to rest. And then he told me to be here after work and hung up the phone, so of course, my brain went into overdrive imagining all sorts, because I know damn well that you wouldn't miss work unless it was really bad. So, spill the tea, Elise, because I need to know why last night changed so dramatically from you coming here to get your freak on to you having a busted lip and bruises on your face, and God knows where else."

And so, I regale her with how my husband tried to fucking kill me.

Chapter Forty-Two

DORIEN

By the time Celeste leaves, Elise is exhausted, and once she's said goodbye to her friend at the door, I walk up behind her and close it, lifting her into my arms and carrying her to the bedroom.

"Dorien, what—"

"Stop squirming," I scold her, and she scowls at me, not having any idea how fucking hot that scowl is.

I take her to the bedroom and put her down on the bed, before I say, "Get changed and get into bed."

And she fucking laughs at me. Really laughs. Laughs so much that she's holding her stomach and wiping tears from her eyes.

"What is so funny?" I ask after a few minutes.

"Just… everything," she replies as she tries to catch her breath. Well, that really fucking narrows it down. She sees the confusion on my face, and she props herself against the headboard. "It's just… if someone had told me that I was going to end up fucking my boss and that my husband was going to completely lose his shit and try to strangle me, I'd have told them to stay off the drugs. Oh, and not to mention how my parents pimped me out to said husband to ensure they were financially secure for the rest of their lives, only for it to all go up in smoke when the husband decided to become a lazy wanker and force me to give up my dreams of a career to scrub floors and make sure the upper class didn't have a bloody crease in their bed sheets. I mean, it's so fucking tragic that if I don't laugh, I'll most certainly cry, and I don't want to cry anymore…" Her voice trails off as her eyes drop to look at the quilt that she starts to pick at, as if there is some kind of fluff she can't get rid of.

"Elise—"

"Oh, and then there's the part where I have no home, can't go to work because I look like I got beaten the shit out of in a boxing match, and now I have to worry about the husband coming back, as well as dealing with the stress the divorce will cause. My mother hasn't even spoken to me since you threw them out of here, and there's still a part of me that can't quite let go of wanting them to be fucking happy for me, proud of me, let me choose my own path without shoving a shitload of guilt down my throat."

She's breathing heavily by the time she's done, and something aches inside of me from hearing her words and watching her putting on a brave face, when I know she just wants to break, even as she fights against it.

"Why do you even want me here, Dorien? Why do you even care what happens to me?" she whispers, and as I stand at her bedside, my hands balled into fists in my pockets from all she has been through, I know that now is the time to be honest. She needs it, and, hell, maybe I do too. I've never been a fan of it, but slowly, she's changing me, and she has no fucking idea.

"Because you're my light, Elise. I saw it the first time we met, and I still see it now."

"There's no light left in me, Dorien," she says sadly, and even as she said she didn't want to cry anymore, the tears come, and I go to her, wrapping her in my arms and letting her cry it out.

"You don't have to be strong around me, buttercup," I soothe, because even as I hate to see her swallowed by her grief and the guilt she still carries due to her parents, she needs to know she doesn't need to be anything but her true self with me.

"I don't want to be scared," she croaks, and it makes me hold her a little tighter. And as I sit there with her, time ticks by, her sobs slowing down and her hold on me loosening as her eyelids flutter closed, but it's her last words before sleep claims her that has me torn in two. "I think I like you, Dorien Dukes. More than I probably should."

Fuck.

When I'm sure she's passed out, I uncurl my arms from around her and cover her with a blanket on the end of the bed. I don't want to move her to get the quilt, so the blanket will suffice for now.

I leave the bedroom, running my hands through my hair as I go to the kitchen and pour myself a glass of scotch. I'm going to fucking need it for the next phone call I have to make. It's not one I ever planned on making, but then, fuck, I didn't plan on meeting her and having my whole world turned upside down.

I step onto the balcony and pull my phone from my pocket, sipping the scotch as I look at the number on my phone.

Do I? Don't I? What the hell will I be signing up for if I do? Should I wait a bit longer? But even as I ask myself these questions, I know I'm not going to wait. I know I would sign up for anything to make her safe and happy. And I know that I've done the very thing I vowed I never would... I've fallen in love. That in turn makes me vulnerable, something I never wanted to be again, not after my parents made me feel so fucking weak and pathetic, but she's been treated the same way. She's lived a life of pain and disappointment because of the very people that should have loved her. And here I am, just as damaged emotionally as she is, but it's happened anyway. I've let her in, and now I don't want to let her go.

And that tragic fucking hope in my chest tells me that I want her to feel the same way about me too.

I hate hope. It always leaves me disappointed, and it's why I gave up on it years ago. And if she doesn't feel the same for me, I know that nothing will ever bring me hope again, because I won't fucking let it. I shouldn't have let her in, but I did, and here I am, about to possibly sign my life away to give her some peace. I can't do shit about her parents right now, but her husband? I can absolutely fucking deal with him, even if I did plan to wait until she'd divorced him so she wasn't caught in the crossfire, but needs must. I just need to find the fucker first.

I hit the call button on my phone and put it to my ear, leaning on the balcony and looking across the city below.

It rings three times before the call is answered.

"Hello," comes the deep voice of the most dangerous guy I've ever heard of. There's ruthless, and then there's this guy, who will fuck you up for putting a foot wrong.

"Nate Knowles?" I ask, the confidence in my voice not wavering in the slightest.

"Who wants to know?" he questions.

"Dorien Dukes."

Silence ticks by for a moment, before he says, "And why would you be calling me, Dorien?"

"I need your help." It pains me to ask for the help, but I can't wait around for the guys I ordered to watch Derrick's arse to find him. He could be fuck knows where by now.

"And how exactly did you get my number?" he asks.

"I'm pretty sure you know that money talks," I inform him.

"It does, so enlighten me, Dorien."

Nate will know exactly who I am by my name alone, but even if he didn't, I'm pretty sure he'd have intel in front of him by now. You don't get a reputation like he's got by being a shit leader of the criminal underworld.

"I need someone found and dealt with," I say, taking another sip of scotch.

"And you're coming to me because…" His voice drifts off, and I have a feeling he's going to make me squirm before I get what I want.

"Because you're the best, and I only ever deal with the best."

"And I don't discuss business over the phone," he says firmly. "I'll be at your hotel tomorrow evening at eight o'clock."

"I own many hotels, Nate."

"Do you really think I don't know which one you're currently staying in?" he asks, but that right there shows me that he is the best in the business, confirming that the rumours are true. "Blue

Diamond at eight o'clock, and I expect a decent table, because I'll be bringing my wife for a meal before we talk business. And it's Mr Knowles, not Nate."

And with that, the line goes dead, and even as I know I'm treading in dangerous waters, I would make that phone call again, because when my plan comes together, her fucking husband is a dead man walking.

Chapter Forty-Three

ELISE

"So, can we speak freely today, or is Mr Bossman around to keep an ear out?" Celeste asks quietly as I open the door, her head peering around while her eyes scan behind me for signs of Dorien, making me chuckle.

"He's not here," I confirm, and she walks in more like her usual self, flopping down on the sofa and declaring, "Thank God for that. Christ, I felt so fucking awkward last night."

I chuckle again as I shut the door and go to the kitchen, carrying in the hot drinks that I made just before she knocked on the door. I place them down on the coffee table and then take a seat in the chair that is quickly becoming my favourite place to sit. I shouldn't even have a favourite chair in an apartment that isn't mine, but he moved me in here for the time being, so I figure I'm allowed to try and live as I would in my own place, mostly.

"He can be a little bit tense," I say.

"A little bit? Shit, Elise, he's like this burly caveman that looks like he's about to drag you off any second and lock you up... which is totally hot, by the way, but, fuck, it's awkward because he's my boss."

"Burly caveman?"

"Oh yeah, he'd rock a club like nobody's business," she says sassily, and I bark a laugh as an image of Dorien dragging a club along the floor comes to mind.

"Yeah, I can totally picture that," I agree, and she nods.

"So, what's the deal with you two?" she asks as she picks up her drink and takes a sip, settling back in for what I think she hopes is an amazing love story of guy meets girl.

"I don't know, Celeste. I mean, he's moved me in here for the time being, he's told me it's not just fucking, and he's been the sweetest as he's looked after me, but as for what we are, I have no idea."

"Oh come on, you haven't had the conversation yet? Seriously?"

"Seriously," I confirm with a nod of my head. "I'm scared to."

"I don't think you need to be scared, Elise. It's fairly damn obvious to anyone with eyes that he cares about you."

"Yeah, but… I don't think I could take it if he didn't feel like…" I stop myself, because I haven't admitted out loud how he truly makes me feel. It would make it more real, more of a bigger deal than I want it to be.

"Oh my god, you've fallen for him," Celeste says, taking the words right out of my mouth, and I close my eyes and shake my head, knowing how stupid I am for falling for a guy when I've just ended a marriage.

"I can't Celeste."

"Can't what?"

"I can't talk about this, because if I do, then it makes it different. If I don't talk about it, then I can keep things the way they are."

She looks at me like I've grown a second head. "You keep telling yourself that, Elise, but we both know that this isn't going to go away."

"But it can be put on pause, for now," I tell her, and she seems to take a few seconds to accept what I'm saying, and then with a nod of her head, she starts to talk about something else, something irrelevant that will take my mind off of the bigger questions I should be answering.

After Celeste left, I spent the rest of the day lounging around, while Dorien has been dealing with hotel business, and I'm finding that I miss him. He's been gone for six hours, and I actually do fucking miss him. Been staying with him for two days and I'm in deeper than I thought I would be.

With a sigh, I go to the bathroom and inspect my face. The bruising has come out more in the last twenty-four hours, the dark purple shades making me grimace. A shitty reminder of my trauma that I hope will fade quickly.

I haven't heard a thing from Derrick since that night, and I hope I don't, but after the way he acted, the silence is alarming. Or maybe it's the fact that he realised he went too far and is now remorseful? I shake my head, because trying to figure out his mind will take more energy than I'm willing to give.

I hear the front door open, and I walk out of the bathroom with excitement bubbling up inside me. Excitement that Dorien is home, because clearly my heart has chosen its path and is winning the battle with my head not to accept that I'm falling for him. I have been since the moment he called me a 'good girl'.

"Hey," I say with a smile when he turns to look at me, and he hits me with the most handsome grin.

"Feeling better?" he asks as I walk right up to him and place a light kiss on his lips.

"The meds help with the aches." I shrug, because I'm not about to darken the mood talking about my mental state, I did that last night and ended up going from laughing to being a bloody mess.

He studies my face, his eyes running over the bruises.

"They're hideous, I know," I say, reminding myself not to bite my lip and hinder the healing process.

"They're not hideous, Elise." He cups my face in his hands and tilts my head. "They're a reminder that you're a fighter."

"I don't feel like one," I admit.

"Well, you are, and even as you hate them, they won't be there forever. They will fade, but your fight won't."

"And how do you know that? Because I have to be honest and say that I feel exhausted by it all."

"Even by me?"

"No," I whisper. "Because you're my light too."

"Fuck," he says before he brings his mouth to mine and kisses me softly, so as not to hurt me.

"How old are you, Dorien?" I say against his lips, and he barks a laugh.

"You mean you haven't already tried to find out by looking me up on the internet?" he asks.

"No," I say as I screw my nose up a little. "I have no interest in seeing what the internet says about you, because I'd rather you told me yourself." I've been tempted to look, of course I have, but if I'd have done that, it would have meant snooping on him, when all I want is for him to tell me things himself—you know, like people used to before the internet and social media came along.

"Does it matter?"

"No, I'm just curious."

"I'm thirty-nine, Elise."

"Oh, wow, I may need to rethink some stuff," I tease.

"Funny. And if you weren't in pain right now, I'd be telling you to get down on your fucking knees for that comment."

"My knees don't hurt," I whisper as I drop down to the floor and move my hands to his trousers.

"Fuck, no, Elise." His voice is stern, but I need to feel anything but fucking helpless. I want to do this because he turns me on and makes me hot all of the damn time.

I ignore his words and undo his zip, my fingers delving in and touching his cock. He takes hold of my wrist to stop me from undoing the button, but I look up at him and say, "Please, Dorien."

He stares at me, his eyes full of hunger and his jaw clenched tight as his grip relaxes on my wrist, and I take that as my cue to carry on. I finish undoing his button and move my hands around to his arse, pushing his trousers and boxers down, freeing his cock.

Immediately, my tongue darts out, licking the tip, and my hand comes back around and fists him. I move up and down, licking and swirling my tongue as he watches me, making it so much fucking hotter.

And even as my lips ache, I wrap them around him, taking him to the back of my throat and staying there for a moment as he growls, "Fuck."

I move back and forth slowly, taking my time, tasting him, feeling how hard I make him. I'd like to be able to sit on his lap and ride his dick until I'm screaming his name, but I know he won't do that just yet, so this will have to suffice.

I hungrily devour him, forgetting about the aches and pains. Dorien's hand goes to the back of my head, his fingers fisting in the strands. Jesus, this guy makes me feel feral for him, and I know that a part of me never wants that to end.

I work him until he's coming in my mouth, saying my name as he does, and I fight the smile that wants to break free as I finish him off, taking everything he's got to give.

He gently pulls my head back, and I wipe my lips on the back of my hand as he stares down at me with a smirk and says, "My fucking turn."

He drops to his knees and has me on my back within seconds, my joggers being removed quickly, and him nestling between my legs as he pulls my knickers to the side and starts to eat me. He rests his other hand on my stomach, to keep me in place, avoiding the bruise at my side as he does.

I moan as his tongue flicks my clit, sending pleasure to every part of my body. It's my turn for my hands to find the back of his head as he pushes two fingers inside of me and makes me come hard on the floor.

"DORIEN," I shout as my body trembles with the release he's just given me. He chuckles against my pussy, the vibrations of that making my body writhe as the sensations become too much.

"Stop," I whisper, and he immediately ceases all contact, moving up my body and hovering above me with a questioning and concerned look on his face. "I'm okay, it was just… too much." It's all I can give without turning the beautiful moment into a possible clusterfuck of feelings that I'm not sure either of us are ready to deal with, even if we are living them daily.

He brings his lips to mine, placing a soft kiss, and I taste my arousal on his mouth. His lips trail over my skin, with him paying particular interest in covering every single bruise on my face and body. He ends up back between my thighs, and he places a light kiss on the inside of one of them before he stands up and offers me his hand. When I'm standing flush with his body, he wraps his arms around me, his forehead resting against mine.

"I have to go out tonight for a business meeting," he tells me, and I feel disappointment hit that we won't be snuggling up together and acting like this whole relationship is normal.

"Will you be gone long?" I'm aware I'm sounding needy, but nothing about being with him has followed any kind of chilled behaviour.

"An hour, maybe two," he says between kisses, making me melt.

"I miss going out," I say with a sigh.

"It's been two days, Elise," he says with a chuckle.

"Yes, but it's the not being able to because, well…" I point to my face with a frown.

"It'll fade soon."

"Not soon enough," I mutter.

"It's only you stopping yourself from going anywhere, buttercup."

"I don't want my work colleagues to see me like this," I admit, but he already knows that—he seems to know me better than I know myself sometimes.

"What if they didn't have to see you?" he says, and I instantly perk up.

"Tell me more," I reply, and he chuckles.

"We could have dinner before my meeting, in a secluded area which I can have cordoned off from prying eyes."

The thought alone is tempting, but I wouldn't want to make him late for his meeting, and I really don't want to bump into anyone I know, so instead of saying yes, I tell him, "Maybe in a few days."

He frowns briefly, but then he swoops down and places another soft kiss on my lips before he leaves to go and get ready, and for the millionth time since I met him, I find myself wishing that I was worthy of his heart, because as much as he gives off 'don't come near me' vibes, I think he's the most wonderful man I've ever met.

Chapter Forty-Four

DORIEN

I'm sat at the bar in the dining area, in the corner, sipping a scotch. I appear to be the picture of confidence right now, which is exactly what I need to face a man like Nate Knowles. He's due to arrive with his wife in the next fifteen minutes. I have no idea if we will talk business before or after their meal, but I'll wait at this bar until I have to, even if it takes all night. I've secured them the finest table of the night, out on the private patio, secluded by lush greenery and dim lighting, paired with outdoor heaters that will keep them warm when the air starts to cool a little more. I am nothing if not the perfect host.

I'm about to get up and go and check once more that the wine cooler is in place and that everything is set how it should be, just to keep my mind busy for a few moments, when a hand braces the bar next to me, making me look out of the corner of my eye to see the Crime Lord himself has arrived.

A waiter immediately comes over and Nate orders a scotch and a glass of the finest white wine we stock, and when the waiter scurries off, he says, "So, what is it you need from me, Dorien? And don't beat around the bush. I have my wife arriving in the next few minutes, and I'd prefer to have this wrapped up so I can spend the evening giving her my full attention."

I presumed his wife would be coming with him, but it's not my place to question anything, so I do exactly what he wants and I tell him what I need. "I need someone found and dealt with."

"So you said on the phone. *Who* is it you want found and dealt with?"

"His name is Derrick Woods," I say as I pull out a picture of him from the inside pocket of my jacket, sliding it across the bar to him.

"Why?"

"He's the husband of the woman I… of one of the maid's that works here, and a couple of nights ago, he beat her out the back of the hotel. Since then, he hasn't been seen, and I don't have time to wait around." I realise I nearly referred to Elise as more than a maid, but I stopped myself before I could voice what I really feel for her. Plus, I seriously doubt that he will give a shit about my love life. He's here for a job and a nice meal, nothing more.

He studies the photo for a moment, and then he says, "Just a maid, huh?"

I clear my throat and drain the last of my scotch to avoid answering.

"And this maid, she knows about this?" he enquires.

"No."

"And how exactly would you want him dealt with?" he asks, and this time, I turn my head to look him in the eye.

"I want him to fucking suffer," I grit out. I don't need to expand, he gets it. "So, how much?"

"Do not insult me by throwing your money around, Dorien," he bites, but I don't waver. I hold my own, my back straight and my eyes boring into his. "I don't *need* money, but what I *want* is a stake in this hotel chain."

I stay silent and unmoving for a beat. When I signed on the dotted line for the merger a few weeks ago, I was elated to be rid of the fucking board that wanted to take my hard-earned money for doing sod all. I was finally free to reign on my own, but if I give him a stake in my business, I will be right back to square one again, kind of. And with a crime lord, no less. But as I ponder his proposal, I already know that she's worth risking it all for.

"Done," I tell him.

"Just like that?" he says, tilting his head to the side, a slight smirk appearing at the corner of his mouth.

"Just like that," I confirm.

"We'll talk details tomorrow," he says as he turns and looks at the entrance to the hotel restaurant. "My wife has just arrived."

With that, he starts to walk towards her, briefly turning back around as I say, "Don't you need more details than his name and a photo?"

He laughs at me before replying with, "You wanted the best, so there's no need to question how I do things." And then he turns his back to me once more and greets his wife, who has one hell of a smile on her face as she takes in her husband.

They walk across the dining area, a waiter leading them out to the private patio space, his attention solely on her. There are two big burly men in front of them, who scour outside before taking up residence just inside the doors that lead out there, and I ask myself what the hell I've gotten myself into by agreeing to go into business with the man that seemingly came back from nowhere after disappearing for five years and still retained the power that he has today.

Nate has more than likely got everything but my dental records at his disposal, but I also did a little digging into his background, and that's how I know he disappeared for a few years, leaving the empire he built behind, only to return two months ago and firmly put himself back at the helm of the criminal underworld. And I'm also aware that if it really came to it, he'd slit my throat without a second thought, but when I picture Elise's face the night of the attack, the pain in her face and the sorrow in her eyes, I know that finding her husband and getting him out of her life is the right move, no matter what happens between us in the end.

I open the door to the penthouse which is shrouded in darkness, except for the TV screen at the opposite end which is casting a dim light over Elise as she picks some popcorn out of a bowl in her lap, the duvet wrapped around her and her eyes glued to the film until she notices me.

"Hey, how did the meeting go?" she asks, and it's such a fucking normal question that it throws me, because her being here feels so normal, her watching TV here feels normal, her being in my life feels so fucking normal, and I know I need to address it. Need to stop being such a pussy and really talk to her.

"It was good." I'm not going to go into the finer details, nor am I going to tell her who I had the meeting with, because if she knows who Nate Knowles is, then she'll know that my meeting wasn't all above board. Not that it could really be called a meeting as such.

"Want to come watch the film with me?" she asks, moving the duvet back and patting the sofa next to her. It makes me smile so fucking wide, and it takes me no time at all to decide that there is nothing else I'd rather do.

"I'll just go get changed and then I'll be there."

"Sure. Want me to make more popcorn?" she asks, but I'm not much of a popcorn guy, so I decline and go to the bedroom to change.

When I've stripped off my suit and put on a pair of jogging bottoms and a loose tank top, I make my way back out to her, the duvet still pulled back, the film paused as she waits for me. I get settled, letting her put the duvet over me, my arm going along the back of the sofa behind her, and her resuming the film. I couldn't really give a fuck what film it is, and I don't even care if it's a chick flick, because being sat here with her, just like this, at peace, together, on our own, is truly something special.

Chapter Forty-Five

ELISE

I open my eyes to see that I'm snuggled into Dorien on the sofa, the glow of the TV dimly lighting part of the room. I look up to see that Dorien has his eyes closed, his head resting on the back of the sofa, his arm wrapped around me.

I study him for a moment, and I feel a flutter in my stomach. I know that what I feel for him is growing by the day, and there is nothing I can do to stop it. I don't even know if I want to stop it at this point. I've never been one to believe in fate, but it's like he was sent to me just when I needed him. The light at the end of the storm. That's him.

My light, just as he said I'm his.

Two damaged souls coming together and figuring out how to learn to let our guards down.

Except, I don't know why he's always been so closed off, only fucking, only doing one night, until me. I figure he may tell me in time, maybe. I gently move away from him, careful not to wake him, but when I push the duvet back, I feel his hands reach out for me, his fingers going to my hips and turning me, until I'm straddling his lap, my hands resting either side of his head on the back of the sofa.

He stares at me for a moment, and then I lower my lips to his, needing to connect with him in the only way we can really seem to express ourselves. Actions, not words. It's easier than voicing what I feel for him, and he seems to feel the same way, so as his tongue moulds with mine, our lips softly moving in sync, I know that he's trying to tell me something, but I'm scared to acknowledge it, in case I'm wrong and he breaks my heart.

His fingers caress my skin, gently tracing over my hips until he pushes his hand up the inside of the leg of my shorts and brushes my pussy. I'm already fucking wet for him, because this is what he does to me. Makes me crazy. Makes me hot. Makes me feel.

I lift up slightly and he pulls my shorts down, our lips still connected as I fumble to move my shorts further down my legs, past my knees, and then Dorien pushes them down to my ankles. I wasn't wearing underwear with my shorts, and as I push my hand beneath the waistband of his joggers, I see that he isn't wearing any either. His dick is rock hard for me, and he lifts his arse up, allowing me to push his joggers down more until his dick is uncovered and my pussy is hovering above.

I grip his cock in my hand gently, and then I slide down on him slowly, until he's filling me completely. Our moans are swallowed as our lips refuse to be parted, and I start to ride him on the sofa as his hands cup my arse.

I don't even feel any pain as I move, my body blocking it out and revelling in everything he has to give.

I gasp in his mouth as I tilt my hips, his dick hitting me perfectly, and his lips move away from mine as he kisses my neck, my jaw, my collarbone, as he pulls my sleepshirt to the side. I grab the hem of my top and pull it off, dropping it beside us as his lips find my nipples in turn over the lace fabric of my bra. I throw my head back, but I keep the slow pace as I ride him, dragging out the sensations, never wanting this feeling to end.

I move one of my hands from beside him and press my finger to my clit, my head coming back up to find his eyes on me, watching me as I move my finger in circles.

"Fuck," he breathes, and then his eyes drift back up and connect with mine. His hands leave my arse and find my hair, gripping gently, and my forehead drops to his as I feel shudders begin to wrack my body.

I climax hard but slow. He moans my name as he finds his release, and then he kisses me softly as he carries me to bed, his dick still inside me as his body settles on top of mine.

And that's how we spend most of the night. Not fucking, but doing something else entirely.

Chapter Forty-Six
DORIEN

As I wait in my office for the arrival of Nate, I double check the documents in front of me, making sure I have everything he needs in order to find Derrick—all the information I have on the bastard, so he can put it to use to track him down, hopefully. I received a call from him early this morning, stating that he would be here at nine o'clock, sharp. I reluctantly left Elise in bed, even as I wanted to stay there with her. Last night was a night I will never forget. The way she rode me on the sofa, and the way in which we spent most of the night wrapped up in each other, signifying that what we have is so much more than either of us asked for. And maybe that's not a bad thing, because she's showing me that I don't just live and breathe work. I live and breathe her. Possibly more than I do owning a successful hotel chain. Never thought it would be possible, but here we are—so fucking pussy whipped, I can't even deny it.

A knock sounds on my door, bang on nine o'clock, and Hayley waits for me to call her in before opening the door and announcing Nate's presence. He walks in, large as life, flanked by two other guys.

"That will be all, Hayley," I tell her, flicking my hand in her direction to dismiss her. She nods her head and leaves, the door closing as the three men stand there, staring at me. The one on the right looks like a Viking with his long blonde hair, and the one on the left has tattoos donning his arms and neck, both of them with deadpan faces and suspicious eyes.

Nate steps forwards and introduces them each in turn. "Dorien, this is Ronan," he says, nodding to the Viking before nodding to the other side and telling me, "And this is Jax."

I tilt my head at each of them, and Nate doesn't bother to tell them who I am because they'll already know. "Do you have everything I need?"

"Yes," I say as I pick up the few sheets of paper in front of me and hold them out to him. Nate steps forwards again and takes them, scanning over them before handing them back to Ronan, who looks them over before passing them to Jax.

"My guys will have him found in the next seventy-two hours," Nate declares, and I raise an eyebrow.

"Can you guarantee that?" I question. I guess most don't question him, and if they do, I'm sure they end up with their throats slit, or in other various states of demise, but as much as they should intimidate me, they don't. Some might call me a stupid fuck, but I refuse to bow down when I'm paying for their services, not to mention I haven't been insulting or rude, so there's no need for me to be sat here like a nervous wreck. And you should never show men like this that you're intimated by them anyway, not in my book. If you show fear, they will eat you alive.

"If I get what I want, I can guarantee it," Nate confirms.

"And if you don't?"

"Then the whole deal is off, you'll owe me nothing, and I will kill the fucker in due course without taking any payment because he doesn't deserve to live," he tells me, and I almost balk at his honesty. I could tell him the deal is off, that I don't need to pay him anything, seeing as he just told me he would end the fucker anyway, but there's no guarantee on when that would happen, and Elise needs the guarantee even if she doesn't know about any of this—not to mention, I need the guarantee just as much. For her.

I sit back and gesture for him to take a seat, which he does, the two men behind him staying where they are.

I open a draw to my side and pull out a contract, sliding it across the desk for him to look at. "That indicates the shares you will have, and I will have the contract finalised once you've agreed," I state, and Nate's curious gaze runs over the paperwork before his eyes lift back up to look at me.

"Twenty percent," he muses.

"It's a good offer," I reply, making him smirk.

"Thirty is better."

"Come on, Nate, twenty percent for a stake in my hotel chain is going to make you thousands per month."

"Not as much as thirty will. And it's Mr Knowles until I say otherwise," he says with that smirk still in place.

"I thought you didn't want the money?" I question, referring to what he said last night.

"Oh, I don't, but thirty percent is non-negotiable." His tone is firm, and I quickly deduce that I don't have time to sit here and fight over ten percent, it's not fucking worth it, so I hold my hand out, ready to shake on it before I call my solicitor and have the contract drawn up.

He raises his hand and shakes mine, and even without the contract, I would classify this moment as a done deal anyway. I'm a man of my word, and I think that Nate is too, even if he's essentially a criminal.

"Pleasure doing business with you, Dorien," he says as he stands. "Ronan will deal with the contract side of things. He's got your number, so he'll call you later today to check progress and give you any details you may need for the deeds."

I nod as he turns and walks to the door, but before he opens it, he turns back around and says, "And now you can call me Nate."

I actually let out a gruff laugh of surprise. "Sure."

And then he's gone, the two men following him and closing the door behind them.

Seventy-two hours and her nightmares could all be over. No need to go through a messy divorce, which I now have no doubt he will fight at every turn, no need to be scared of him ever coming back to hurt her again, and I can't even tell her any of this, because I have no idea how she would react. We can't even talk about how we feel, so how the fuck would we talk about me meeting with a fucking crime lord and shaking on a deal for him to find Derrick and kill him whilst receiving a stake in my business? The thought makes me laugh out loud, but another knock at the door has me running a hand over my face and saying, "Give me fucking strength," before I tell whoever it is to come in. And when the door opens, I wish I hadn't, because it's fucking Hayley, and I could do without her bullshit right now. Although, I do have a big fucking bone to pick with her, so maybe now is the right time to do it.

"Dorien, do you have a moment?" she asks as she walks on in, closing the door behind her.

"Come on in why don't you?" I mutter, and I know she hears me when her footsteps falter.

"I can come back later if now isn't convenient?" she says, batting her eyelashes in a way that I presume is supposed to do something, but it just falls flat.

"Sit down, Hayley," I order, and she complies, crossing her legs and giving me dopey eyes.

"Everything okay?" she asks, tilting her head to the side.

"I haven't had a chance to ask you something that has been on my mind, so I'll cut right to the chase. Why was Elise out the back of the hotel three nights ago, on her own, taking out a bag of rubbish?"

She looks at me blankly for a moment before replying, "The chute was blocked on the first floor where she was finishing up her shift, but maintenance sorted it that evening."

"And it's part of the employee safety to take rubbish out at night, is it?" I question, and I see her gulp.

"Well, it's the staff entrance too, so I didn't think it was a big deal," she replies innocently, but we both know she's far from innocent.

"The staff use that entrance between the hours of seven a.m. and five p.m., because that door is monitored during those times. At all other times, they come through the front entrance, just like they do in my other hotels. So, tell me why you would send her out there with no security and no one watching?"

"I didn't think it was a big issue." She shrugs her shoulders, enraging me further.

"Well it is, Hayley, and as of this moment, you are relieved of your duties here," I inform her, because her reasons aren't good enough. I get the feeling there is more to this than meets the eye, but I just want her out of my fucking sight.

"Excuse me?" She balks, her mouth dropping open and her eyes narrowing.

"Get your things and get out. You will be paid until the end of the month, call it severance pay, and you will no longer be welcome in any of my hotels."

"You can't do that," she screeches.

"I just fucking did." My face is deadpan. This isn't up for discussion, my mind is made up and she needs to get the hell out of here before I lose my patience with her.

"Is this just because you're fucking her? Is her pussy really that good?" she sneers, shocking the shit out of me with her words, but I keep my face neutral, not showing her how infuriated I am that she has dared to speak to me in this way.

"Who I am fucking is none of your business, and let's be honest here, Hayley, your treatment of the staff is appalling most of the time. This was just the cherry on top of the cake."

"And what the hell has she got that I haven't?"

"Pardon me?"

"I mean, she's a maid, Dorien," she says with a scoff, and I feel my blood boil. "How on earth could you ignore me in favour of her? A maid, for fuck's sake."

Is she being serious right now? The fucking audacity of her, to sit there and belittle another person just because they work a job that she believes is beneath her.

"Is your jealousy the reason that you set her up for her husband to beat the shit out of her, Hayley?" I say, trusting my gut instinct, unable to keep the darkness out of my voice. She has the decency to look a little sheepish as I see her gulp. "Or have you always been a narcissist?"

"I am no such thing," she defends, but her words hold no meaning. She's out for herself and fuck everyone else.

"So what would you call it when things don't go your way and the whole world doesn't appear to revolve around you? What would you call it when you actually arrange to have another person hurt because you can't stand not being the centre of attention?"

"You can't prove I did anything," she says, and right there shows just how stupid she really is.

"You've given yourself up with your words alone," I inform her, my jaw clenching as I contain my rage.

"She's got you wrapped around her little finger, hasn't she?"

I don't answer. I refuse to get into a piss-poor slinging match with someone who has no relevance in my life. "Hand your key cards in to security on your way out." I turn my attention to my phone, ready to call security and reception, making sure they're aware that Hayley no longer works here. She'll be logged out of the hotel system within the next ten minutes, once I put the call in to my tech guy, and I'll give the deputy manager the call of a lifetime when I inform him that he will be running the show until I have finalised my plans for the a manager to take over.

"Oh, and, Hayley," I say, making her turn her attention back to me before she opens the door. "I suggest you go quietly, keep your head down and your nose clean, because if I get one sniff of you trying to cause any kind of trouble, or if you dare to ever show your face again, it'll be the last thing you ever do." I don't mince my words, because when you're dealing with crazy, there is no point in trying to be reasonable.

I watch her shoulders slump as she knows she's been defeated. There is no point in going up against me, because she won't ever win.

"We could have been good together," she says quietly, just showing how delusional she really is.

"Not in this lifetime or the next," I tell her. "Or any lifetime, actually."

"Goodbye, Dorien," she whispers before she leaves the room, closing the door quietly behind her.

I blow out a puff of air and start to make the phone calls needed. I know that I won't see her again. Call it a hunch. And there was never going to be any point in threatening me, which I think she quickly realised, because if I wasn't threatened by Nate Knowles, then Hayley sure wasn't going to fucking scare me.

Chapter Forty-Seven

ELISE

"Hey," I say as I answer the door to see Chantel stood there.

"I saw Dorien going into his office earlier, and I thought you might want some company," she says with a smile.

"Oh, sure." I step back from the door and she walks past, pulling a bottle of wine out of her handbag. "Too early for a drink?"

I look at the clock to see it's just after one in the afternoon. "I can't, I'm still on these damn pain meds." She pouts and puts the bottle away. "Cup of tea?" I ask.

"I suppose it'll do until we can paint the town red," she says, and she follows me into the kitchen and takes a seat at the island in the middle as I fill the kettle and flick it on.

"You staying here for a while?" I ask as I get the cups out of the cupboard, putting a teabag in both of them.

"For another few days. To be honest, it's been a nice change of pace from the world of fashion."

"You work in fashion?" I ask, suddenly excited to know more.

"Honey, I don't just work in it, I run my own fashion powerhouse," she tells me with a grin. "Ever heard of CG Parks?"

"Oh my god, I love that fashion line," I exclaim.

"Well, that's me," she declares with her arms held wide, chuckling.

"Holy shit. I had no idea."

"I tend to hide away in the wings, working on new creations and keeping out of the spotlight. I have a partner that fronts it all, you know, to be the face of the brand, but I don't care for the attention. It's a pretty sweet deal, I get to remain anonymous except to those closest to me, and my partner, Jules, does all of the public stuff."

I quickly ask how she takes her tea, and then I carry the mugs to the island, placing them down and sitting opposite her, absolutely rapt by the fact that I am in the presence of fashion royalty.

"I won't tell a soul, I promise," I assure her.

"I know you won't, otherwise I wouldn't have said anything."

"And how do you know that? You've only met me once," I say with a laugh, but she has a serious expression on her face as she answers.

"I've always relied on my gut instinct, and it's never failed me. When I met you the other day, I knew instantly that you were genuine, real, and didn't have one fake bone in your body."

Huh. Pretty fucking deep for someone I've only met twice, but I like her perception of me.

"Anyway," she continues, breezing past her assessment of me. "I see that sparkle in your eye, so tell me, you like fashion?"

"I really do. I mean, I haven't been involved in anything, because I never got the chance to, but back when I was in college, I was studying fashion design."

"Ooooo, do you have any drawings?" she asks, but my face falls.

"Not anymore. Derrick, my husband, made me get rid of them when everything went to shit and I had to give up my dream to become a maid to keep us afloat. And I guess, after that, I stopped hoping and gave up on admiring gorgeous creations, because I didn't see the point in wishing for something that wasn't ever going to come true."

"I'm sorry," she says, but I wave my hand, not wanting to put a downer on her popping in here.

"It is what it is." I shrug.

"And what is the dream, Elise?"

I allow myself a moment to wander back to a time when I had hope and my dreams weren't crushed to dust. "To create. To see my designs come to life. To see them being worn and be proud."

"Not for the fame?" she asks, and I screw my nose up.

"No, I don't think I'd be comfortable with being on show, so to speak. I mean, I'd show my face if I had to, but it was never about fame for me, I just wanted to design," I tell her truthfully.

"You know, that's exactly what I wanted, and I never thought I'd be able to stay hidden, but ten years later and I'm doing okay." She smiles, and much as I did the other day, I feel a connection with her. Like we're meant to be friends.

"I bet it's magical to be able to see your designs come to life."

"It really is. But it gets a bit much sometimes, the constant need to keep producing new pieces and putting home life on the back burner because a celebrity has paid an extortionate amount of money to have a one-of-a-kind creation. So when Gabe and I are able to get away from it, we pick one of Dorien's hotels and we just relax, shut our phones off, and we take the time to appreciate one another."

"That's sweet." It really is, and it's obvious to anyone with eyes that they both adore one another.

"Makes you realise that work isn't always the be all and end all." She's being very open right now, and I get the feeling that maybe she needs a friend too. "You should come to my studio one day."

"Seriously?"

"Yes, seriously, Elise," she says with a chuckle.

"Wow, yes, oh my god, I'd love to," I ramble.

"We'll be sure to make it happen." She winks, and then she asks me a personal question. "Any news on your husband?"

I hate that he gets to be called that. Husband. He never deserved the title in the first place. "No. I haven't heard from him, and I don't really want to either."

"That's understandable." She nods her head, and I sip my drink. "You know, Elise, I've known Dorien a long time. I've given him so much shit over the years for not settling down, or for putting all of his energy into work and not caring about having a family, a wife, or, hell, even a girlfriend. But seeing him with you, I know why he waited."

I stare at her, not sure what to say from the unexpected flip in conversation.

"You're special, Elise, and I know that may sound weird coming from someone you barely know, but Dorien needs someone special, and I'm pretty sure he's found it in you."

Her words bring unshed tears to my eyes. I've never been called special. I've never been loved for just being me, so hearing her say something nice is throwing me all off.

"I don't mean to make you upset," she says, her tone now sounding worried.

"I'm not upset," I tell her as I swipe a hand under my eyes. "It's just… I've never really felt like I've belonged before. My parents made me marry my husband, and they did it for their own gains. They always made me feel like I was never good enough, and now you're saying nice things and it's just hard to hear after so many years of nothing." And now she's going to think I'm a silly twat for spouting all of that to her when, like she said, we hardly know each other.

"None of them deserved you, Elise." She reaches across the island and takes my hand in hers. "Truly, they didn't deserve your beautiful soul."

Fucking hell, now there's no stopping the tears from falling. "My parents haven't even tried to contact me since Dorien threw my mother out of this hotel."

"He threw her out?" she asks, shocked.

"Yeah, when she came here with Derrick and tried to make me go back to him."

"Oh damn, you gotta tell me that story at some point, because I've seen Dorien pissed, and I can only imagine how he told her to 'do one'."

"Oh yeah, it was, um…"

"So Dorien?"

"Exactly," I reply, my tears subsiding as I laugh quietly.

"He's a hard man to love, Elise, but when he lets you in, it's so worth it. And I say that just as a friend, because I'm madly in love with my husband," she reiterates, but I never thought anything of the sort. Their close bond was apparent the first time I saw them here.

"I'm scared, Chantel," I whisper, because she fucking knows him and she probably has more of an idea of what he feels for me than I do. My head is all over the place with the whiplash I'm giving myself over whether he feels what I do.

"But sometimes, that's the best kind of feeling, because it shows you just how much you want it, and when it's returned, it's magical." She's speaking like she knows, and maybe she went through something with Gabriel before they figured it out so she's speaking from experience. "Be fierce, Elise, and never settle."

Be fierce.

Never settle.

And the first step to doing that is to admit to myself what I've been trying to ignore for a while.

I am totally in love with Dorien Dukes.

Chapter Forty-Eight

DORIEN

"Elise," I call when I get through the penthouse door. I've got food being prepared to be sent up here for us, and I need to ask her a question that has been on my mind all day.

"Yeah?" She pokes her head out of the bathroom, and I fucking drink her in. She's so fucking gorgeous. And so fucking mine.

"Come, I need to talk to you."

"Is everything okay?" she asks warily as she makes her way towards me.

"It will be," I say before I swoop down and kiss her lips. Fuck, I've missed her today. Just another confirmation that this woman has my dick in a vice. Her hands find the back of my neck, her fingers delving into the hair at the nape, and I pull her flush against me, taking my time reacquainting my tongue with hers. And then a bastard knock comes to the door.

"For fuck's sake," I grumble, and her answering chuckle has my dick ready to stand to attention. I know it will be the food I ordered, but still, crappy fucking timing. I pull open the door and take the trolley from the porter, saying thank you and waving them away quickly.

"In a rush, are we?" she says as I close the door and wheel the trolley over to the table by the windows.

"Yes, because I've not had my cock in you since the early hours of the morning and I'd like to remedy that," I admit. It's been a fucker of a day, and losing myself in her is the best way to unwind.

"And who says I want your dick in me?" she sasses.

"Are you going to pretend that you don't?"

She just smiles at me and takes a seat at the table as I uncover the dishes on the trolley and pull two warm plates from the bottom. I ordered steak, chips, onion rings, salad, and different sauces, because I didn't know which one she would want—the fucking works.

"That smells amazing," she says as I gesture for her to start filling her plate.

"Eat, and then we'll talk," I say as I sit down and dish my own food.

"And then we'll fuck?" she asks cheekily, and a roar of laughter leaves me.

"Yes, Elise, then we'll fuck, and I'll eat your pussy for dessert," I tell her, which earns me a grin.

"Will you tell me to get on my knees?"

Oh, she's goading me, and if she carries on, we won't be eating, and we won't be talking, because she'll be too busy with my dick in her mouth to hear what I have to ask her.

"Will you be a good girl?"

"Aren't I always?" she says playfully, and I fucking love this side of her. It brings out the best in me too, her playfulness, her sass, and her smart fucking mouth that unleashes more and more with every day that passes. Her smile, it's the fucking light I need amidst all of the dark.

We continue to eat our food in contented silence, and once we're done, I sit back and get straight to the point of what I want to talk about, because the sooner it's done, the sooner I get to take her to bed.

"I fired Hayley today," I blurt out, and maybe it wasn't a good idea to say it when she was sipping her drink, because it makes her splutter. I quickly round the table and rub her back as she controls her breathing. "Jesus, are you okay?"

"I'm fine." She waves her hand and turns on her chair to face me. "You did what?"

"I fired Hayley."

"Why?"

"Because she fucked up."

"Oh my god. But… what did she do?" she asks.

"She's the reason your husband attacked you," I state, and her mouth drops open.

"Dorien, come on, she can't be blamed for that."

"Can't she?"

"Well, not really. I mean, she sent me out there, yes, but she didn't know that Derrick was going to be waiting there for me."

"Think about it, Elise," I say as I lean down, one hand braced on her chair, the other on the table. "Fucking convenient that the chute was blocked on the floor you were working on, and that you were asked to go out there, where Derrick was waiting at the right time to get you on your own."

"He could have been waiting there for a while, and he would know when my shifts ended," she points out.

"Yes, that's true, but it doesn't account for the fact that he showed up five minutes before she found you and asked you to go out there, it doesn't account for the fact that the security camera at the staff entrance was turned off, and it doesn't account for the fact that she'd had phone conversations with him, and the odd text."

I don't think I could have shocked her more if I'd tried. Her eyes are wide with surprise as she processes what I've just said. "No, you must have it wrong."

"Except I don't." I spent the remainder of the afternoon on the phone to my tech guy, where he delved into Hayley's phone records. Call me a paranoid fucker, but after she gave herself away in my office earlier, I needed to know exactly what Hayley had been up to. I knew there was something shifty about it all.

"Fucking hell," she exclaims. "I mean, why would she do that?"

I just give her a look, and it doesn't take her long to catch onto my meaning.

"Oh god, this is because I'm here, isn't it? This is because I'm here with you," Elise deduces, and all I do is nod my head, because there's no point in sugar-coating Hayley's actions. She would have no other reason to go after Elise, even if she is a first-class bitch regardless. "Had you and her——"

"No." I cut her off before she can even finish the question. "Never."

"Jesus, this gets more complicated by the day," she mutters, her eyes falling closed for a moment, and I decide I may as well hit her with the next thing I want to ask.

"So, I need a new hotel manager," I begin, and her eyes spring open.

"Dorien, no."

"No?"

"You're not thinking of asking me to manage this place, are you?"

"Of course I am."

"Dorien, I can barely manage my own life right now, how the hell do you expect me to run a hotel when I know nothing about how to do that?" she questions, but this is all irrelevant crap that can be worked through.

"By learning on the job." It's the best way. Qualifications get you so far, but working from the ground up is what I've found works.

"I can't do it," she says softly, but I didn't get where I am today by backing down. I crouch in front of her, taking her hands in mine.

"Elise, if I didn't think you could do it, I wouldn't be asking you. I'm a businessman through and through, so I'm not going to make decisions on a whim, and this has nothing to with the fact that you are in my bed every night. This is about trust, and I need someone I can trust to not fuck me or any of the employees over." It's honest, and that's all I can be with her. "I can be here to help to start with, if it makes you feel better."

Her hand comes up to cup my cheek as she says, "You're being totally serious, aren't you?"

"Deadly." I hold her gaze, waiting for her to give me the answer I want.

"Can I think about it?" she asks.

"Of course. You have forty-eight hours to give me your decision."

"You're putting me on a time limit?" she says with a chuckle.

"Did you expect anything less?"

"No," she tells me, before pushing her lips to mine and finally giving me a taste of her. "You're a special man, Dorien Dukes," she whispers, and the time for talking is over, for now. I pick her up from the chair and carry her to the bedroom, where I plan to make her scream my name so loud that the floor downstairs will hear us.

Chapter Forty-Nine

ELISE

My phone rings on the bedside table, rousing me from sleep, and I lazily pick it up, only to spring up in bed at seeing my mother's name on the screen. I can't deal with her before I've had coffee, especially as it's been a few weeks since I last had contact with her. I'm sure she's phoning to berate me into going back to Derrick, but nothing could make me go back to him. Ever.

I put my phone back on the side and get out of bed, padding my way to the bathroom before going into the main room to see Dorien sat at the table with breakfast laid out ready. He's drinking a coffee and reading something on his phone. Such a simple thing has me smiling.

"Morning," I say as I walk over to him after finishing admiring how delicious he is.

"Good, you're awake," he says as I get to the table and pour myself a cup of coffee. "Got an answer for me yet?"

I chuckle and roll my eyes. "So impatient."

"You already know this about me," he states, and I take a seat whilst enjoying the gentle banter we seem to be building up between us more and more with each day that passes. "I have something else for you, actually." I pause with my cup halfway to my mouth as he picks up an envelope from beside him and passes it to me.

I take the envelope and narrow my eyes on him a little. "If this is a contract to become the manager, I haven't decided yet."

He laughs, and it warms me to hear it. "It's not that, but it is a document of sorts."

Intrigued, I open the envelope and pull out the contents, my eyes scanning the first page and nearly bugging out of my head. Fuck me, it's divorce papers. For me. And Derrick. What the hell?

"I had my legal team draft that for you, so you don't have to wait," Dorien informs me, but I am incapable of saying anything for a moment. "You don't have to use them, but they are the best, and they are there any time you need to speak to them. Their number is on the card inside the envelope."

I still have no words as I scan the next page, my coffee forgotten on the table.

"I need to go to another hotel this morning, so I'll leave you to look over that and then we can talk later, if you need to," he says, getting up from the table and coming round to give me a kiss before he's taking off without another word.

Who the fuck is this guy? He seems to think of everything, and I'm not going to lie, it's all a little overwhelming. I mean, I've gone from not being given a fuck about, to feeling like I'm pretty much the centre of someone else's world, even though we haven't discussed anything about what happens when I leave here and return to Celeste's, or how he expects things to work if I keep working here, especially if I take the manager role.

Oh lord. I need to offload all of this on someone, because my brain hurts. My first thought goes to Celeste, but I know she'll be busy working, and as much as she'd bunk off to come and help me sort through my muddled thoughts, I also know that she can't afford to do that, and I wouldn't expect her to. So, without thinking too much about it, I dial Chantel, who gave me her number yesterday before she left.

"Hey, Elise," she answers brightly.

"Hi, um, I was wondering if you were busy today?"

"I don't have any plans as such, but I have a feeling I'm about to," she says with a chuckle.

"Do you wanna maybe grab some lunch?" I suggest.

"Sure, want me to come to the penthouse?"

"No, I'm sick of being stuck in here. I thought we could go to the restaurant downstairs, maybe sit out on the patio, so I don't have everyone staring at me the whole time," I say, because the thought of them wondering why I'm having lunch instead of working fills me with dread, but I need to get out of this place, even if it is just to go downstairs.

"Leave it with me and I'll get it booked. I'll meet you by the lifts at twelve."

"Sounds good. See you soon."

"Looking forward to it," she chirps before we hang up. I'm well aware that the bruises are still on my face and neck, but I'll cover them up as much as possible. I can't keep hiding out in here, and I'll be returning to work soon anyway, to see the looks on everyone's faces when they see me and wonder where I've been. Might as well let them gossip before I return.

"So, what's going on?" Chantel says as we take a seat at a secluded table on the patio outside. The waiter hands us the menus and then disappears, saying he'll be back in a few minutes. I didn't fail to notice the looks some of the staff gave me as I walked by, but I knew that was going to happen, so I was kind of prepared for it.

"Dorien."

"Oh boy, what's he done now?"

"Well, he's only gone and offered me a job working here as the hotel manager, because he fired the previous one yesterday. And then he pulls out divorce papers for me this morning, which he said were a rough draft, and then he told me that his legal team are basically at my disposal."

Her eyebrows shoot up a little as the waiter returns and we quickly scan the menu to order food. I choose the chicken salad with extra fries, and Chantel picks the same. I pour myself a glass of water as the waiter takes the menus away and leaves us on our own again.

"You know, Elise, I've seen Dorien in all types of situations, but never this one, with you. And as much as this may be a little overboard, this is how he is. A powerful man who would absolutely put his life on the line for those he—"

"Don't say it," I interrupt, but she ignores me.

"Loves."

"He doesn't love me, Chantel."

"He so fucking does. He may not have said it, and he may not be great with voicing his feelings, but he does, whether you want to hear it or not."

I groan, because this isn't how any of this was supposed to go. I was supposed to leave Derrick and find myself, not fall in love with a man who would move heaven and earth for me.

"And you love him," she finishes.

"Fuck." I sit back and blow out a breath. I can't even deny it. I do fucking love him. But I also know I've jumped from the frying pan into the fire. I also know there is an age difference. I also know that I am going to be accused of sleeping my way to the top. And I also know that I can't fucking fight how I feel any longer. I don't have the energy to stop myself from being consumed by Dorien Dukes.

"One thing at a time, Elise, you don't have to conquer the world in a day," Chantel says gently, as the waiter brings over our food, our conversation paused until he's disappeared.

"I feel so out of my depth here," I admit.

"And sometimes that's not a bad thing. Feeling out of our depth pushes us to do things we wouldn't have the guts to do normally. It forces our hand and makes us do things we never thought possible. I know you've got a lot of shit to sort out, but ask yourself this question… is he worth it? If the answer is yes, then everything else will fall into place."

"And if the answer is no?" I whisper, waiting with bated breath for her answer.

"Then he wasn't something worth having in the first place."

Chapter Fifty

DORIEN

I get back to The Blue Diamond hotel, feeling stressed as fuck. I visited another hotel in my chain today, and to say the running of it underwhelmed me would be an understatement. I need to hire someone else to keep a check on things, like a shark who rotates when they check on different hotels and who can replace staff without having to fucking bother me about it. Yes, I'll add that to my agenda for tomorrow, but for now, I just want to relax, preferably balls deep in Elise.

I open the penthouse door to darkness, except for a lamp on in the far corner of the room. My eyes try to search out Elise, but there's no sign of her. I deduce that she's either in the bedroom or bathroom, because the kitchen is empty too.

I kick the door closed behind me, tossing the key card on the side table by the door, and then a movement to my right catches my eye. The dim light shows me Elise stood there, in nothing but lacy underwear and a long, silk dressing gown flowing behind her. She walks over to the table by the window, where I see a chair has been moved to sit on its own between the sofa and the table.

"Sit," she commands, and I raise one eyebrow at her. She doesn't move, doesn't even attempt to say anything else as she holds my gaze and keeps her finger pointing at the chair. Curious, I make my way over, sitting down and wondering what she's got planned. Her hair is framing her face, and her eyes sparkle with mischief. I could get used to this side of her—carefree. It's sexy as hell when she takes me by surprise, and watching her come into her own more and more just adds to that.

She moves to the side, picking a remote from the table and pressing a button, music starting to filter through the room. I recognise it, the sensual rhythm and blues beat seeming to set the tone, and I watch as she puts the remote back on the table before turning away from me as she moves her body to the music.

I watch, fucking rapt, as she sways her hips from side to side, revealing her back as she drops the dressing gown to the floor and starts to grind her hips. Her hands move down her stomach as she turns to face me, skimming over her pussy before she's coming towards me and giving me a lap dance. Mother of fuck.

She rotates her hips, her hands brushing over my chest as she starts to undo my shirt buttons. I'm hard as fucking rock for her. I'm mesmerised by her. I'm infatuated with her.

When she's undone my shirt, she pushes it off my shoulders, along with my jacket, and then she steps back, admiring my abs, biting her bottom lip as she moves her hands behind her and unclasps her bra, letting it fall to the floor. And then her hands move to the sides of her knickers as she hooks her thumbs underneath the fabric, teasing me, tempting me. There are equal parts of me that want this to hurry up and be over so I can touch her but also wanting the song to play on repeat because I don't want this to end.

She pushes the lace fabric down her legs, and then she's kneeling before me and running her hands up my thighs, slowly, sensually. She finds the button on my trousers, undoing it and pulling my zip down, reaching in my boxers and fisting my cock, before uncovering it and teasing the tip with her tongue.

Her other hand comes up and her nails rake over my chest. Something feral ignites inside of me, and I struggle not to fucking haul her up off the floor and plunge my dick in her. She's clearly enjoying being in control here, and as much as I usually take control, I want her to have this moment, until I bend her over and fuck her hard, that is.

She bobs her head up and down as she takes my cock to the back of her throat. Jesus. She looks up at me from underneath her lashes, and seeing her like this, my cock filling her mouth, is just fucking everything. I'm not going to be able to control myself much longer, even as I tell myself she needs this, because she's too fucking beautiful to not touch.

She can see my internal struggle, I'm sure of it, because she moves back up my dick and lets it fall from her mouth as she pushes up and straddles me. My hands instantly find her hips as she grinds to the music, making my cock jerk with every movement. Her lips connect with mine, and that is where I lose control. I fist the hair at the nape of her neck as I devour her. I lift her as I stand and move us to the window, pushing her against it as my cock enters her dripping wet pussy. I fuck her there as she wraps her limbs around me, not seeming to be able to get close enough, even as there is no space between us.

She pants in my mouth but I refuse to break our lips apart.

She grabs my hair and cries out loud as she comes hard, my punishing strokes not letting up and taking her to another fucking level.

"Fucking take it all, Elise," I grunt as she clenches around me. She cries out again as I push her towards another orgasm, the clenching of her pussy telling me she's on the verge. And then I say something I never thought I'd say to a woman ever… "I fucking love you." She screams my name, my words taking her over that edge and me following right behind her.

Her lips crash back onto mine again, and I carry her through the apartment and to the bedroom, where I lie her down and take the rest of my clothes off, her eyes watching my every move. I know she heard me in there, when I said I loved her, and maybe that's why she's looking at me the way she is. It's a look I can't quite decipher as I cover my body with hers, kissing her softly, a complete contrast to what we just did in the other room. My dick doesn't take long to harden again, and I slide inside of her, moving slow.

"Dorien," she whispers against my lips as my hips rock into her. "Is this real?"

"Every single second of it," I whisper back.

I see her eyes glisten as I make love to her, my forehead resting on hers, our bodies moving in sync, our fingers entwined as I hold her hands above her head.

And when she orgasms again, she doesn't look away from me, the look of pure ecstasy on her face making me come hard.

I place a light kiss on the end of her nose as I move to the side of her and lie on my back. She immediately curls up to the side of me, her head resting on my chest, her arm hooking around my waist and her leg doing the same to my thigh.

Silence descends, only the sounds of our breathing to be heard, until she breaks the silence.

"Dorien," she says, and I look down at her. She moves her head, resting her chin on my chest to look back at me. "I'm scared."

"Scared?"

"Scared of loving you so much that I lose myself."

Fuck. This woman.

"You love me?" I ask, because I didn't realise how much I needed to hear her say it until now. I didn't realise I fucking need to hear the words leave her lips to complete me.

"I love you," she whispers, and I move so I'm back on top of her again.

"Say it again."

"I love you, Dorien Dukes."

"Fuck." My lips are on hers as I claim what's mine. I've waited a fucking lifetime to find her, and now that I've got her, I'm never letting go.

Chapter Fifty-One

DORIEN

The phone call comes at five a.m.

I hear it ringing from the other room, and I untangle myself from Elise, so as not to disturb her. As I pull on a pair of joggers that are strewn across the floor, I pad my way out to the main room, ready to tear whoever is ringing me at this hour a new arsehole. The phone stops ringing as I reach the coffee table, but when I see who the missed call is from, I know that there will be no new arsehole needed.

Nate Knowles.

It's been nearly forty-eight hours since I met with him. Forty-five since I had the contract drafted, which I gave to Ronan, for Nate to become a partner in my business. And it's been forty-three since he signed on the dotted line and the deal was finalised.

I'm yet to discuss anything further with him, and if he thinks I'm going to change the way I run things, then we're going to run into major issues, because I know success, clearly, I've made fucking millions from my hotels and business deals, and I wouldn't expect him to question me, just like I wouldn't question how he runs the underworld.

But my gut is already telling me that this isn't related to hotel business, and as I dial him back and put the phone to my ear, he answers on the first ring with just three words.

"We've got him."

I left Elise in bed, got dressed, putting on a suit, and then I left the hotel and got into my car, driving to the location Nate gave me, ready to put an end to this part of Elise's life.

I feel in control as I park in a space at the back of an abandoned warehouse, away from the main road, and hidden by trees that make it look like nothing is here but woodland.

I pick up the envelope I brought with me and exit the car with my game face on. I've been waiting for this moment since he attacked her, and my adrenaline is pumping through me as my mind urges me to keep my cool façade.

Ronan is waiting for me at the back entrance as I approach, and with a nod, he turns and leads me inside. There's one of the big burly fuckers stood inside the door, and when we're through, he closes the door and bolts it, standing guard as Ronan continues to lead me through a small room and into a big open space, which is the main part of the warehouse. I see Nate and Jax are stood in the middle of the room, with a man hunched over in the chair he's been tied to just before them, with his back to me. I clench my fist at my side as my other hand struggles not to crumple the envelope.

"Dorien," Nate greets as I stop behind Derrick, fighting the desire to kill the bastard myself.

"Nate," I reply, my jaw clenched as I rein in my anger for a little longer. "Jax."

Jax just grunts in response, his fingers clenching at each side of him, like he's ready to do some damage.

"If you have anything to say to him, I'd do it quickly," Nate says, before he nods at Derrick and finishes with, "Because Jax is ready to unleash."

I move around Derrick as he lifts his head to look at me. "You," he breathes, and a few feet away from him, I smirk and say, "Yes. Me."

"From the hotel… you… you threw me out," he rasps.

"I did."

"Why are you here?" he questions.

"To watch you pay," I tell him, keeping it vague, seeing his legs twitching nervously. I want the fucker to squirm before he dies.

"For what?" He really looks like he doesn't think he's done anything wrong, but I'm here to enlighten him.

"Is there a table in here?" I ask, turning to look at Nate, who nods at Ronan. Ronan disappears for a moment, into the dark corner of the warehouse, before he's bringing over a folding table and passing it to me. "Thanks."

I take the table and unfold it, putting it in front of Derrick and slapping the envelope down.

"What's that?" Derrick asks.

"That is the ticket to your wife's freedom," I tell him, and his eyes shoot up to look at me as they widen.

"What? Elise's freedom?"

"Yes, Derrick, her freedom from you." I could just stop all of this and tell Jax to get on with ending his life, but that wouldn't ensure Elise's own financial security, whereas this will. I pick the envelope back up and open it, pulling out several papers which detail everything about her being granted a divorce and retaining the assets she's entitled to.

I place the papers down in front of him and pull a pen out of the inside pocket of my jacket, taking the lid off and placing it to the side.

"What is this?" he demands, but if he's reading it correctly, it's pretty fucking obvious what it is. I know the dim lighting isn't great, but he's not fucking blind.

"Divorce papers. You're going to sign every single piece of paper that needs signing, and then I'm going to walk out of here and give Elise her life back," I tell him.

"I'm not signing anything."

"You fucking are."

"Did she put you up to this?" he questions, and I laugh in his face.

"Does she seem like the type that would ask anyone to do this?" I growl, because if he has to even ask that question, he never fucking knew her at all.

"I'm not signing anything. She's *my* wife."

"You've got pretty big balls for someone who is tied to a chair in a room with men who are ready to kill you," I sneer, and he trembles harder, his Adam's apple bobbing up and down.

"You're not going to kill me," he says pathetically, unsure of the words even as he speaks them.

"I'm not, but they will," I reply, flicking my head back to Nate and Jax behind me.

"Who the hell are you people?" he whispers.

"That doesn't matter. What matters is you put your hands on your wife when she didn't want you to. You attacked her, at my hotel, and I can't ever forgive that," I tell him.

"It was you, wasn't it? On the phone that day when I called her, when she was clearly having sex whilst I was trying to speak to her." Good God, give him a fucking medal.

I laugh callously as I say, "I wasn't having sex with her. I was eating her pussy as she spread her legs on my desk."

"You bastard," he says as he tries to fight the restraints on his wrists.

"I did something for her you never did, and I've been doing it ever since," I goad, because I fucking can.

"Untie me, I need to see her," he demands, but he hasn't got a hope in hell of leaving here alive.

"Sign the papers," I grit out.

"I can't very well do anything with my arms tied to the fucking chair," he spits sarcastically. I narrow my eyes on him as I look up at Ronan. He comes up behind Derrick and pulls a knife from his pocket, putting it by Derrick's wrist and saying, "Don't get any smart fucking ideas," before he slices through the ties and frees one wrist. Derrick immediately ignores Ronan's warning and starts flinging his arm out, his hand balled into a fist, which Ronan dodges easily.

"Fucking moron," Ronan says as he grabs hold of his flailing arm and pins it behind him, Derrick screeching as he does, but that's nothing compared to the moment when Ronan picks up the pen I laid down on the table and stabs it through his other hand. Derrick screams, his skin going pasty white as the blood oozes from his hand. I watch on, not at all repulsed by the violence. He deserves this and so much more.

"If you're going to kill me, why the fuck does it matter if I sign the papers or not?" Derrick wheezes as he screws his eyes shut and breathes deeply through the pain.

"Because you're a cunt who made sure that she will get nothing if she divorces you, not to mention her parents will become entitled to everything if you die," I say, my anger resurfacing.

"How do you know that?" he whispers.

"I'm a powerful man, Derrick. I can find out anything I want, including how you fucked her over every which way you could to make her feel like she was worth nothing. You made her give up her career, her dream, and then you punished her for your failings because you're a fucking parasite. I know all about how you lost your job, how you sexually harassed female workers and was asked to leave quietly so as not to bring any negativity to the company you worked for. And then there's the fact that they made it so you couldn't find employment again, so you made Elise suffer for your sins."

His eyes widen, but I'm not done.

"There's also the issue of you having fucked her mother, behind her and her father's back, and the devious bitch made sure to gain financial security until you fucked it all up, and then she just hated you for it as she continued to take out her jealousy on Elise—jealousy that she's harboured for years over her only daughter."

He has the decency to remain quiet as I simmer with rage.

"It poses the question of why her mother didn't divorce her father and marry you instead, but you wanted a younger model to compete with the other office wankers that were marrying younger women left, right and centre, so you both came up with a plan as her mother dangled herself in front of you like a goddamn carrot, ready to sleep with you at a moment's notice, and also having the power of being able to tell Elise about your seedy relationship if you didn't do what she wanted. She knew that if she mentioned it, Elise would never have married you, and you knew it too. You also knew that it was a golden opportunity to bag that younger wife and keep up with the other office workers, because you were nothing if not materialistic. So, Elise's mother, Karen, convinced Elise's father to go along with it, omitting the details about you two fucking, of course, and then you all watched as Elise's life became miserable but none of you cared enough to do anything about it.

"You all made her feel so much guilt over something that never should have happened in the first place. And don't worry, her parents won't get away with this, they'll be left with nothing if I have my way, and nor will the company that you used to work for, because they made the mistake of covering up the fact you're a seedy wanker."

"Who the hell are you?" he asks, shocked I've just recited how truly pathetic his life was.

"Your worst fucking nightmare. Now, sign the fucking papers," I order.

"You can't make me do anything," he says, but he underestimates me, clearly. I let the fucking anger overtake me as I pull the pen out of his hand and wipe it off on my suit jacket to the sounds of him screaming again. And then I take his restrained arm from Ronan, and I make him hold the pen as I put it to the papers in from of him and force his hand to sign every part he needs to.

My fingers crush his as he cries like a fucking baby. I watch as he signs away all of his rights, handing the house over to Elise, as well as her parents'. Their names were never on the deeds, because this sneaky fucker made sure he had her mother dangling on a carrot too, just as she did with him about being able to rat them out over their disgusting affair. And even as her dad wasn't involved in the shadier aspect of all this, he still watched as they treated her like crap, and he still used her for his own gains.

When he's done, I let his hand go as he whimpers like a dog, and I pick up the papers, depositing them back in the envelope before I walk to Nate and say, "Hold these for a sec, please." I speak calmly, coolly, but when he's taken the papers from me, Jax bristling beside him, I turn back around and clench my fist as I draw my arm back and plough it forwards, straight into Derrick's jaw. He yells, spitting blood as I do it again, the second punch forceful enough to knock his chair back so he's lying on the floor.

I stand above him before I crouch down, and I grab him by the scruff of his T-shirt, spitting in his face as I shout, "You never fucking deserved her. None of you. And I'll meet you in hell where I'll fuck you up all over again." I throw him back down, his head banging against the concrete floor before I stand up, adjust my jacket, and go back to Nate, taking the papers from him.

"Do your worst," I tell him, but I don't need to. He's got a wife, and if anyone ever touched her, I'm sure my actions would be fucking tame compared to his.

I walk towards the exit, feeling somewhat lighter than I have done since she was attacked, and when I get to the door, I turn back around to see Jax stood waiting, ready to strike as Ronan unties Derrick from the chair and holds him there, dragging out the seconds until he receives his true punishment.

I watch as Jax cricks his neck before he throws a few punches in Derrick's stomach, Ronan keeping him upright so he doesn't drop like a sack of shit to the floor. And then I see Jax pull out a pair of pliers, and as much as I may want to watch Derrick meet his end, I find that I don't need to. I have what I need. Elise's freedom. Something no one else has ever given her.

I push the door open and walk out towards my car as I make a mental note to send a bonus to my private investigator who dug up all that shit on Derrick, as well as Elise's parents. I have no idea how he got that information, and I don't fucking care. I don't need to know how. As for dealing with her mother and father, I'm not sure that's up to me, so I'll bide my time for now, until Elise truly lets them go.

Chapter Fifty-Two

ELISE

Waking up to Dorien's arms around me is my new comfort zone. Last night was incredible, he is incredible, and I don't know what I did to deserve his love, but I'm so fucking thankful for him. He's changing me, for the better, showing me who I want to be—someone who owns what they want, goes after what they desire, and doesn't let anyone keep them down.

I spent years having my self-esteem bulldozed, and it's almost crazy to me that he's changed my mindset in such a short amount of time.

But my bliss is short lived when my phone rings on the bedside table, my mother's name appearing on the screen. I never called her back. I almost don't want to, but that damn guilt rears its head once again.

I've never ignored her like this, never had the guts to determine my own path. Dorien has helped me more than he will ever know, and I don't know if I will ever be able to repay him for that.

With a sigh, I snuggle back into him, and his arm tightens around me, holding me close. Considering it's just after ten in the morning, I'd have expected him to be up by now, possibly not even here as he runs his empire. But he is, and I'd do anything to just prolong this moment—this happiness that is threatened by everything left unsolved in my life.

"Morning," he grumbles into my hair, before his lips find my ear, his teeth nibbling softly on my lobe. I sigh with contentment and link my fingers through his.

"Morning, yourself." My phone goes again, and Dorien's head peeks over my shoulder.

"Someone's keen," he comments, and my sigh this time isn't so content.

"It's my mother." Silence ensues for a beat. I don't know what he thinks of my parents, and I honestly don't know if I care enough to try and rescue the opinion he has of them, because I know it'll be negative from what I've told him.

"I'll go make coffee," he says, giving me a kiss on the cheek before getting out of the bed, leaving me with a feeling of missing him even as he stands there and pulls on a pair of joggers. I roll my eyes at myself being so ridiculous. It doesn't stop me from looking at his arse as he walks away, though. The man is a fucking god.

The phone rings again and I drag myself out of bed to splash some water on my face before I go and drink my coffee and work up the strength to call my mother back.

When I enter the main room, Dorien is walking in from the kitchen area with two mugs. I smile when he passes me mine, and we both sit at the table, the sun filtering through and casting the room in a warm glow.

"So, I was thinking, I'm going to go back to work on Monday," I say, before I take a sip of coffee as I wait for him to respond.

"As the manager," he replies, his face giving nothing away.

"No, as a maid, you know, the job I was doing before you decided to try and land me with the pressure of running this place." I speak in a light tone, because the offer is extremely nice, but it's just not for me.

"Mmhmm," he mumbles. "And I'm guessing that I can't change your mind?"

"You guess correctly." I give him a bright smile, hoping he'll just let this go.

"I thought that might be the case," he comments, stumping me, because I thought I'd be doing more arguing about it than this. "Which is why I decided to put a manager position in place for housekeeping. You will have control over the rotas, the shift patterns, the general running of the maids only, and you will also be able to allocate a deputy, who will step in when I'm too busy fucking you." He winks at me, and my shock is replaced with a fluttering in my stomach. Oh, he's good.

"As wonderful as that sounds, I'm not sure it's appropriate for you to just decide to fuck me at a moment's notice," I tease, but really, the thought of him doing just that is rather thrilling.

"But I'm the owner, and ultimately, your boss," he says in a dangerously low voice.

"You gonna reprimand me?"

"You better fucking believe it," he says before I shoot off my chair and run for the bedroom, him hot on my heels and making me squeal like a damn schoolgirl.

He grabs me around the waist before I can shut the door and lock it, and he hauls me over his shoulder before dropping me to the bed and pinning me there, my limbs trapped by his.

I stop squirming and look at him, my expression more serious as I say, "Go on then, boss, show me just what you'll do if I misbehave."

The smile he gives me is devilish, and it makes me so fucking wet for him.

"Challenge accepted."

After Dorien has devoured me and gone on his merry way, I pluck up the courage to call my mother. I can feel the tension rising as I hit the dial button and wait for her to answer. She does so in two rings.

"Elise, where the hell have you been?" she says, not even bothering to greet me nicely before she goes off on one.

"Hello, Mother, so good to hear from you," I say sarcastically, because I can't help myself.

"Don't get fresh with me, young lady. Where the hell are you? We have things to talk about," she declares, as if it is her God given right to order me about. Maybe once upon a time it worked, but now, not so much. I feel brave being in Dorien's world, and I need to channel that into dealing with my parents.

"And what exactly do we need to discuss?" I ask, knowing her next sentence before she's even said it.

"When you are going to stop this charade and return to your husband." And there it is, Team Derrick through and through.

"I'm not going back to him, Mum."

"You bloody well are."

"You can say that all you want, but it won't make it come true."

"If you do not go back to your rightful place, by your husband's side, then you'll be dead to me," she spits, and I can imagine her red face and irate stance on the other end of the phone.

"Did you ever love me?" I ask, and the line goes silent for a moment. "I mean, you've always made it seem like you hate me, and I've always tried so hard to make you proud of me—hell, even to like me. So what did I do? Did I do something horrible when I was little that I can't remember? Because I have no idea where all of this hate came from. I have no idea why you made me feel so much guilt, or why you pushed me into marrying a man I never loved."

"Stop being so dramatic, Elise," she says, but I hear the waver in her voice, so I push on, because I have a feeling this is going to be my only chance to be honest with her.

"I spent my whole life being belittled, being made to feel like I could do more, because it was what you wanted. And I never really understood what narcissistic behaviour you had until I walked away."

"How dare you, you ungrateful little bitch," she shouts, and if she were a bird, she'd have her chest all puffed up, raring for action. The thought almost makes me laugh.

"Prime example," I say. "I just want to know, Mum, why you ever had me if you didn't want me?"

"You know what, Elise, I have no idea," she says, and unshed tears start to clog at the backs of my eyes. "I don't think I could be more ashamed of you than I am right now."

"Wow," I say on a breath, her words hitting far deeper than I should let them.

"You always wanted to be the centre of attention, monopolising everyone's time, and it was pathetic to witness," she continues. "And then you finally did something we could actually be happy about. Marrying Derrick. Securing our futures, until he became a layabout and you couldn't even muster up the decency to get him back on his feet."

I scoff, because what the hell? I did everything I could think of to get his lazy arse back to work, even as I hated him, because I thought it was the right thing to do. I now see the right thing to do would have been to walk away from them all the first chance I got.

"He was a good man until you changed him. He was a decent man until you brought him down. He was everything this family needed..." Her voice trails off as I hear her sniff, and my heart starts to race a little faster, because this feels like we've gone into new territory but I'm not quite sure what.

"He could have been great, with the right woman behind him, but he needed someone younger, someone who could compete with the office sluts," she spits, and I get a feeling of dread building inside me.

"He could have had the best, a woman who worshipped him and just wanted to love him, but no, he had to choose someone younger, someone prettier—"

"Oh my god," I say, cutting her off. "Did you..." I can't even ask it because it's too ridiculous for words.

"He was supposed to choose me," she whispers, and I hear the emotion in her voice, something I haven't heard from her... ever.

I can barely think straight.

My mother and my husband?

Together?

No, this is some kind of sick joke, surely?

"Did you love him?" I ask quietly, needing her to confirm what I'm thinking and stop me from feeling so disgusting for the thought entering my head.

"Of course I fucking loved him. And then I watched him wither away from the man he once was to what he is now. And it's all your fault," she accuses.

"Does Dad know?" I whisper, tears clogging my throat and making it hard to talk.

"Of course he doesn't know. The stupid fool."

How did she become this person? So bitter. So twisted. So evil. But then, this has always been her, and it's only now that I'm realising it.

"I don't understand why you guilted me into marrying him when you…" My voice trails off as I struggle to form the words needed. I feel like I'm in some kind of sick and twisted film. My mother and my husband… Jesus Christ.

"Because then I could keep him around," she says quickly, and I wonder if she's finally lost her mind admitting all of this to me. I mean, she can hardly expect to tell me to go back to him now, but then again, I don't understand any of this—how she could be so disgusting, how she could essentially pimp out her own daughter for a fucking house and some money, and how she could fuck my husband for God knows how long. "If he didn't marry you, he could have married some young tart who would never have let me see him. This way, I saw him whenever I wanted to."

I struggle not to retch. This is madness. Absolute madness. I've never heard of anything so fucked-up.

"He should have chosen me," she croaks, and as she falls apart on the phone, sobbing as if her world has ended, I finally get the closure I needed.

I don't need to hear anything else. There is no coming back from this, and there is no reasoning with her kind of crazy, because that's what she is, crazy for even thinking that any of this would ever be acceptable. It's betrayal of the worse kind, and of the sickest.

And as I finally shut down the guilt I've lived with since I can remember, I say the last two words I will ever say to the woman who gave birth to me. "Goodbye, Mother."

Chapter Fifty-Three

DORIEN

I made it back to the hotel this morning before Elise even woke up, and I made sure to hold her a little tighter as she slept. I have no regrets over Derrick's death, and I'm yet to show Elise the papers that will release her from the life she hated for so long. I figured I'd do it in a day or two, when Derrick's suicide note has been found, so as not to arouse suspicion. I know it's lying to her in a sense, but if I tell her that I was the reason he was murdered, she would become an accessory, knowing about it, and she's had enough hurt and drama for a lifetime.

It's my job to protect her. I feel it. She's mine to love and care for. She's awakened something primal inside of me, and I'll always fight for her.

I've been out all day, working, having to spend time away from her, but my last stop before I go home is the most important. As I pull up to the back of the club, Purity—the club that Nate's sister, Zoey, owns—I know that I owe Nate, Jax and Ronan a big fucking drink for their part in finding Derrick and making him disappear. He may have taken a stake in my business, but it's a small price to pay for Elise's state of mind.

I'm truly putting someone before my own selfish needs, and I never intend to stop.

I walk into the club, being waved past the queue outside by the big fuckers on the door. I guess that means I'm on the guest list. People start to grumble behind me, but I pay them no notice. I couldn't give a damn if they have to wait all night. I just need to get this done and get back to Elise.

I walk into the main room, the dance floor packed with people and the bar three deep. Fuck's sake. I run a hand through my hair before I feel a tap on my shoulder, and I turn to see Jax stood there, his tattoos on show and his face still fucking deadpan.

"This way," he barks, and he turns before I even have chance to respond.

"Nice to see you too, fucker," I mutter quietly, the music loud enough to cover my sarcasm.

He leads me down a corridor, where I come to three separate doors, and then he opens the door to the middle one. It reveals an office, with Nate behind the desk, looking at something on the monitors.

"Sit down, Dorien," Nate barks as Jax closes the door, leaving just the two of us in the room. I do as Nate says and take a seat, and he leans back in the chair, his attention fully focused on me for the time being. He opens a draw beside him and pulls out a small pile of papers, and I instantly recognise the print, it's the contract for the hotel. My brow furrows, because I thought this was all done and dusted.

Nate smirks as he looks at me, and then he picks the contract up and rips it to pieces. I can't stop the stunned look I give him. What the fuck is he doing?

"I'm not giving you a bigger cut, we made a deal," I tell him, before he can even ask, and he starts to laugh.

"I don't want a bigger cut. I don't want any cut," he informs me, but I'm still fucking clueless. "I'm a businessman, a man who doesn't make allowances for many very often, but I no longer feel the need to take a slice of your pie, Dorien."

"But we made a deal," I say, wondering whether this is the

moment where one of them blows my fucking head off in some kind of twisted game.

"We did, and now I'm un-making it."

"But why?" I have to ask, because this makes no sense.

"I don't need the stress, and I don't need to add anything to my plate," he says with a shrug of his shoulders.

"But you weren't going to be doing anything, anyway," I stress. "You were going to be a silent partner."

"Pah. Do you honestly think I would ever be a silent partner?" he questions.

"Probably not, but we'd have duked it out," I reply, not at all fazed by who he is. He's just another guy, a powerful one, yes, but he's still just a guy who had an agenda and made it work.

"We both know I could kick your arse into next week, Dorien, so let's not fuck about," he replies, but his tone is anything but menacing, for reasons I'm still yet to fully understand. "You proved last night that you did what you did for one reason and one reason only. Her. The one. And there aren't many men who would do that, not from where I come from anyway. Usually they're out for themselves, with little thought for anything or anyone else. So when someone comes along who will put themselves on the line and get their hands dirty, to a certain extent in your case, then they automatically gain some respect from me. They gain even more respect when they don't cower before me because of who I am."

I still have no fucking idea where he's going with this, so I remain quiet.

"I no longer want shares in your empire, but what I do want is exceptional service when I stay at your establishments, and, of course, you'll foot the bill."

I don't even need to hesitate as I answer. "Goes without saying."

"Good. Now, get the fuck out, I have work to do," he says, and I shake my head from side to side with a smile on my face.

"Pleasure doing business with you, Nate." I get to the door, but he stops me one last time.

"Dorien." I turn to face him, my hand resting on the door knob. "Look after her."

"I will," I say with more certainty than ever before. He nods, and I leave, Jax still waiting outside the door.

"See you soon, fucker," he says, and I can't help the deep laugh that leaves me. So he did hear my comment earlier. His answering smirk tells me he doesn't have an issue with me, and I guess I gained a little of his respect too.

I walk out of Purity feeling like everything is how it's supposed to be.

As soon as I walk in the penthouse, I know something is wrong, my eyes zeroing in on Elise sat at the table by the windows, looking out onto the balcony. She doesn't even look my way as I close the door, and she looks ghostly white.

"Hey," I say softly as I crouch in front of her and take her hands in mine. She finally turns her head to face me, her eyes showing me how exhausted she is by whatever has happened since I've been gone. "What's wrong?"

She closes her eyes and takes a couple of deep breaths, before opening them and telling me, "I spoke to my mother."

Oh shit. She doesn't know the extent of her mother's betrayal, and I dread to think how she would react if she did.

"She… I…" She's struggling to form words as she blows out another breath. "She slept with Derrick."

Oh fuck, so she does know. Jesus. What a mindfuck.

"She lost it on the phone, calling me selfish and all the usual bullshit she used to chuck my way, and then it was like she forgot she was talking to me as she said he should have chosen her."

"Elise—"

"She loved him, and she was jealous of me, which turned to hate in the end." She lifts her eyes and looks at me as she says, "They never deserved me, Dorien. And I'm so pissed at myself for not realising it sooner. I'm pissed I threw away years of my life and wasted my opportunities to try and please people that never fucking loved me in the first place."

I let go of one of her hands and reach up, cupping her face.

"But I'm also a little grateful to them," she continues, and I frown as her lips pull into a soft smile. "It sounds weird, but if they hadn't been the way they were, then I may never have worked here, and I may never have met you."

Fucking hell, she's killing me. For a guy that felt nothing a short time ago, I seem to feel fucking everything with her.

"I love you, Dorien, and I love that you don't try to change me," she whispers, and then her arms are wrapping around me as she hugs me fiercely, like I'm her lifeline. I hold her close to me, knowing that our story didn't start conventionally, but it's one I wouldn't change for anything, because it gave me her. She was in room twenty-nine on that first morning I met her for a reason, and it will always stay in my mind as the best room service I ever had.

Chapter Fifty-Four

ELISE

My life has been like a whirlwind for the last couple of weeks, but as I stand in front of the bathroom mirror in my new suit, which I got for my new duties as the housekeeping manager, I feel lighter than ever. It may not be my dream job, but I'm not going to give up hope that one day I may get to design clothes that will be worn around the world. I'll never let myself stop believing again, and Dorien is the reason for that.

I smile at myself in the mirror, the bruises that are fading no longer reminding me of the pain I've endured, but more what I have survived.

There's a knock on the door as I enter the main room, and I know it'll be Celeste, who I appointed as my deputy when I called her over the weekend.

"Morning, boss," she says breezily, the excitement radiating from her.

"Stop with the boss talk," I tell her, but there is no wiping the smile from my face at seeing how happy my best friend is.

"Well, you are, technically."

I roll my eyes, because it sounds so ridiculous right now. I'm sure I'll get used to it, eventually, maybe. "Coffee?"

"Please."

I lead her over to the table by the window and pour us each a cup, taking a seat while Celeste walks onto the balcony to gaze over the city.

"Wow, that is some view," she says when she comes back in and sits opposite me.

"It's incredible."

"So, you and Dorien..." She lets her voice trail off, and I laugh at how unsubtle she is.

"We're good."

"Is that all I get? Good? He's had you holed up in here for over a week, and all I get is good?" Come on, give me something else, let me live vicariously through you," she says, making me laugh and nearly spit out the mouthful of coffee I just took.

"He's amazing," I gush. "He's changed me, Celeste."

"I can see that. Your eyes sparkle again, and you look like you want to live," she comments, nothing but joy on her face.

"I do. I really do."

"I'm so happy for you, Elise. You deserve it more than anyone I know," she says genuinely, and my heart fills with warmth. The feeling of being loved is coming more naturally with every passing day.

"I cut ties with my mother," I tell her, and her eyes widen slightly. "It's a good thing. Turns out, she was fucking Derrick before I even married him."

"What the hell?"

"Yeah. Pretty shocking, but it's given me the closure I needed. My parents were nothing but money grabbers, out for themselves, my mother even more so than my father."

"Have you spoken to your dad?" she asks, and I shake my head.

"No, and I don't want to. He may not have a clue about her and Derrick, but he watched and played a part in guilting me to ensure they were okay, and I can't forgive that," I tell her honestly. "It's not like I ever had a close bond with him, not really, it was always my mother calling the shots and pulling the trigger."

"Fucking hell, Elise," Celeste exclaims, shocked. "Are you sure you're okay?"

"Totally. I mean, I can't even say I'm surprised, not when I think back on it. She was always on Derrick's side, always belittling me and making him look like he was the most amazing man to walk the earth. I guess, to her, he was. But then she got nastier, hated me more, and her jealousy took over any love she may have felt for me once upon a time."

"God, she doesn't deserve to have you in her life."

"I know that now," I say with a smile, and Celeste's watery eyes stare back at me. "All I have to do now is divorce the bastard, and then I'll be free."

"Hell yes. And you know we're having a divorce party," Celeste says, blinking her eyes rapidly as I try to lighten the mood before we start work in our new roles. Today isn't about sadness, it's a day to celebrate where we are now. I'm done looking back.

"I'll drink to that," I say as I raise my coffee cup, and Celeste does the same, both of us laughing as we finish our drinks and head out of the penthouse.

"So, at risk of already knowing the answer," she begins. "Are you coming back to stay with me anytime soon?"

"I'm planning to," I say, because I can't live in a penthouse forever, nor do I want to.

"Pfft." She scoffs as I push the button for the lift. "He's not going to want you to leave now."

And even as we travel down to the ground floor where our joint office is located, I know that she's right. And if I'm being honest, I don't want to leave him either.

My first day as manager went pretty well. Celeste and I worked together most of the day to get everything in order, and I feel like we're going to be people that the staff can come to because we can relate to them more than someone coming in here straight from an office job or something similar. Working from the ground up gives us that insight into how the staff are treated and how we can make it better.

I have a pep in my step as I walk into the penthouse, seeing Dorien is already here. He's at the table, working on his laptop, but his focus turns to me as I walk towards him, going behind him and resting my arms over his shoulders until my head is beside his. I kiss his cheek, and then he captures my lips with his.

I moan into his mouth, having missed the feel of him all day long. I'm totally obsessed with him, and I'm okay with it. The feeling seems to be mutual, and I move around him until he's pushing his chair back and I'm sat in his lap.

"How did your first day go?" he asks, his lips brushing mine, tempting me, teasing me.

"It was really good," I reply with a smile.

"Glad to hear it, and I'm about to make it even better," he says, and I quirk an eyebrow at him.

"Oh yeah?"

He chuckles. "Not in that way, not yet anyway." He winks and then reaches around me, picking up an envelope and handing it to me. My brows furrow as I open it, and when I read the contents, I'm astounded.

"Dorien… this is—"

"Your divorce. All signed and sealed," he finishes.

"How did you… when…" Words fail me at seeing Derrick's signature signing everything over to me, as well as my parents' house and any possessions we had.

"You're welcome."

I move my eyes from the paperwork, staring at him like he's the key to my soul. Which I guess he is.

"But, how?"

"It doesn't matter how. What matters is that you have your freedom, Elise. No more ties."

"Oh my god," I exclaim as I wrap my arms around his neck and hold him tight. "Thank you," I whisper, with tears in my eyes. I don't have to deal with Derrick ever again. Dorien has made it so that he's out of my life once and for all.

He truly is a remarkable man.

"All you have to do is sign and then we can get it filed with the courts. You shouldn't have to do anything else, because he's not contesting anything," he continues, and I let a tear fall.

"No one has ever done anything on this scale for me before," I whisper, pulling back to look at him.

"No one has ever loved you like I do," he tells me, and I fucking melt.

Dorien Dukes went from a man with no feeling to the one that sits before me, giving me every part of him that he kept hidden.

"I love you," I whisper, my lips meeting his and hoping for a lifetime of happiness with him.

Chapter Fifty-Five

ELISE

I should know by now that happiness is short-lived, but with my newfound zest for life, I decided to try and push all negativity away. Until I opened the door to two policemen.

"Can I help you?" I ask, and they introduce themselves, following with needing to speak to me about Derrick Woods. Puzzled, I invite them in, showing them to the sofa as I take the chair.

"Derrick and I are divorced now, so I don't know why you would need to speak to me," I tell them, really not wanting to hear anything they have to say about my ex-husband.

Ex-husband. Sounds so fucking good.

"Miss Woods—"

"Just Elise is fine," I interrupt, because I don't want to use my maiden name either, it's just as toxic as my married one.

"Elise, we're here to tell you that your husb—" The police officer stops himself before clearing his throat and continuing. "Your ex-husband is believed to have committed suicide."

Time stops for a moment.

"Pardon?" I question, because I must have heard them wrong.

"A note was sent to your mother, and she called us to report it.

Derrick's body hasn't been found yet, but we're looking as we speak. There aren't many leads to go on, but as his next of kin, we had to inform you."

Derrick's dead?

Suicide?

Note sent to my mother?

What the hell?

"We realise this is shocking news, Elise, but we need to ask if you can shed any light on where he might possibly have gone to…"

"To kill himself," I finish as his voice fades off.

"Yes," he replies with a nod.

I sigh and give them the only response I can. "Derrick hasn't left the house in years, preferring to spend his days as a couch potato. In all honesty, I'm surprised he even had the energy to get up and top himself." Their eyes widen, but I don't care. I have no feelings for him, and if he's truly taken his life, then it doesn't mean anything to me. Callous, possibly, but I put up with a world of shit because of him, and I refuse to let it impact my future.

Just then, the door opens, and I turn to see Dorien walking in, his eyes narrowing on the men sat on the sofa.

"Who are you?" he questions, taking his jacket off and throwing it over the back of my chair before putting his hands in his pockets in a dominating stance.

"Uh, we're here on police business," the older looking guy says, and I bite my bottom lip. Dorien won't like the vague answer.

"I asked who you were, not what line of work you're in," Dorien demands, and fuck me, even in this bizarre situation I find myself turned on by his tone.

The officer clears his throat before introducing the two of them and explaining they are here to talk to me about Derrick. I notice the slight shift of Dorien's body, but that's only because I know his body's reactions. I question it as he keeps his face deadpan, his eyes boring into the officers.

"They came to tell me that Derrick has committed suicide," I say. "They thought I might be able to help with where to find him."

Dorien's jaw is ticking. "And can you?" he asks me, but he knows

I don't, so I shake my head. "Then this conversation is redundant," he barks.

"And you are?" the officer asks.

"Dorien Dukes, but you already knew that before you got here," Dorien replies, giving his focus back to the officers.

"And the nature of your relationship with Miss… Elise is what?"

"None of your business. I'll show you out," Dorien says, ending any further questions they may have.

My mouth drops open a little at how abrupt he's being, but this is the Dorien that I first met. No feelings, no emotion. He has no time for the men asking questions about a man from my past, and neither do I.

"If you think of anything, give us a call," the one officer says, handing me his card, but Dorien quickly takes it before I can, barking, "She won't."

"Nice to meet you, Elise," he says before nodding his head and going to the door, which Dorien is now holding open for them.

When they've gone, Dorien closes the door and marches to the bedroom, tension radiating off of him as my stomach starts to swirl, and not in a good way. I follow him, getting to the bedroom as he's taking off his tie, his back to me.

I watch as he removes his shirt, flinging it on a chair to the side of the room, that tension seeming to grow by the second.

"Dorien," I say loudly, making him freeze, but he keeps his back to me. "Dorien, look at me." I keep my tone firm, even as my mind is racing.

He turns slowly, his hands going to his trouser pockets, his head lifting, and his eyes connecting with mine.

I walk towards him, stopping a few feet before him. He's keeping his shield in place, but it's too late, he's already let me see him, and I know that he's been caught off-guard by the police showing up here.

"Dorien, why would the officers be questioning our relationship?" I begin.

"Because they're nosey fucks."

I study him, knowing that there is more to this than meets the eye. "And the reason for you being so abrupt is?"

"I don't have to justify myself to anybody."

"You do to me," I say firmly. "You got Derrick to sign the divorce papers and hand everything over to me, which means you've seen him. So, I'll ask you this once… Did you have anything to do with his death?"

Time seems to stop as we stare at one another, my heartbeat in my throat as I wait for his answer.

He crouches down a little, so we're eye level, before he says, "No." One word, nothing further, and I know he's lying. I can see the storm brewing deep in his eyes that have captivated me for weeks.

And even as I know he's lying, I can't feel anything but love for him. He's the reason I'm free. He's the reason I'm becoming the woman I always hid away. He's the reason for colour coming back into my life, so how can I possibly do anything but be grateful to him when he's given me so much?

I move forwards, my arms wrapping around his neck as my lips hover over his and I say, "Thank you," before I kiss him with everything I have. My hands find his hair, entwining through the strands as my tongue meets his and his arms hold me tightly. I pour my love for him into my actions, and he lies me down on the bed, covering me with his body before he makes love to me over and over again. No words. No breather. It's just us amid all of the bullshit we've come through.

Chapter Fifty-Six

ELISE

I laid awake for the remainder of the night, when Dorien wasn't inside of me, thinking about what he's done. I got caught up in the moment before it truly hit me that he was involved in Derrick's death, which means it wasn't suicide. It was murder. Because of me. Because of me, I've tainted the man I've fallen madly in love with. Because of me, he's risked everything, and I have no idea how to deal with that. I don't know how to process how strongly he loves me. There is no doubt that he does, but at what cost? His sanity? His morals?

I worked quietly all day, Celeste thinking that my less than enthusiastic mood was down to hearing that Derrick was dead. But it's not for the reason she's thinking, I'm not sad about Derrick, I'm sad about Dorien. About how I've changed him, but maybe it's not been for the better. Maybe he was right when he said at the start that no feelings worked, that one night was all he could give... until he gave me more.

Is it selfish of me to keep him?

Can I really walk away from him so as not to taint him anymore?

Can I really give him up?

I enter the penthouse quietly, and there's no sign of Dorien in the main room, until he walks out of the bathroom, reminding me of how he takes my breath away. I know with certainty that I would do anything for him, just like he's seemingly done for me, but isn't that unhealthy? Isn't it toxic?

The worst part is I can't talk to anyone but Dorien about this, because the last thing I would ever want to do is get him into trouble or change anyone's opinion of him.

"Hey," he says as he walks towards me, stopping when he sees the expression on my face.

"We need to talk," I tell him quietly. His jaw ticks as we stand there, him waiting for me to continue. "We need to talk about what we're doing here."

"I thought that was obvious, Elise. I love you, you love me, so what is there to question?"

"Dorien, last night…" My voice trails off as his head drops, and without him looking at me, I say what I think we both need in order to find out who we truly are. "I didn't ask as many questions as I should have, but I'm guessing that you were involved in having Derrick's suicide note sent to my mother." He just looks at me, but I know the answer, he doesn't have to tell me it was his idea. "I think we should take a break."

His head flies back up, and he looks at me like I just gave him the most devastating news he's ever heard. "What?"

"I… I think we should pause whatever this is," I say pathetically.

"Whatever this is?" He looks enraged. "And what exactly does that mean?"

I take a breath, steadying my erratic heart as it threatens to beat out of my chest. "We need time, Dorien, to figure out who we are."

"I know who I am, Elise. I'm a man that felt nothing before you. I'm a man that refused to let anyone in. I'm a man that relied only on himself… until you."

The tears threaten to creep up on me, and I blink rapidly, knowing I need to get through this without breaking. I can break later, but not now.

"I just… I can't be the reason that you become someone that

you never wanted to be," I say, not making much sense as I struggle to explain what's going on in my head.

"You're going to have to spell it out for me, Elise, because I'm not following."

"You played a part in Derrick's death, and I don't need to know what that is, but you did that because of me. You put yourself in a position where you could possibly face prison because of me. You had the police sniffing around here yesterday because of me, and I can't be the reason you fall, Dorien. I *won't* be the reason you fall."

"Elise, you need to cut this shit out and start thinking clearly," he demands, but I think this is the clearest I've seen in my whole life. The pain I feel in this moment hurts, my head is screaming at me to not fucking do this, but even as my heart aches, I know this is what needs to happen in order to save myself. To save him.

"I could get lost in you forever, Dorien," I say softly, walking towards him until I'm stood in front of him, my hand cupping his cheek. "I could lose myself completely to just be with you, but it wouldn't be fair to either of us. I appreciate everything you've done for me, I truly do, and I'll never be able to show you just how much you've freed me."

He brings his head down, his forehead resting against mine, his hands on my hips, and my other hand resting over his heart.

"But I need to live without you." I almost choke on the words as I close my eyes and feel the tears falling down my cheeks. "You need to be without me, too. We've been so wrapped up in one another and all of the drama, that I think our judgements are clouded."

"Elise, don't do this," he begs, his voice breaking as he speaks.

"You need this just as much as I do, and then, if we're meant to be, we'll come back to one another."

"This isn't a fucking fairy-tale, Elise," he says, his voice a little more firm than a moment ago.

"But it could be." I open my eyes and feel like I'm looking into his soul. "And it could be the most beautiful fairy-tale ever written." I push my lips to his and kiss him, pouring everything into this moment, because if this doesn't pan out the way my mind has showed me, then I may never get a chance to kiss him again. He holds me tight, not wanting to let me go, and I allow myself to feel every bit of sadness that wraps around my heart, my lungs, and every fucking organ in my body.

I know I'm going to regret this the moment I walk out of here—hell, I already do regret it, but I also know we both need it, even if he doesn't understand that right now.

I break my lips from his and look into his gorgeous eyes that I will remember forever. "Thank you for everything you've done, Dorien."

He stays silent and his arms drop to his sides, a cold feeling washing over me. I go to the bedroom and pack the few things I have here, and then I walk back out to the main room, Dorien standing in the same spot. His hands are in his pockets, his head hanging down. My heart thumps wildly as I walk past him and put my hand on the doorknob.

"I'll make sure Celeste takes over my managerial role." The role I've had for only forty-eight hours.

"Six months," he says, making me frown as he lifts his head and looks at me, the electricity zinging between us, like it always has. "I'll give you six months, and then I'm coming to find you."

I smile softly, having no doubt that he will keep that promise. "I hope you do. But if not, I'll always love you." I had to say it one last time before I opened the door and walked away from the only man who has ever loved me for me. And in doing this, I'm ensuring I save the man I love from becoming a version of himself that he never asked for.

Chapter Fifty-Seven

DORIEN

I let her go. She walked away. I'm shit at goodbyes, and I had no intention of dragging it out. I feel pain like no other shoot through me, and I grab a bottle of scotch from the kitchen, taking it onto the balcony and swigging it straight from the bottle rather than fucking about getting a glass. My eyes are pinned to the street below as I wait for her leave the hotel, and when she emerges, my fucking heart goes with her.

I get that she needs a moment to process all of the shit that she's been through, but all it does is fucking hurt that she's walked away from me.

I swig the scotch until she's out of sight, and then I turn and hurl the fucking bottle at the window, causing it to shatter in pieces at my feet. The window is made of sterner stuff, but the bottle is like me. Broken.

It's funny how she was the broken one to start with, and all I wanted to do was to give her one night where she could forget, and yet here I am, standing on this balcony with my heart ripped into shreds. And I guess I'm the broken one after all.

Chapter Fifty-Eight

ELISE

One month later

Everything has moved so quickly, apart from that first week which was hell on earth. I cried so many tears, I felt pain slicing through me all the time, and even as I still feel pain now, it's not as prominent as it was back then.

I allowed myself a week of living on Celeste's sofa to give me time to grieve everything that had taken me to this point. I allowed myself to miss Dorien, to ache for him, to scream out loud that I wasn't with him, to punish myself for making this decision to walk away. And then I stopped and picked myself back up.

I made this choice, and I need to give it my best shot, because otherwise, it was all for nothing. So, I sold the house I used to share with Derrick, and I used the money to rent a small apartment on the outskirts of the city. I enrolled in art classes at the local college that's a small walk from where I live. I took a part-time job as a cleaner in the evenings, just cleaning some offices after the workers had finished for the day, and I really only did that to keep my mind busy. In my spare time, I draw, pouring my feelings onto the page, putting it into designs that act as a kind of therapy for me, in a way.

I also signed over the deeds to my parents' house to them, because I didn't want anything to do with it. I didn't see them to do this, and my solicitor handled everything. I'm sure my mother was just pleased to have gotten something out of her fuck-up of a daughter and the man she harboured a secret love for, but I fail to give them the headspace. They don't deserve it.

I gave the police my new contact details, in case they needed to get in touch with me about Derrick, but I've not really heard anything further. No body has been found, and I doubt they'll ever find it now.

I speak to Celeste most days, and she fills me on how much she is loving her new role, but she doesn't speak about Dorien. She tried when I spent that week on her sofa, and then when she saw me get up and dust myself off, she stopped.

Every time I speak to her, I'm dying to ask if she's seen him, how he is, what he's been doing, but I don't. It would only hurt more to know if he's moved on. I'd rather remain in ignorant bliss.

I heard from Chantel in the first week, but I was too numb to speak to her, so I'm yet to make that phone call. I don't know if I should. She's Dorien's family. Maybe I'll pluck up the courage one day, but by the time that comes, I'll probably have left it too late.

I've made a couple of friends living here, two of them also staying in this apartment block, but they're into the clubbing thing and hooking up on the weekends, whereas I'd rather stay in and draw.

And so, my new life is simple, which is a stark contrast to my mind.

Chapter Fifty-Nine

DORIEN

Two months later

It's been three months since she left, and I mark every fucking day on a calendar. The more I mark off, the closer I am to going after her.

I've been a miserable bastard for most of it, but about a week ago, I let go of the anger that had consumed me since the moment she walked out of the door. I know she didn't do it to hurt me, but fuck does it sting. I guess it helped that Hayley, the previous hotel manager, got her comeuppance. I was never going to let her get away with what she did, and now, she's begging for scraps, because no respectable employer will touch her with a barge pole. She deserves to rot for the part she played in Elise's ex-husband hurting her. She deserves to suffer for all of the years she talked down to people and made them feel like they were nothing. She deserves it for hurting the only woman I've ever loved.

Chantel and Gabriel have been checking in on me, and I hate the fucking pity in their voices even as they try to hide it. I've reverted to my go-to mode of business and nothing else. I haven't entertained going back to my one-night trysts because even the thought makes me feel sick. I'm just hoping she's worked through her shit in the next three months, because once that's over, I'm not letting her go again, ever.

Chapter Sixty

ELISE

Four months have gone by, and each day I feel more at peace, more in touch with who I am and who I want to be. My art course is going well, and I finally plucked up the courage a week ago to phone Chantel back. She never gave up trying, and I have to admire her determination. So, here I sit, at a café by the beach, which is about an hour away from my apartment. I don't want anyone but Celeste to know where I am, not until the time comes for Dorien to find me, if he still wants to.

I sip my iced coffee and look out at the calm waves, the sun beaming down on me. It's glorious, and it feels so refreshing. I've found myself just appreciating the simple things in life, something I never allowed myself to do before.

And then I see Chantel walking towards my table, like a ray of sunshine all in herself. She's stunning in an off-the shoulder sundress, paired with wedges and a large hat.

I feel nervous all of a sudden, but I needn't, because she walks straight up to me and leans down to give me a hug. We may not have had much time to get to know one another, but I know she's a good one, a loyal one, which is why I'm unsure about her trying to get in touch with me for so long.

"You are a hard lady to get hold of," she says as she takes a seat, the waiter quickly coming over and taking her drink order.

"Sorry, it's been a crazy few months," I reply shyly, dreading the moment she brings up Dorien.

"I'll say. So, at risk of diving straight in, tell me what's been going on with you."

I blink at her for a moment. I was expecting to be grilled about why I left, but she's just smiling at me, waiting for me to tell her what I've been doing the last four months. So, I do, omitting the part where I spent a week at the beginning wallowing in self-pity. The waiter brings her drink over and she continues to listen as I tell her about art college, my passion shining through.

And when I'm done, she asks, "Can I see some of your drawings?"

"Oh, um…"

"You don't have to show me right now, Elise." She chuckles. "I was thinking you could bring them to my studio, if you wanted to…"

"Yes, oh my god, yes," I reply immediately, but then I mention the elephant in the room. "But isn't it going to be weird because of…"

She sips her drink, and her eyes look at me with a sparkle in them. "No, it's not weird, because you two will find your way to where you're supposed to be."

God I hope she's right.

Chapter Sixty-One

ELISE

"These designs are gorgeous," I comment as I look at what Chantel is working on, as well as nosing through her portfolio.

"I just love the lace trim on this one," she says, pointing to an elegant evening dress.

"It's stunning." I can't take my eyes off of the way she's captured exactly what this dress shows—class and understated beauty. I am in awe of her work.

"And yours are fabulous," she says, pulling a couple of my sketches out of the folder I left by the door. I abandoned it there the moment I walked in, totally focused on her stuff rather than mine.

"Oh." I blush. No one has ever seen my work before, except for the people at the college, and my teacher.

"Wow," she breathes as she looks at a sheer silk wedding dress I drew for an assignment. "Elise, this is perfect." She takes the drawing to a table by the window and studies it whilst I feel proud and excited that she seems to like my work. "Look at the detail." I designed it to look simple, whilst retaining a delicate pattern on the bottom half. "How much?" she says suddenly, and I look at her puzzled.

"Sorry?"

"How much to come work for me?"

I open my mouth a few times like a fish out of water. "Me? Work here? For you?"

"Yes, Elise. I want you to work here, with me. Hell, it doesn't even have to be under my own fashion line, we could put these designs under a new brand name, market it, get it on the runways and watch as the world falls in love with your work."

"Chantel, wait a minute… I haven't even finished my college course yet, and I'm nowhere near your level of expertise." She can't possibly be serious.

"I know a brilliant designer when I see one, Elise. I am one. And your style is so on point right now."

"Right now… what if that changes?" I question, hardly daring to believe that this isn't some kind of dream that I'm about to wake up from.

"You'll evolve over time anyway, and you can finish your course at the college and work for me part time."

"You're not joking, are you?"

"Not even a little bit," she says adamantly.

"I don't want things to be awkward," I say, biting my bottom lip.

"Elise, this is simply a business decision based on incredible designs. By all means, finish up your course and then come and talk to me if that makes you feel better. The offer isn't going anywhere," she assures me, and then she breezes on to showing me more creations, letting me feel different fabrics that she's testing out, giving me more insight into a possible future doing what I love.

Chapter Sixty-Two

DORIEN

"Gabriel, you need to stop fucking checking up on me," I scold. "I'm fine."

"See, someone who couldn't give a shit would believe you, but I've known you too long, Dukes."

"Fucking busy body," I mutter, but he just laughs.

I walk around my home, the one I've never shared with anyone, the one that only Gabriel and Chantel know exists because I like my privacy, but I wish Elise knew about this place too. I can just picture her on the decking, looking out over the vast garden, admiring the flowers that are tended to by the gardeners. I can imagine her sipping coffee and looking at me like she wants me to devour her. I can see me telling her to get on her fucking knees, just like I did at the beginning, before I take her to the king-size bed and eat her until her limbs turn to jelly.

Soon, Dorien. Soon. I've reminded myself daily to bide my time, give her the space she said we both needed. I've taken time away from work, holed up here for a few weeks and shut myself off from everything and everyone. Except this little visit from Gabriel tells me that my time of solitude is up.

"She's doing good, you know," he says, and I pin him with my gaze.

"She is?"

He nods in response as I wonder how he knows, and me being me refuses to be kept in the dark anymore. "Where is she?"

"I can't tell you that, but I can tell you she's doing really well."

"You can't fucking tell me?" I question. "May I remind you who your loyalty lies with?"

I could have found her myself, in time, but I've resisted, even as the urge has consumed me daily. I've been a fucking saint abiding by her wants, her needs, even as it's killed me to do so. But I know that she'd never forgive me for not taking the time to find myself or whatever. I never needed to find myself, I just needed her, but I have realised that work is no longer something that I care about as much as I once did. I've let go a little more, become less overbearing with how things are run. These last couple of weeks I've simply been here, doing not a lot and replaying my past in my head. The women, the nights where I thought I was fulfilling my needs, but in reality, I was just waiting until she came along to show me what life was all about.

"It's not about loyalty, Dorien," Gabe says, interrupting my thoughts.

"When did you see her?"

"I haven't."

"Then how do you… Chantel," I say, and I scoff a laugh. Of course Chantel has seen her, bloody nosey woman that she is. "Is that why she isn't here with you, because she's hiding her guilt?"

"Take it down a notch, Dorien," he warns me, and I rein in my frustration. "She isn't here because she's working, and you know as well as I do that Chantel has only got your best interests at heart, so she doesn't need to harbour any guilt."

"Sorry," I mumble, even as I feel like they've gone behind my back in a round-about way. "I just fucking miss her."

"I know, but your story isn't over," he says, and I feel it in my gut. It isn't over, not by a long shot. I've got one more month until I find her, and until then, I better work through my remaining shit, so she gets the best of me. The part only she will ever get.

Chapter Sixty-Three

ELISE

The summer break from art college begins, but I have more than enough to be getting on with until we return in the autumn. I took Chantel up on her offer, quit my cleaning job, and true to her word, she hasn't told Dorien anything, because if she had then he would have rocked up already, I'm sure of it. I refuse to believe he isn't ready to unleash his anger at me for walking away, but it's truly helped me to learn who I am on my own, which is exactly what I wanted.

I'm also very aware that the six months break is nearly up, and a part of me wants to break it now, a few days early, because my heart just wants to be near him, but I'm also scared that I've hurt him so much that he'll deny me.

Out of everything I've learned on my journey of self-discovery, it's that the only person in the world who can truly hurt me is him, because I never let him go. So, because I'm scared of his reaction to me just turning up and begging him to take me back, I'm being a coward and waiting to see if he comes to me, just like he said he would.

Chapter Sixty-Four

DORIEN

Six months to the day she left, and I find myself on the phone, calling up the man I didn't think I'd ever have to ask for a favour from again. Because actually, that's what he did for me previously, if you think about it, once he ripped the contract to be part of my hotel chain up.

"Well, well, well," Nate says as he answers the phone. "To what do I owe the pleasure, Dorien?"

In the last few months, I've seen Nate in several of my hotels, with his wife, and sometimes Jax and his sister, Zoey, too. I've even had dinner with them on a couple of occasions, so I guess you could say we have a very tentative friendship of sorts.

"I need you to find someone," I tell him, but I don't even need to say her name, because he knows I'm calling about her. I spilled my drunken guts about her leaving at the beginning, when he was at the bar ordering drinks one night at The Blue Diamond, the place that holds so many fucking memories for me.

"Consider it done. I'll call you by the end of the day." And then he hangs up, our conversation over. He'll find her quicker than a private investigator would, and I don't have any more time to waste.

Chapter Sixty-Five

ELISE

I get in the door after going for a drink with Chantel, once we'd wrapped up the latest design we've been working on together. It's late, but we had to go and celebrate, because it was the first piece that had been commissioned from the new line we've just launched. As promised, Chantel didn't push me to be the face of it, and it's just an extension of her and Gabe's brand, but fuck, it's one of the best things ever. The long hours have been worth it, and I can't wait to see what the future holds.

It's also been good to be busy, because today marked the end of the six months. The six months where Dorien said he would find me, but there's been no sign of him. The disappointment hits me even harder as I kick off my shoes and close the front door, reaching for the light but finding that the room is still bathed in darkness, except for the glow of the moonlight coming through the lounge window. I groan as I feel my way to the other side, to switch on the lamp, but as I reach the table the lamp sits on, I hear a sound, my ears instantly picking it up and my body going on high alert. Fuck. If it's an intruder, I'll scream bloody murder. But then, music starts to play, coming through the speakers at the corners of the room, and my heart pumps for a totally different reason.

As the song I once played for him in the penthouse begins, the one where I commanded him to sit as I gave him a thank you, of sorts, on the same night when he first told me he loved me, I know that he's here. He came for me. And when I see a shadow moving on the other side of the room, I struggle to keep my trembling legs from collapsing. He walks further into the room, until the moonlight lets me see the side of his face, the power in his stance, and the way his jaw ticks as he looks at me.

For a moment, I think my eyes are playing tricks on me, my mind having some kind of fucking breakdown and showing me what I want to see. I drop my head and turn to the table, placing a hand on it to steady myself, but then I feel him behind me and I straighten myself up, anticipating the moment he decides to touch me again.

His fingers touch the skin at the side of my neck first, his fingers brushing my hair back as his lips whisper in my ear, "Time's up, buttercup."

And just those words alone has my heart fit to burst.

His body brushes against mine, and then his hips are moving to the beat as his hands find my hips and moves me with him. He grinds against me, and my eyes fill with unshed tears. He came. He's here. He didn't give up on me.

He turns me around and holds me as we dance to the music, and I feel like all of my dreams have finally come true.

"Have you found yourself, Elise?" he asks, his eyes boring into mine.

"Not entirely," I whisper, and I feel his body tense a little at my answer. "But that's because the last part of the missing puzzle is you. I'm not me without you, Dorien." It's the honest to God truth. Even as I spent months doing what I needed to do, I was always missing the piece of my soul that only belongs to him. "I'm sorry I—"

"Shhh," he says, placing a finger on my lips to stop me from speaking. "No more apologies, Elise. You have nothing to apologise for."

"I do," I say, even as his hand cups my cheek and his thumb runs over my lips. "And I'll never stop trying to make up for it."

Our hips move in sync as his lips lower to mine, and I finally taste what I've missed for so long. He moves me back and pins me against the wall, my hands held above my head as our tongues meet, desperate to make up for the time we've missed.

And when he breaks his lips from mine, he smirks and says, "Get on your knees."

A laugh bursts out of me from pure happiness. We can talk later, if he wants to, because there is nothing I will ever hide from him, not now, not ever. I found my peace in him, and the time apart has only made that stronger.

And as he lets go of my hands and I drop to my knees, I look up at him, totally mesmerised by him as he says, "Good girl."

I quickly undo his trousers, freeing his cock and devouring him. He grabs the back of my head, his fingers fisting in my hair as he fucks my mouth, but before he can come, he pulls me off him and back to a standing position, walking me to the sofa where he tells me to, "Bend over," the end. I don't need asking twice as I fold my body over the arm and thank fuck I put a skirt on this morning. He lifts my skirt up and runs his hand over my arse, before I look behind and see him crouched down, his tongue running over the lace covering my pussy, making me moan out loud.

"So fucking wet for me," he says, tasting me, feeling what he does to me. Only him, always.

He pulls my knickers to the side and buries his tongue in me, my cries of pleasure echoing around the apartment, mixed with the sensual music that continues to play. My senses are heightened, every part of me trembling with my need for him. He eats me from behind, squeezing my arse cheeks, and then he pulls away and tells me, "Sit on my face, Elise." I push myself off the sofa to find him laying on the floor, waiting for me to straddle him, but I'm obviously taking too long as he pulls me down until my pussy is in line with his mouth, his fingers ripping the material of my underwear which he throws to the side.

"Hold your skirt up and watch as you fuck my face," he demands, and my body heats from his words alone. I watch as he pleasures me. I watch as I come from his mouth. I watch as the man

I love more than anything in this world takes everything from me before I explode on his tongue. And then he carries me to the bedroom, stripping me of my clothes, and me stripping him of his, before he makes love to me. Claiming me all over again.

"I love you, Dorien, so fucking much," I say as he brings me to orgasm, and then his words push me over the edge.

"I love you more, buttercup."

Chapter Sixty-Six

DORIEN

Three months later

I watch as she walks down the aisle, looking absolutely fucking stunning in a silk wedding dress that she designed. Neither of us wanted to waste any more time than we already had. I proposed to her two weeks after I took her home, to the place where I envisioned her during our time apart. I was right, she looked like she belonged the minute she walked through the front door. I proposed on the decking, with fairy lights all around us. She didn't even question how fast I was at popping the question, and it showed me just how far she'd actually come.

I may not have understood her reasons for taking that break, but now I do. I've watched her daily as she's exuded confidence and radiated happiness. She has truly come out of her shell since the very first time I set eyes on her. She credits me for most of that, but I think she underestimates herself. I've also opened up to her about my past, why I was so closed off for so long, how my parents treated me as nothing more than a bank balance, and how I didn't think it possible for me to love or be loved. We both have shitty pasts, but we've got something beautiful out of all of the hurt—each other.

She's been through more shit than she should have, and I'm here to make sure she doesn't endure anymore.

She thought she was tainting me, but really, she showed me who I wanted to be.

Her protector.

Her fucking heartbeat as she is mine.

And yet, we both run our own businesses, keeping work life separate from home life, and it works. I miss her when I'm not with her, and I can't wait to see her at the end of the day. I don't work as much as I used to, and I make sure I'm home to greet her when she's been designing, something I'm so fucking proud to see her do. Our weekends are spent lazing around or having dinner and drinks with Celeste or Chantel and Gabriel—hell, we've even had dinner with Nate and his wife, Kat. She's come back into my life so effortlessly, in such contrast to when she first arrived.

She truly has given me a new lease of life.

And now, as she walks towards me, ready to become my wife, I know that we're rock solid. There are no doubts, no questions about what we are or who we want to be. We coexist to make each other the best versions of ourselves.

I once told her that she was the best room service I'd ever had, to which she smacked me across the chest and then I fucked her on the floor of the lounge, but it's true. There is a lot to be said for unexpectedly finding your heart on the floor of your hotel room, on her knees, cleaning up after you, and there's a lot to be said for a man who shut down emotion until he found a woman that was worthy of it all.

THE END

Note from the author

I hope you enjoyed Room Service and loved Elise and Dorien's story as much as I did. What was supposed to be my shortest book ended up being my longest, because these two wanted to tell their whole story, and I'm so glad they did.

They've consumed me for weeks, and I enjoyed writing every single part of them.

And if you haven't yet read about the infamous Crime Lord, keep reading for the first chapter of Wrecking Ball, where Nate Knowles first appeared.

And there's also the first chapter of The Untouchable Brother, which is Jax and Zoey's story.

I never intended for Nate and co to rock up in this book, but they did, and I think that there was a reason for that… to show me that I am not done with the Wrecking Ball world *winky face*

Thank you for reading, and I hope you continue to enjoy my books, because I write them for you, my readers.

Much love,

Lindsey

Wrecking Ball

Chapter One

Kat

Every girl dreams about it.

Every woman plans it.

The white dress.

The pretty flowers.

The handsome man waiting at the altar.

And that is the most important part.

The guy. The one you want to spend the rest of your life with. The one that will cherish you, love you, protect you and make you feel like they would move heaven and earth to make you happy.

Yeah. That guy.

Except, I'm not marrying that guy.

Instead, I'm stood next to the devil with a fake smile plastered on my face.

I'm wearing the dress and I have the pretty flowers, but that's as far as it goes. The rest has all been fabricated.

You see, I'm stood here because of a debt. A debt I stupidly thought I could repay with money, but no. Instead, I'm paying with my life, and it's all my fault.

I lost and gambled away my own future.

Crazy, huh?

That it may be, but it's happened and here I am.

I'm not marrying the man I love; I'm marrying the most dangerous guy in the country.

Nate Knowles.

Number one asshole and blackmail extraordinaire.

I had a debt with the most powerful man in the crime world, and I truly believed that I could have paid him back… until I didn't.

One wrong choice was my downfall.

And that choice I made was for love. A love that turned out to be false. The man I thought I loved turned his back on me and left me to rot.

And now, here I am.

Bowing down to the crime lord where his world involves popping a bullet in someone's head as if it is as normal as eating breakfast.

Playing ball is what will keep me alive.

Acting the part is what will stop me from being fifty feet under.

So, even as I hate Nate Knowles with a passion, I will smile and say the right things in public, but in private, all bets are off.

I need a plan, a way to get the hell out of this nightmare.

I need to suss things out, ingrain myself so deep that he will never see it coming.

Role of a lifetime.

Good meets evil.

And I will take down the monster.

You just see if I don't…

Keep reading here:

http://viewbook.at/WreckingBall

The Untouchable Brother

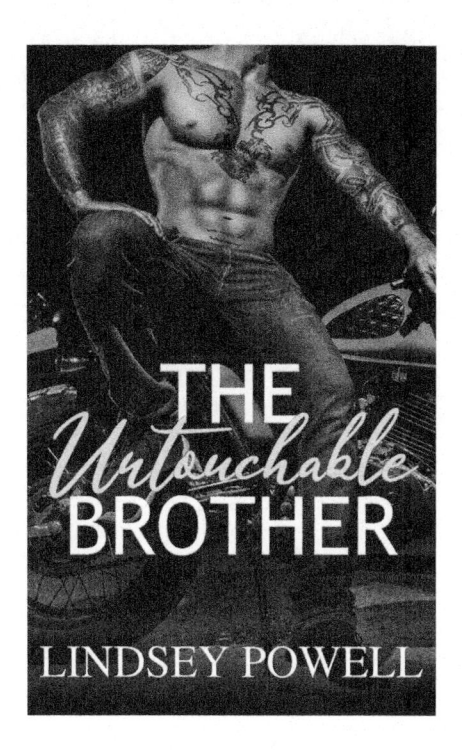

Chapter 1

Zoey

Sitting on the beach and looking at the waves rippling softly, I remind myself how lucky I am.

I'm living a dream life in idyllic surroundings, and the beach just so happens to be my back garden.

Living on a beautiful island, away from all the chaos of my previous life has been wonderful. I had been looking for an escape, a place where no one knew who I was or who my brother was.

You see, my brother is Nate Knowles, notorious crime lord who ran the streets for a long time. It was in his blood, and he had taken over when our parents had been killed years before. It was all he knew, until Kat Wiltshire—now Knowles—walked into his life. She turned his head away from what he knew and showed him what it was like to love hard and to put that one person above anything else.

I am so thankful that Kat came into our lives, because if she hadn't, then I don't know what my brother would be like now. I mean, he was ruthless back then, but with time, I'm sure he would have become even harder, if that was at all possible.

Kat is my best friend and the sister I never had. Once we met, it was like we just clicked, and our bond is so strong that nothing could break it. She's my family, and not only does she make my brother happy, but she has given me the most beautiful niece to love and cherish. In fact, I can hear her squeals of laughter from where I sit, and it makes me smile as I close my eyes and appreciate the fact that I am still alive.

When we came here five years ago, it was just for a holiday, but Nate quickly made a dream a reality when he bought a house out here and said that it was our home.

It was the escape I had been looking for.

A way out of the life I left behind.

The grief and the guilt that plagued me has taken years to push to the back of my mind, but the death and destruction that we left behind still leaves me with guilt to this day, hidden in my subconscious.

I lost someone that I could really have fallen for. Someone who made me feel alive and wanted, cherished but would give me a run for my money at the same time. Jason Jones is the biker that I lost, the man that died helping me. And I don't know if I will ever truly forgive myself for asking him and some of his crew to help on that fateful day…

I was so confident when I walked in here. I had a plan, a way to deal with the problem that had been fucking with Nate and Kat for weeks—possibly months, I'm not entirely sure, because my brother kept me out of the loop. I know he always thinks he's protecting me, but I'm a big girl who can roll with the best of them.

Sure, I may seem like more of a party girl, but underneath, I can be cold-hearted too.

But then I guess that's what big brothers are for—to protect their younger siblings and take the brunt of any danger that comes their way.

Nate being a crime lord meant that he had to always be on his game, on top form, ready to strike down anyone that threatened him or anyone he cared about.

That had only ever been me until Kat came along, and now she's here with me, chained to the wall like a fucking animal whilst the enemy stares at us from across the room.

Motherfucking Jessica.

A woman who Nate trusted and who has totally stabbed him in the back.

"Zoey," Jessica says, as if this is a friendly meet. "What a surprise." Ugh, I always did hate her fucking voice. So whiny and high-pitched. How the hell Nate kept her around, I'll never know—other than maybe feeling sorry for her, I can't see the pull. But then, he did find some guy kicking the shit out of her outside the strip club she used to work in years ago, so maybe he did show the heart that he buries deep down inside on that particular night.

"Quite," I reply deadpan. Other than sticking a knife in this bitch, I want nothing to do with her.

"So, to what do I owe the pleasure of this visit?" she says, standing there, thinking she's lady fucking muck with her arms crossed over her chest and a smirk across her face.

"Oh, you know, just thought it would be good to catch up," I tell her, the sarcasm clear in my voice. And then she laughs, and it makes me cringe. Ugh. I hate everything about her.

"Don't tell me you miss me?" she asks, and I lose any patience I may have been harbouring.

"Cut the bullshit, Jessica. We both know I came here to end you," I snarl at her.

"And you brought along a treat," she says as she turns her attention to Kat. She stalks forward, and I take a moment to appreciate just how different the two women are.

Jessica has short blonde hair and dark grey eyes which are almost squinty, like she's got the sun glaring at her constantly, whereas Kat has long brunette hair and beautiful blue eyes that—usually—sparkle with happiness and mischief. It's why we clicked so well, because I can see a rebellious spark inside of her that lives inside of me too.

But that spark has landed us in trouble, and it's all my fucking fault.

"So, you're the one he chose," Jessica says to Kat as she looks her up and down like she's a piece of shit on her shoe. But the truth is, Jessica was always a jealous bitch, and it's so obvious that Kat is way above her and totally in a different league. The really creepy part about all of this is the fact that Jessica and Nate were never an item—not to my knowledge anyway. He would never have gone for her, and this is just the ridiculous play of a bunny boiler who thinks this is going to get her the life that she always wanted. Pah. Yeah. Good luck with that when Nate gets here and releases me to end your sorry existence, Jessica.

"Tell me, does it feel good to fuck what belongs to me?" Jessica says, continuing her perusal of Kat. She continues to witter on, and I will my big brother to get here and save us from the mess I have made of this mission. I guess that's why he's the brains and I've never been at the forefront of operations in the underworld, because I clearly don't think shit through enough before acting.

"Rock hard abs, thick thighs, and the best ass I've ever seen... I don't like when others play with my toys," she continues as I zone in and out, but that is where my patience for this crap ends.

"Jesus, Jessica, can you cut it with the details... that is my brother you're talking about," I snap, and the next thing I know, one of her fucking guard dogs—and by that, I mean gross, sweaty men—comes over and sticks tape over my mouth.

"Always had a motor mouth that one," Jessica says in reference to me. Bitch. And with my mouth taped, she witters on some more before her next words have my heart trying to beat out of my chest...

"I think Mrs Knowles needs a taste of what it's like when you take something that isn't yours... Have your fun first before you finish her off," she instructs her men, and then they are quickly tying rope around Kat's legs. No, no, no, they can't take her.

"And if you're thinking about those biker men coming to rescue you, then don't. They're all dead," Jessica says, and I swear the fucking pain in my heart is like a knife ripping me apart, but I don't have time to process anything more when Jessica says, "Ruin her," as they remove the cuffs and get ready to carry Kat out of here.

I wildly thrash my arms and legs around, praying to a God that I don't believe in to throw me a fucking bone or some shit to get out of this and help Kat, but instead of a bone, I see the fucking devil has answered my silent plea.

Because there, stood in the doorway, looking as evil as ever is my brother, Lucas. The brother that killed our parents. The one that always put his needs before anyone else's. The man who thrives on pain, suffering and power. Fuck.

"Hi, sis," Lucas says, a smirk crossing his mouth, and my panic from moments ago multiplies ten-fold. "It's been a long time." Yeah, it sure has, it's just a shame it's not been even longer.

At Lucas' request, the tape is removed from my mouth by one of the guard dogs, and I struggle to form words.

"You didn't really think I'd just disappeared never to be seen again, did you?" he says. Well, I lived in hope, but fate obviously had other shit in store, clearly. Lucas turns his attention to Kat and then starts to give her a quick intro to who the hell he is. He admits to killing our parents and then makes his hatred and jealousy of Nate known—something I always knew. He always wanted everything Nate had, and I mean everything. Women, school friends, grades, even the fucking lunchbox that our mum used to pack his sandwiches in.

"Turns out, no one really liked me much, and they all chose Nate over me. So, I bided my time, went underground, kept silent, and now, here I am, ready and waiting for him to come here to rescue you both… and he won't even see the trap as he comes in here. He won't be thinking clearly, and it will pave the way for me to capture him and torture him before he meets his maker," he says to Kat as I try to pull myself out of the shock my body currently seems to be in.

"Just think how he will cope without his wife and his sister. Doesn't bare thinking about really, does it?" he taunts, and the thought shatters my heart. It would kill Nate to be without us both, I know it would, and I know that he would give up and let Lucas do whatever he wanted to him. Tears sting the backs of my eyes and I furiously blink them back as they start to distort my vision.

"It'll make him careless to know that I have you both," he says with a grin.

"Lucas, please don't do this," I plead, trying to reach some part of my brother that may still be somewhat human.

"Why not? Because we can all be one big happy family?" He laughs at me. "I don't fucking think so. Now, take her away and make sure we hear her screams," he says to the two guys, and then he's stepping aside and the guard dogs are taking Kat from the room. I scream and thrash about, but I'm rendered useless, and I know that I won't be able to live with myself after this. I know that if they hurt Kat and Nate doesn't get to her in time then I will never forgive myself.

"Now all we have to do is wait for the big bad crime lord to show up, and then the real fun starts," Lucas says as he walks into the room and stands beside Jessica. She looks at him with a mixture of fear and lust. Ugh. She really has no morals.

"Please, Lucas, I'm begging you to let Kat go. Please," I try to reason with him, but I already know it's pointless.

"*I have absolutely no interest in rescuing some tart of Nate's,*" he replies, looking bored as fuck. "*She's just bait, and you were an added bonus.*"

"*And you wonder why everyone hated you,*" I grit out, anger running through my body at this whole situation.

"*Oof,*" he says sarcastically, pretending I've wounded him by placing his hand on his heart.

"*Why didn't you just stay away, huh?*" I continue. "*You're a fucking parasite—*"

"*And you're a fucking bitch,*" he shouts at me, cutting me off. Good, I appear to have pissed him off. If I can keep him talking, then it may distract him so Nate can come on in here and kill the bastard. "*You always did suck up to fucking Nate. Everyone did. He was the best, he was the worthy one, meanwhile I'd just be stood there wondering what the fuck I ever did wrong.*"

"*Really? You actually asked yourself that question after all the years of taunting and hurting me and Nate?*" I ask incredulously. "*All of the times you laughed at us when we fell over, or what about when you would push us and act like it was an accident—and then there was the time that I busted my lip because I came off of my bike after you rammed the front wheel of yours into the back of mine.*"

"*That was just child's play,*" he retorts. Figures. He never did know how to show remorse.

"*You can call it what you want, Lucas, but I call it bullying.*"

He stares long and hard at me, but I don't back down. If he's going to kill me, then I want to look the fucker right in the eyes as he does.

"*Baby sis, I'm sorry it had to end like this… well, actually, I'm not really, and I will take great pleasure in finally bringing Nate to his fucking knees. It's his turn to beg for mercy, beg for life, but I'll never give him that.*

"*I'll torture him until he struggles to breathe, and then I'll rip out his fucking heart and lodge a bullet in his brain at the same time, because I couldn't decide which ending was better, so I'll just go with both.*" He's clearly done with the slight recap on our childhood, and I guess this is where it all ends. There is no reasoning with him, and my time is up.

"*Lucas, you promised me that I could have my fun before you ended him,*" Jessica says.

"*And you can. You can jump around on his dick as much as you like until I decide that it is enough,*" Lucas says, and I can hear the warning in his tone.

"You two are fucking sick," I tell them, disgust clear in my voice.

"You always knew this about me, sis, and I never pretended to be anything else," Lucas replies. "And you know what else, dear sister of mine?"

There is a pause as he takes a step towards me.

"I'm going to make sure that I retell the story to him over and over again about how his pretty little wife was raped repeatedly as she begged for her life."

His words make me shudder. Kat is the sister I never had, and I hope to God that by some miracle she gets out of here safely.

And it looks like my prayer has just been answered as Lucas' features go slack and he drops like a sack of shit to the floor, to reveal Nate stood behind him with a gun in his hand. Oh thank fuck.

Nate turns the gun on Jessica and her mouth drops open as her eyes go wide. "Nate," she whispers as her hands come up in front of her. "Please… I didn't… Please don't…"

"Spare me the fucking pity party," Nate snarls as he walks into the room. "You fucked with the wrong brother," he says, and I see that he's getting ready to pull the trigger, and I shout, "No, Nate."

He pauses and looks at me questioningly.

"Let me do it," I tell him, because I want to do this. I want to take this burden from him and end it once and for all. I worry he will never get over killing a woman, it's not something he's done previously, and I don't want him to take this on when it's my fault anyway.

"Get the key, let me out of these cuffs, and then I'll kill her," I say, determination running through me. "It won't be my first time," I add on, shocking the shit out of him. Yeah, I've killed and kept it secret, but I don't have time to answer the questions that I know will be rattling around his head right now. We can talk later, but now is the time for action.

"Where's the key?" he barks at Jessica, and she quickly goes to get it and then frees me from the chains.

"Oh, I'm going to enjoy this," I say as it takes me less than half a second to plough my fist straight into her face. She drops to the floor, and I walk over to Nate, taking the gun from him and pointing it at her. "Bye bye, Jessica. Sweet dreams." I pull the trigger, and it's lights out for her.

Silence fills the room for a beat before Nate turns to me and says, "Where's Kat?"

The pain of that day is still very real. I will never forget the way my heart beat uncontrollably, or how it broke when Nate, Kat and I finally left the place where it all went to hell and drove past the dead bodies lining the driveway. Every single biker that came to help me died. And when I saw Jason, I don't know how I held myself together. His eyes were open, looking up to the sky, his mouth hanging open slightly, the life gone from him.

And that will forever be the last image of him ingrained in my memory.

It taints everything that came before that, and I know the image will never leave me.

I can't take back what happened, but if I could rewind the clock, I would.

Instead of staying and facing up to what had happened, I ran away. I came to this idyllic island with Kat and Nate, and I never looked back.

But the urge to return is there. It always has been. And working through my grief has made that urge so much stronger.

I couldn't face it before. I know that their deaths were my fault, but I couldn't accept it fully when my heart was breaking too.

But now I can.

I've had some therapy, and I've worked through as much as I can here, but in order to truly heal, I have to go back and face the demons that may await me.

All I have to do now is tell my big brother and hope that he doesn't block me from truly allowing my heart to heal.

Keep reading here:
http://mybook.to/UntouchableBrother

About the Author

Lindsey lives in South West, England, with her partner and two children. She works within a family run business, and she began her writing career in 2013. She finds the time to write in-between working and raising a family.

Lindsey's love of reading inspired her to create her own book series. Her favourite book genre is romance, but her interests span over several genre's including mystery, suspense and crime.

To keep up to date with book news, you can find Lindsey on social media and you can also check out Lindsey's website where you can find all of her books and her newsletter:

https://lindseypowellauthor.wordpress.com

facebook.com/lindseypowellperfect

twitter.com/Lindsey_perfect

instagram.com/lindseypowellperfect

bookbub.com/authors/lindsey-powell

goodreads.com/lpow21

tiktok.com/@lpowperfect

Printed in Great Britain
by Amazon